Brazen Desires
Desperate Hours

J. Saltwick

ISBN 978-1-64079-815-1 (paperback)
ISBN 978-1-64079-817-5 (hardcover)
ISBN 978-1-64079-816-8 (digital)

Christian Faith Publishing, Inc.
832 Park Avenue
Meadville, PA 16335
www.christianfaithpublishing.com

Printed in the United States of America

1

With a figure that turned men's heads, the fifth-generation rancher set out on early-morning rounds to check the stock and the men who worked for her. Alone in the pickup, Kate Clark motored up the hill of the once-mighty ranch of historic proportions. Amassed by her great-grandfather and decimated by her grandfather, it was three properties shy of returning to its original size. From as far back as she could remember, Kate had made it her lifelong ambition to continue what her parents started and return the Clark family ranch to its magnificent stature.

A mile up from the main ranch compound, Kate came upon a wrangler as he swung a club at one of her steers. Slamming on the brake, she leaped from the cab. "Stop that," she yelled as the club came down hard across the animal's face. *Crack!* came the bone-shattering report. The steer stumbled and staggered back. "What the hell are you doing?" she demanded. This was her ranch, and no one mistreated her animals, especially not one of her wranglers.

"It tried ta gore me. It's gotta be taught a lesson," he said, reeling about.

"No, it doesn't. It's just a steer. You're fired. Get off my ranch now," she said.

"You can't fire me," he sneered. "I don't work fa you. I work fa Gene. He hired me," he said with slurred speech, referring to Kate's foreman who had hired him. Stumbling, he swung the club in her direction.

That's it, Kate resolved. "The hell, I can't!" Catching the wood with a gloved hand, Kate wrenched it out of his grasp. Grabbing his hand, she bent it back painfully between his shoulder blades. He tried to yell but couldn't when her other hand closed on his throat. He gasped as she marched him to his pickup. "Now you and your pile of junk get off my ranch. Go to the office and collect your pay." She shoved him inside and watched as he dug out and drove down the hill.

"So much for you," she muttered. Dusting off her hands, she reached into her truck for the radio microphone. "Dolores, I need someone up to area three with a trailer to haul in a steer. Jake just clubbed it, and it needs to be butchered. I fired the miserable no-good drunk. Soon as you pay him off, tell Gene I don't ever want to see him on my land again."

"Will do, boss," replied the woman who was married to Gene and lived with him and their twelve-year-old son, Dusty, in the foreman's house, not far from the Clark family home.

"Soon as I finish loading the steer, I'm going down to work Billie B," Kate said, referring to one of the many roping horses she was bringing along.

Dolores was quick to point out, "Remember, you have that cattle ranch owners association meeting today."

"Thanks for the reminder. I should finish in the arena with time to spare." Turning, Kate watched as the truck with trailer made its way up toward her. Some folks in town referred to her as that "spinster owner of the ol' Clark family ranch." She, on the other hand, preferred to think of herself as the not-yet-married owner of one of the most successful operations in the state. A marital status she planned to rectify as soon as the man who lived with her became more interested in matrimony and less in his new diesel-powered pickup and big shiny tractor.

Minutes later, with the steer loaded, Kate drove to the building with the large domed roof. Grabbing the saddle, she swung up onto Billie B. Backing the filly into the starting box, she called to the man at the head of the chute. "Hit it," she said. The steer broke for its freedom. Her bootheels came down on the horse's flanks. A couple quick twirls of her lariat, and the loop settled over the animal's head. Leaping off, she raced down the taut line to the steer. Grabbing two handfuls of thrashing calf, she jerked the animal off its feet. Dust choked the air as she collected three legs and cinched them together. Flinging her arms back, she sprang to her feet. "How'd I do?" she called to the man who ran in her direction.

"Great time, boss—8.9 seconds," the man replied.

"Good, but not good enough," she said, realizing the best male time was a good second faster. "Bring on another calf. I want to run her again."

A number of steers later, she handed the horse off to the man who ran the starting chute. "Cool her down. I'll check her out again in a couple days. With luck, she should bring top dollar." Glancing at her watch, she hustled toward the exit. "I have to get going, I have a Montana Cattle Ranch Owners Association meeting to attend, and I need to get cleaned up." Rather than open and close the big gate at the far end of the building, she put a foot up on a rung and vaulted over on her way to her pickup.

Parking behind her house, she dashed across the broad porch to the most unlikely of Montana ranch houses, a white-columned antebellum mansion straight out of the old South. Built by her great-grandfather, it was his monument to having assembled the largest ranch in the state. Without pause, she passed through the kitchen toward the bedroom floor above. If she hurried, she'd have time to visit with Wylie, the man who lived with her, before she had to leave.

Finished showering, she was picking out what she was going to wear when her next-door neighbor, Patty Mitchell, ground to a stop behind the house. Owner of one of the three properties Kate needed, her best friend made her way to the back door. "You decent?" Patty called out.

Inches shorter than Kate, Patty had been friends with her since before grade school. Not waiting for an answer, Patty headed across the empty kitchen. A couple months shy of thirty-four, she was a few weeks older than Kate and noticeably heavier. Helping herself to coffee, she turned in search of the powdered creamer on the kitchen table. Set toward the end, where the day's mail had been neatly sorted, she stirred in creamer and spied *The Nation's Meat* magazine on the top of one of the stacks. A sedate trade publication directed toward producers of beef, pork, and poultry, it was not known for flashy covers. Patty's eyes widened when she saw the man pictured on the cover. Wearing an all-too-brief swimsuit and a luscious bronze tan, he was at the controls of an open-cockpit speedboat. Drenched in spray, his sculpted chest glistened, as did his washboard abs. Below his picture, the caption read,

> Jarrett Sinclair—bachelor, playboy, entrepreneur
> Chairman of the board and owner of AJS Foods
> America's fastest-growing meat wholesaler

"Whew. You're something else." Patty whistled softly.

"Good morning," Kate said as she dashed past on the way to her office. "You say something?"

Patty held up the magazine. "You sell big-time to AJS Foods. What can you tell me about this guy, Jarrett Sinclair? He's on the cover this month. He looks delicious."

Kate checked her answering machine and seeing no blinkers, turned back. "Not much. All of my dealings are with Karl Schneider. He's my AJS account manager."

Patty's expression brightened. "Have you ever met Sinclair?"

"No," Kate replied.

"Too bad," Patty said. "He's handsome and rich. He flies around in his own private jet. He owns hotels and office buildings all over the place. He produces movies. Award-winning ones. A month seldom passes he's not featured in some tabloid with a gorgeous woman clinging to his arm at a movie premiere or building dedication. He's Mr. Excitement." Her eyes glowed. "A real hunk," she said, licking her lips.

"Forget it," Kate replied. "He's a big corporate mogul, and I'm just a little ol' rancher from Montana."

"From what I've seen of him in the tabloids, he's drawn to good-looking females, and let's face it, you're more than that." Patty assessed her friend dressed in a tailored tan Western shirt, matching Western-cut trousers with razor-sharp creases and golden-brown custom cowboy boots. "What's with the fancy duds? Where are you off to? Obviously not just the grocery store."

"Right," Kate said. "I'm going to the quarterly ranch owner's association meeting."

"Oooh," Patty mumbled. "I forgot about that." She paused. "If you're going to that meeting, why aren't you wearing a skirt and blouse and high heels? Lord knows you've got the figure for it." Her brow furrowed. "Kate. Once in a while, try dressing like a woman." She studied her friend. "Speaking of which, do you even own a dress?"

"Yes, I own a dress," Kate snapped back.

"Oh, really? When was the last time you wore one?" Patty asked.

"I wore one to mom's funeral. That was three years…" Her voice trailed off. *Wrong. I wore one to…,* she thought. *Forget it. That's beside the point.* Sensing she'd been a bit abrupt, she made with a lighthearted chuckle. "Hell." She grinned. "I'm a tough, hard-nosed rancher and breeder of horses and not one of those fancy floozies you find in your tabloids and fashion magazines. I'll leave the girly stuff to them." Having had it with the questions, her eyes narrowed as she focused on Patty. "What exactly are you here for?"

"Oh. Yeah, that. My nieces are with me. They wanted to check out the university in Missoula, so I let them use my convertible. Right now I'm stuck with Wylie's old gas-guzzling pickup. I forgot about your meeting today and was hoping you were going to town so I could ride along. I hate refilling his tank when gas costs this much. Obviously, you're not, so I guess I wasted a trip over here."

"I guess you did."

Patty drained her mug and looked toward the yard. "Speaking of Wylie, where's his crew cab?" There was a glint in her eye and sparkle in her voice she could not disguise. She was secretly in love with William, Wylie Lewis, the man who lived with Kate; and at times, it showed. "I didn't pass him on my way in, and he's not parked out back."

Kate pointed toward the stables. "I sold a mare to the Hendersons. He and Dad are over there loading her into the trailer."

"So he'll he be back today?"

"Yes," Kate said. "After they deliver the mare, Wylie's coming back so he can get an early start tomorrow working one of his fields." Kate looked toward the door. "I have a long drive ahead of me, and I really need to get going."

"Hey, I'm out of here," Patty said and left.

Patty's dust had barely settled when Wylie rolled up with trailer in tow. "I'm ready to go," he announced on entering. A large man with massive shoulders, no neck, and upper arms the size of most people's thighs, he owned one of the three properties Kate needed to restore her ranch to the largest in the state. The third property she needed was to the north of hers owned by the Wilsons. All three properties had been in the many parcels her grandfather had sold off to support his love of art, mostly painting, a passion he had practiced in the attic for years. "The horse is loaded. Is there anything special I need to tell them?" A couple of inches shorter than Kate, he had an easy smile and, fortunately, a calm disposition.

"No, I can't think of a thing. Gretchen's going to use her barrel racing. She's aggressive, quick off the line, fast, and turns well."

"You should know. You barrel raced and won a ton of awards." He turned to go. "Get home early if you can. I don't like you driving out here late at night. No telling what might dart out in front of you in the dark. It was all I could do to keep from hitting a moose and her calf three nights ago."

Kate smiled. She appreciated his concern. As always, he had her best interest at heart. "I'll try my best, but I've those two committees I'm on, and one runs through dinner."

It was late when the second committee adjourned. On her way toward the exit, Kate was stopped by Monty Parks, a rancher from down around Yellowstone. "Kate, I think I better tell you, a developer out of Denver has been nosing around in my area. Word has it they were looking to acquire a sizeable tract of land on which to build a colossal resort. They weren't able to find what they were looking for in my area and might be coming your way. With you owning the largest private wilderness on the east side of the Rockies, it's best I tell you."

Kate's expression chilled. "Thanks. I appreciate the warning."

"You better watch out. I heard they are big and powerful and have a lot of money."

"So do I," she snarled sardonically. "We'll see who blinks first."

From off to the side came a rancher's sarcastic whisper, "You tell him, fella."

Ignoring the man, she left.

2

The first light of day streamed through the master bedroom windows. Up on one elbow, Kate pushed back the tangle of hair that lay across her face. She had not slept well. The fact some developer might be heading her way gnawed at her. *How dare they consider building a resort here?* She scowled. *They can take their money and go ruin nature somewhere else.*

About to roll from the bed and let Wylie sleep, she saw the clock on the nightstand beside his head. "Whoops!" she called out and gave him a shake. He'd left a note in the kitchen, telling her he was going to set his alarm for five-thirty so he could get an early start working his field. It was now five minutes to six. "Darling, it's time to get up. Your alarm didn't go off."

"Huh," Wylie grunted. Forcing an eye open, he groped for the clock. He fumbled for the alarm. "Dang, I forgot to pull the plunger," he growled. Yawning, he rubbed the sleep from his eyes. When he saw the state of her hair, he blinked. "Have trouble sleeping?"

"You could say that. According to Monty Parks from down around Yellowstone, a developer out of Denver has been looking to buy land to build a big resort. They weren't able to find what they were after in his area and now might be coming our way."

Wylie's expression brightened. "Great!" he glowed and pushed up on both elbows. "So someone might be interested in doing something with this land other than raising a bunch of dumb cows. With beef prices down along with demand, it's all most of us around here can do to break even."

Kate did not comment. While a lot of the smaller ranches around her were having trouble, she was not. She looked at him. To get in a conversation about ranch profitability would only lead to a heated discussion, which she was not up for this early in the morning. Tossing the covers aside, she rolled from the bed. Dressed in a plain knee-length sleep shirt, she dashed to the dressing room. "If you want to get in your field by seven, you better get moving."

"Yeah, I hear you," he mumbled and tugged the sheet back over his body. "When you finish, I'll get up."

Minutes later, dressed in jeans, a Western shirt, and thick boot socks, she stopped by the bed. Just as she had expected, he'd drifted back to sleep. She gave him a shake. "See you downstairs," she said and waited for his eyes to open. "I'll have coffee ready when you get there."

With the coffee brewing, Kate stepped over to the table and picked out the magazine that had caught Patty's attention. When she saw the cover, she stopped. What drew her in was not the brevity of the man's attire but rather Sinclair's eyes. Taking a breath, she felt he was looking at her. "Whew," she whispered. The sight of his gaze brought on a glow she had never felt before. Her juices were flowing, and not just a little. "Get a grip," she mumbled. "This is only a picture. He's not looking at me." Exhaling loudly, her expression eased as she laid the magazine aside. About to go check the coffee, she stopped and reached back for the publication. She studied the cover. Again, the hot rush welled up within her. She swallowed hard. Spray ran down his sculpted chest and over his powerful tanned arms. She agreed, *Patty was right. You are something else.*

Below the picture, the word *playboy* caught her attention. *You don't look much like a corporate president if you ask me. A playboy, yes... a corporate president no.*

Behind her, the coffeemaker gurgled. The pot was a little over half full. In a couple minutes, it would be finished, and Wylie would be there. Flipping to the feature, she scanned it quickly.

Like on the cover, the lead picture inside had him at the controls of the open-cockpit speedboat. Unlike on the cover, two bikini-clad females with overflowing breasts hung over his shoulders. One look at the caption told Kate a lot. "Accomplished driver of high-powered ocean-racing speedboats, the most eligible Mr. Sinclair approaches life and business the same way he races—aggressively, inches from the brink of danger." Kate rolled her eyes. *Obviously, the writer has geared the article for the publication's predominate male readership.* Exhaling slowly, she glanced down the page. A sentence in the first paragraph caught her attention: "A star athlete in college, his promising football career was cut short when, following a concession, the school physician barred him from all further contact sports. Not to be deterred, Sinclair took up racing boats, both power and sail."

She muttered, "So much for sports." Turning the page, she stopped at the last picture in the spread. Seated at a desk, Sinclair's suit coat was draped over the back of his chair, and his sleeves were rolled up. Under the picture, the caption read, "Through Mr. Sinclair's hands-on management style, in five years he has taken AJS Foods from bankruptcy to one of the most profitable meat wholesalers in the nation." Kate mouthed, "That's more like it."

Behind her, the coffeemaker made one last noisy burp. Hearing that, she turned back to the cover. Seeing Sinclair's eyes, she stopped. The warm rush returned. She studied his picture and slowly shook her head. "You're hardly my type." She snorted and set the magazine aside. Stepping away, she looked toward the floor above. From overhead came the sound of Wylie tromping down the hall. She smiled. *You're my type.*

Kate filled Wylie's mug as he entered the room. "Coffee's done." She beamed. "It's hot and black and strong enough to kick-start you and your fancy tractor." They both knew what she was referring to: the giant articulating quarter-of-a-million-dollar eight-wheeled machine he'd purchased less than twelve months before. It was taller, wider, and more expensive than any of the decades-old Caterpillar tractors she owned. While any one of her big crawlers were as powerful as his wheeled machine, her Caterpillars had none of the modern conveniences like soundproof air-conditioned cabs, complete with plush shock-absorbing seating, CD players, and Bose speakers.

Wylie took a gulp of coffee and a bite of a sweet roll. Swallowing hard, he eyed Kate in faded jeans and a long-sleeve Western shirt. "Are you planning on working cattle today?"

"No. Soon as I finish a couple things here, I'm going to saddle Ramrod and check on my high-range summer grazing area. I'm afraid the snowmelt runoff and the heavy spring rains have raised havoc with the road and trail leading up there. The winter range is about down to nothing, and I have to move my premium cattle now." As she spoke, she hooked an arm around his and walked him to the door. "Have a good day and plow the heck out of your field."

"I plan to," he said and gave her a peck on the cheek.

She watched as his pickup roared to life and disappeared over a nearby rise. Stepping back into her office, she checked e-mail. Seeing nothing urgent, she crossed to the kitchen side of the room just as Patty's dust-covered Sebring convertible rolled up. Smiling, she went to the door. "To what do I owe the pleasure of your company? You were here only yesterday." Leading the way into the kitchen, Kate pointed at the coffeepot.

Patty nodded yes to coffee as she pulled out her cell phone. The screen was blank. "It fell in the washer last night. I'm heading into town to get a new one. I stopped by to see if you wanted me to pick up anything while I'm there. I figured after all the driving yesterday you might want to hang close to home." She studied Kate when she handed her a mug. "What's with the working duds? Are you planning on running cattle today?"

Kate shook her head and told Patty how she was going to check on the trail leading up to her summer range. With mug in hand, Kate settled in across from Patty. As she did, Patty reached for the creamer and beamed when she saw *The Nation's Meat* magazine. Picking it up, Patty tapped on the picture of Jarrett Sinclair. "Now that's what I call a real man. With that tan, his face looks like its cast in bronze."

She held the magazine up next to Kate. "Yes! You two would make a beautiful couple."

"No way," Kate replied and shoved the magazine aside. "Unless you've forgotten I already have a man, and we're really quite happy."

Patty arched her brow. "Are you?" Patty asked. When Kate said nothing, she turned back to the magazine cover. "Too bad. Your kids would be gorgeous."

Kate's eyes flared. "Yes, we're happy. And for your information, Wylie's and my kids are going to be plenty good-looking."

"Re-re-really!" Patty blurted out. Her face was aglow. It was all she could do to get the words out. "Is there something I should know?" she sputtered. "Are you pregnant?" she asked.

"No, I'm not pregnant," Kate replied. "Trust me, you'd be the first to know."

Patty again held up the picture of Sinclair. "I still say you two would be beautiful together." When Kate did not respond, Patty set the publication aside. Easing back, she studied her friend. "How are things with you and Wylie?"

Kate glared. "What's that supposed to mean?" Sensing she might have overreacted, she forced a quick smile. "Things are just fine."

"Are they?" Patty remarked. She waited, and when Kate did not reply, she continued, "You're the old-fashioned type. No marriage, no commitment, no kids. If you don't mind my saying so, you two are no closer to getting married now than when Wylie moved in here. That was what…three years ago?" Kate nodded. "Right," Patty continued. "Unlike me, you want children. I detest the little buggers. Kate, you're going on thirty-four. In case you haven't noticed, your clock is ticking. If you want children, you'd better start pretty soon. What good is it building this big ranch if you have no one to pass it down to?" Patty waited and, when no response came, continued, "I sense Wylie's still not keen on fatherhood?"

"He has his toys," Kate replied. "At the moment, he's more interested in playing with his new pickup and fancy tractor than having children, but he'll get over that."

Patty rolled her eyes. "Will he?" She waited, and when Kate said nothing, she turned to the magazine and tapped on the cover. "When you're finished with this, can I borrow it? It says Sinclair's not married. If that's the case, I might send him a résumé."

"It's yours," Kate said and shoved the magazine in her direction. "I've seen all I want of him." Across the room, the telephone rang. "Damn!" Kate snorted and ran to her office. "The phone always rings when I want to get away."

Grabbing the magazine, Patty reached for the door. "See ya," she mouthed.

Kate waved. When she finished the call, she grabbed leftovers from the refrigerator. Stuffing them into a canvas tote, she made for the barn. On entering the stables, her horse whinnied. "Morning, big guy," she called out on seeing her prize-cutting horse. Leading Ramrod out, she saddled him quickly. Grabbing her rifle, she hung it from her saddle, and they were out the door. If she'd been in a hurry, she could have hauled Ramrod up to the area she wanted to inspect in a trailer; that started just beyond the place they called the Meadow. Flat and treeless, the Meadow was roughly a mile wide. From there, the mountains rose to the west. But she wasn't in a hurry and wanted to enjoy her horse. Not only was he a gold mine in stud fees, he was a pleasure to ride.

Just as she had expected, not far past the meadow, the road and trail turned bad. The heavy spring rains, on top of the near-record winter snow, had taken their toll. Between pauses to record the damage, she caught herself being drawn back to the memory of Jarrett Sinclair. Not just to his face but his eyes. Unconsciously, she sensed he had been looking at her. A surge of excitement raced through her. The hot feeling she had sensed earlier welled up again. Moments later, she forced herself to settle back in the saddle. *That's ridiculous. He wasn't looking at me. That was only a picture.* Exhaling loudly, she shook her head. *Forget him. I don't know him, and it's not likely I ever will.*

Farther up, they approached a massive washed-out section. A major part of both the road and trail were gone. Photographing the damage, she tapped Ramrod, and he didn't move. She whapped him again, and still nothing. Something had caught his attention in the brush ahead. He stirred nervously beneath her. "Easy, big guy," she whispered as she reached down for her rifle. Whatever was there had to be either a cougar or a bear. Either could spook her horse. Focused on the brush, she pulled up her carbine and levered in a round. The growl of the bear ripped the air. Ramrod reared. Aiming high, she squeezed off a shot. The bear whirled about and disappeared through the brush. She grinned. "Get going there, little guy, and spook someone else."

With the threat gone, Kate eased Ramrod past the washed-out section and up the hill to a clearing. Though spotted with trees, there were no clumps of brush or outcropping of rocks large enough to conceal another bear. She tied Ramrod to a nearby branch and took a seat on a fallen log. She munched her way through leftover chicken and gazed at the miles of rolling plains that made up her high-range summer grazing area. Everywhere she looked was a sea of lush green. "God, I love this country," she called out.

With lunch gone, she took a bite of an apple and gazed at the sky. Off to the west, a small high-wing plane was flying by in a southerly direction. Unable to make out much more than its shape, she finished the apple.

As Kate climbed on her horse, Ramrod whinnied. Rested, his hormones kicked in. His long legs stretched out as he bolted ahead. She grinned. She loved his spirit and let him run. After a mile or so, she settled him to an easy trot. They crested one knoll and another and then another. Everywhere she looked, the grass was thick and tall. *I won't need to truck up hay this year.*

From up ahead came the sound of a small plane. Stopping, she stood tall in the stirrups. It was coming from the south, right out of the sun. Whipping off her hat, she used it to block the glare. The little plane was a couple thousand feet up and coming her way. With high wings and a single engine, it looked like the type many ranchers used to search for lost cattle. She shook her hat defiantly at the plane.

"Go away," she called out. "If you've lost stock, I'll have my people do the looking." Settling back, she followed the plane as it flew north. After a few seconds, it banked sharply and turned her way. Now lower, it zoomed overhead and disappeared into the sun. With it gone, she gave Ramrod a tap with her heels. They had one more knoll to pass over and a couple miles to go to reach the southernmost point of her upper range.

Kate stood in the stirrups and surveyed where she had been. She'd seen enough. With miles to cover to get down to her house, she decided not to go back to the trail she'd come up and instead took the more direct route down through the trees. Rugged and bold with a scattering of streams and pristine lakes, it was some of the last untouched wilderness in Montana.

Well down the hill, she slowed Ramrod to a walk. The heady fragrance of the tall pines hung in the air. She took a deep breath and let out a whoop. "It's hot. I'm going to go for a swim."

Ahead, the sound of water tumbling down the hill could be heard. Her old swimming hole wasn't far. Winding her way through the trees, they broke out into a clearing. There was her lake, the place where she had taught herself how to swim. Kicking off her boots, she stripped down and dove naked into the water "Yeeyoow!" she called out when her head broke the surface. Fed from a distant glacier, the water was freezing. Facedown, she stroked hard for the shallow area. Bathed in the sun, the water there was comfortable. She rolled over on her back and floated with her arms outstretched. When she was young, she'd come up here and float and dream of the day the ranch was going to be all hers. *With the little bit I have yet to get from Pop, the ranch is now all mine.*

Flicking her fingers, she moved along. After a couple of strokes, she stopped. Something caught her attention. There was a sound. She was not alone. She cocked her head and listened as the small plane burst into view. It was flying level and straight a few thousand feet up. Suddenly its nose dropped. The engine noise grew. The plane banked hard and dove toward the lake. Staying within the clearing, the plane zoomed overhead. Now barely a couple hundred feet up, Kate studied it as it flashed by. She blinked. There were round ports in its smooth underside. "Yoow," she called out and almost jumped out of the water. It was a photo-survey plane. "Get out of here," she yelled. "Get off my ranch." As quickly as it appeared, it was gone. "Damn it." She snorted. It had to be employed by that development company. Rolling over, she kicked hard toward the other side of the lake. Pulling on her clothes, she raced down to her house. She had to find out who hired that plane.

In her office, she punched in the phone number for the service center at their local airport. If anyone would know anything about that plane, it would be Gus Collins, the service center owner. A fully qualified airframe and engine mechanic, he knew aircraft and would be a good place to start.

"Gus, a survey plane flew over my place today. What can you tell me about it?"

"If it's the one that stopped in here for fuel a bit ago, it's owned by Bronson Tagree of Tagree Aerial Survey out of Missoula. He topped off his tanks before heading back to base."

"Did the pilot say what he was up to?" Focused, Kate waited for his answer.

"He said he was hired to survey a sixty-plus-mile stretch of the east slopes of the Rockies."

Her eyes narrowed. "Did he say who hired him?"

"No, and I didn't ask. I didn't figure it was any of my business," Gus responded.

"Too bad," Kate replied. "I'd really like to know who ordered a survey of our land and why."

"Well, if you're that interested, you're welcome to call him. If you want, I can give you his number."

Kate was and wrote the number down Gus gave her. "Good. I'll give him a call."

3

Kate looked toward the west. The air surveyor had just left and wouldn't be back to Missoula for a couple hours. By then it would be too late. *I'll call him tomorrow*, she thought and headed for the floor above. It was after five. Wylie would soon be there. She needed to get cleaned up. Showered, she pulled on a tank top and shorts and went down to the kitchen. If the plane had flown over her property, it had to have flown over his along with Patty's and the third bordering ranch she needed to the north.

Down in the kitchen, Kate looked out as Wylie's pickup roared up and slid to a stop in a cloud of dust. She blinked. That was most unlike his normal approach. With dust being an everyday problem in Montana, everyone, including Wylie, took care to stir up as little as possible. Leaping from the cab, he bolted for the door. Without so much as a *howdy* or *how are you*, he stomped past her and grabbed a beer from the refrigerator.

Catching a whiff of him, she backed away. "Whew," she announced, "darling you're a mess." She checked him quickly. "You're soaked with diesel fuel. Did you have a problem?"

He growled. "You can say that." Twisting open the bottle, he took a big gulp. "The fuel pump on that stinkin' new tractor crapped out. Fortunately, it's covered under warranty, but now I have to haul the damn thing into the dealer." Taking another swig, he wiped his mouth with the back of his hand. "After I drop it off, I'm going to Glendive and give Lindsey a hand. I'll be gone a couple days. I called the dealer, and it will take that long to fix the pump. They have to order one in."

Making a point to avoid brushing against him, she pulled a plate of chicken from the refrigerator. "Come, follow me out. It's too hot to cook in here. It hit a hundred today."

Wylie grabbed another beer on his way outside. "How was your ride up to the high country?" he asked as she pulled the barbeque from the bear-proof storage cabinet. "Is the trail going to need much repair?"

"It is. It's going to take a couple days with the Caterpillars to get the trail ready to just push the cattle through." With the barbecue started, she turned his way. "While I was up there, a survey plane flew over. When I got back, I phoned Gus. He said it was hired to photograph a sixty-mile stretch of the east slopes of the Rockies. It had to have flown over your place before, and after, he flew over mine. Did you see it?"

Wylie considered what she said and then shook his head. "Nope. I was too busy with the tractor to notice any planes flying over. Why all the concern?"

"Monty Parks from down around Yellowstone said a development company was coming our way, and this just might be them snooping about."

Draining the first bottle, Wyle growled as he opened the second. "The way I feel right now, if a development company offered me a nickel for my place, I just might take it."

Kate blinked. "You don't mean that!" she said. "If you sold off any of your land, that would put an end to my restoring this place."

Wylie held up his hand. "Whoa there," he said. "Don't get so excited. With all the wilderness on this side of the Rockies, chances are, we won't even get a call."

"We better not," Kate resolved.

Early the next morning, Kate dialed the number Gus gave her the afternoon before. "Hi, I'm Kate Clark, and I'd like to talk to Bronson Tagree."

The man on the other end yawned and was slow to answer. "I'm Bronson," he mumbled with a strained voice. "How can I help you?"

"According to Gus, our Clarkston service base operator, he fueled you up after you did a survey of the east slopes of the Rockies in our area. Is that correct?"

The man was slow to respond. "Yes, I surveyed that area yesterday. What about it?"

Kate continued, "I'd like to know who you were working for."

"Who wants to know?" he replied.

"I would. I'm Kate Clark. A ranch owner in the area."

"So?"

"Like I said, I'm a ranch owner, and you flew over my place and my neighbors', and I want to know who you were working for and what they wanted you to do."

"Sorry, lady, I can't divulge that. Confidential information."

Kate pressed on, "Then what can you tell me?"

There was a pause. "Lady—"

"Kate Clark," she interrupted.

"Fine, Kate Clark," he said. "I'm exhausted. I can't tell you a thing. After doing that daylong survey of your area, I had to fly the digital files of everything I took to the customer. They wanted the unedited results immediately."

Kate settled back. *Maybe a different approach would be better.* She smiled. "Wow. That had to make for a long day." She recalled how Monty Parks said the developer was out of Denver. If he acknowledged he had flown to Denver, she would know where to start her search. "Having to fly all the way to Denver after surveying our area had to be quite an ordeal."

"Denver...who said anything about Denver? I flew to LA. Burbank, to be exact. A hell of a lot farther than Denver."

"LA?" she asked. That did not match what Monty had said.

"Yeah, LA," he responded. "Now I have said more than I was supposed to."

"I'm sorry," Kate apologized. "So what kind of survey did you do? Surely you can tell me that."

He hesitated. "I guess so. I did the standard topographical fly over, straight and level, so they can study the individual images and piece them all together to get the big overall view of the area."

"So you did the joined overall view? That must have taken some time."

"No," he replied. "I didn't do that. They didn't want me to edit or view any of the images I took. They're a rather secretive bunch." He yawned, and his voice sounded more relaxed. "And yes, that is normally part of my standard package. But because they didn't give me the authorization to do it or the time and were paying big bucks, I tossed in a little extra. When I saw anything of local interest, I'd do a low-level pass and snapped it. You know, human-interest stuff, the flora and fauna of the area." He chuckled. "That was a freebie."

"Interesting," she said, recalling the plane's low-level pass over the lake. "What kinds of pictures did you get?"

"I got pictures of all sorts of things. Elk herds, bears, bighorn sheep, what appeared to be an old homestead cabin. I got pictures of a guy standing beside a bright shiny tractor and some gal standing in the saddle on a horse waving her hat at me." He chuckled. "And oh yes, I got some pictures of someone swimming in a lake."

Kate gasped. He had taken pictures of her standing in the stir-rups and floating in the lake. She had to find out what all he saw. "You saw all that. What exactly did you see of the person in the lake?"

"What?" he asked.

"The person in the lake. What did you see?" she pressed.

"Oh, that," he said. "Really not much. I was mainly focused on not hitting the trees around the lake. It was a small area, and I didn't want to crash."

"I don't blame you," she said. "So you don't know even if you got any pictures?"

He laughed proudly. "Oh, I got pictures, all right. I can tell you that much. With the high-def cameras I have, I can make out eye color from two hundred feet up."

Kate gulped. She had to know who he sent the pictures to. "So did those pictures go to the customer as well?"

"Yup." He yawned again. "But like I said, those were a freebie. Most customers ignore the flora and fauna. They're only interested in the topographical and forget the rest."

Kate thanked him. She could only hope the customer responded like others before and did not look closely at the pictures of her floating in the lake.

4

Three days later, Kate pushed back from her desk. There had been no calls from the developer. She let out a satisfied sigh. It was after six. Her business day was over. If the developer were to have called, it most likely would have been during business hours. Maybe Wylie had been right. Could it be the developer was not interested in her ranch? She grinned. *How nice that would be.* She glanced toward the yard. It was after six-thirty. Wylie had called an hour before and said he'd gotten a late start leaving his cousin's, but he'd still be home in time for dinner.

The telephone rang. It had to be Wylie calling to tell her of an additional delay. She grabbed the phone without checking the caller ID. "Hi, hon, how's it going?"

"Hello, Kate Clark. Karl Schneider here."

"Whoops," Kate mumbled on hearing the voice of her AJS account representative. Roughly her age, they had met a half-dozen times at cattlemen's conventions, but that was the extent of their acquaintanceship. "Hi, Karl. I was expecting a call from Wylie. He's due back any minute," she said. "What's on your mind to be calling so late?"

"I just finished going over our recent purchases and felt like giving you a call. We never get a chance to visit during business hours." He paused. "You are finished for the day?"

"I am." Leaning back, she put her feet on her desk.

He continued, "You're so busy these days with all the different things you have going. Do you ever break away and ride up and look over the upper part of your ranch where you raise all those great cattle we get, where you have all those beautiful lakes and wilderness?" He sighed. "It must be a gorgeous sight. In fact, do you ever take out time to swim in any of those mountain lakes?"

Kate looked at the phone. *This was hardly the conversation I'd expect from Karl, but...*

"Swimming occasionally. When I rode up there the other day, it was hot. I stopped at my old swimming hole to cool off. It's been years since I swam there, and it brought back a flood of great memories."

"I bet it did," he said. "I envy you living there with all that beautiful country. Do you and Wylie go up there often?" He cleared his throat. "You two are still a couple, aren't you? Or are you two already married?"

Again, she stared at the phone. If she didn't know better, it almost sounded like he was fishing for information. "No, we don't get up there often, and yes, we're still a couple. And no, we aren't married yet. We will, though, one of these days."

"Speaking of one of these days, I'd like to come by and ride up there and see some of those mountain lakes and wilderness areas."

"Anytime. Give me a call, and I'll be glad to show you around." Dust swirled up as Wylie's pickup rumbled by the open kitchen window. Kate jumped to her feet. "Whoops, got to go. Wylie drove up, and I have to close a window before my kitchen fills with dirt. Call me anytime, and we'll go riding."

Dashing across to the kitchen side, she caught the window before the dust blew in. She smiled on seeing Wylie. On his way to the refrigerator, he dropped a large envelope on the table. "Did I catch you in the middle of something?" he asked.

"Not really," she said and motioned toward her office. "I was just on the phone with Karl, my AJS rep."

Reaching for the refrigerator, Wylie stopped. "At this late hour? Did they panic and have to order more beef?"

"No," she replied, "nothing like that. It was just a friendly call."

Pulling back, he looked at her. "A friendly call?" he asked with a raised questioning brow. "Come on now. No customer calls at this hour to just gab."

"Well, he did," Kate said. "He'd like to come by sometime and ride up to the upper range. He'd like to see the wilderness area and the lake where I used to go swimming."

Wylie pulled the bottle down. "How does he know about where you used to go swimming? That was your private retreat."

"I don't know. I must have mentioned it in the past." Taking his arm, she gave him a squeeze. "Forget Karl. How was your time with your cousin?"

"Great. We got a lot accomplished."

She pointed at what he'd dropped on the table. "What's in the envelope?"

"Oh, that," he said. "Those are the aerial pictures Lindsey had taken of that recreational campsite he and I are working on." Setting his beer aside, Wylie leafed through the photographs and pointed out where they worked. He stopped at the last prints. "As a bonus, Lindsey had the guy make a low-level pass over his place. He got these pictures of his house and his kids playing in the yard. Isn't that something? With the high-definition cameras they use these days, the pilot said it is almost possible to count the individual hairs on a person's head from a couple hundred feet up."

"Really!" Kate grabbed the pictures. If that were the case, she had a problem. She'd been floating naked in her mountain lake. Studying the photographs, her cheeks flushed. She could see the seams in the shirt Lindsey's daughter was wearing. Exhaling loudly, she settled back. Her only hope was that the aerial survey customer ignored the flora and fauna extras. If they didn't she didn't know what she would do.

Saturday afternoon, Kate carried two beers out and joined her foreman on the porch. "It's been a long week," she said and settled in across from Gene. She liked the man, and they worked well together. A second-generation foreman, Gene had grown up together with Kate. "Now that you have the trail cleaned up, are the cattle getting through okay?"

Taking a swig, he wiped his mouth. "Yup. Roughly half of them are up so far. The road's still pretty bad, but the trail's okay. I should have the last of them up there Tuesday of next week. Wednesday at the latest." He looked over to where Wylie normally parked. "Where's Wylie? I haven't seen him all day."

"He's gone up to Kalispell to visit a friend. He's due back tomorrow." From inside the house, a telephone rang. "I better get that. It's probably him calling now." Dashing for the door, she grabbed the call before it went into the answering machine. "Kate here."

"Hello, Kate Clark. Karl again."

Surprised to hear Karl's voice, she settled into her office chair. "Are you heading my way to go riding, or are you working overtime?"

"What?" He paused. "Oh, the latter. Management wants customer profile reports on all our major suppliers, and I have to have mine in first thing Monday. What I need to know is, are you attending that weeklong government cow disease prevention, detection, and control certification seminar in Billings this Monday?"

"No," she replied. "I attended that months ago. I went to the first one they had. I'm sure I mentioned it to you at the time."

There was a long pause. She could hear him clicking his pen— *click, click, click, click, click, click.* "You're right. I got it right here." He continued, "Did Wylie go with you?"

"No. He's going to the one in Billings this coming week."

"Good. I can check that off my list." He hesitated. "Will you be going with him?"

"No, I have too much to do here," she said, and the call was over.

It was Sunday evening when Wylie returned. On her way to Gene's to get the lettuce Dolores had picked, Kate called to Wylie. "Welcome home. Pull out the barbecue and get it heating. I'll be right there to start dinner."

Minutes later, with the bowl of lettuce in hand, Kate passed through the vestibule and gave Wylie a kiss. "Nice to see you home."

"Good to be back." He set his empty bottle on the counter and reached into the refrigerator for a second beer.

Kate grabbed his arm. "Not tonight. One's enough. Remember you have to leave early tomorrow to go to Billings?" When her comment drew a blank, she continued, "Don't you remember? I signed you up for that last seminar on cow diseases months ago."

"Oh, no kidding." Wylie sagged back against the kitchen table. "Do I really have to go? After all, you've already attended. Isn't that enough?"

Kate shook her head. "For my ranch, yes. For your ranch, no. Every ranch owner has to show completion of that course. Because you run yours and Patty's cattle together, your attending covers both places. It's the last one they're having before the new regulations take effect. You need a clear head and an early bedtime."

Later, Wylie served himself a second helping of pie when the telephone rang. Kate took the call. "Hi, Patty." She listened, and then her expression changed. "Sorry to hear that. I'm sure she'll be okay. I agree you need to be there. Hold a second. Wylie's going to Billings tomorrow." She put her hand over the mouthpiece. "Patty's mother had a stroke and was admitted to the hospital in Billings. She needs to get to her. Why don't you take her along? She can keep you company while you drive. What do you think?"

"Sure. Tell her I'll be by her place at four to pick her up."

⋯⋯⋯⋯⋯

Up early the next morning, Kate was down in the kitchen and made enough coffee to fill a large thermos and still have plenty left over. She secured the stopper as Wylie entered the room. "I poured you a cup to wake up with." She held open the tote bag she had on the counter. "I put in some Danish, a couple of mugs, napkins, some sugar, and powdered creamer. The thermos is full. That should be enough so you two won't have to stop for breakfast."

Wylie looked in the bag. "Did you include earplugs? That girl can talk the ears off a brass bull."

"Now, be civil. She means well. Take the time to discuss something other than the latest baseball scores, and you might be surprised." She ignored the fact she was pairing them together for the drive to Billings. Patty was her best friend and wouldn't try anything with Wylie without clearing it with her first.

"Whatever," Wylie said. Grabbing the tote, he made for the door. Moments later, his truck disappeared over a nearby rise.

Turning toward the house, a chill swept over her. With Patty going along, she'd be alone with only the hired help and her father as company. Kate shook her head. *Sometimes this place is a little too solitary,*

It was almost noon Monday when Kate returned to the kitchen. The last of the cattle in the winter range were being rounded up and would soon be ready to move. After lunch, she'd ride up and check on the progress. With the bread out, she was starting to make lunch when the telephone rang. "Kate Clark here."

"Hello, Kate Clark, Karl again."

She blinked. This was his second call in two days and the third in less than a week. Generally, his orders came via e-mail or fax. "What's up, Karl? Need more beef?"

"Always need more cattle, except that's not the reason I'm calling. We—I mean, AJS Foods—are having a regional quarterly meeting of our beef marketing division in Spokane tomorrow. The chairman of the board will be there, along with the president of the company and all the regional managers. I've been informed they want their account managers like myself to invite all our largest suppliers to the meeting. Now I know this is short notice, but with you being one of my primary accounts, I'd like it if you can attend."

Kate's jaw dropped. She looked at the work on her desk and then back at the phone. "Short notice! No kidding, Karl! I don't know if I can find the time. My desk is piled high, and I'm moving the last of a major herd right now. Even if I can free up everything, I doubt I can make a plane reservation. The early-morning flight through here to Spokane is always full and impossible to book less than days in advance."

"You don't have to make the reservation. I already have. I have you booked on the early flight. We'll be covering market trends and projected demands. That will be followed by a brief talk from the chairman of the board."

"Jarrett Sinclair," Kate mumbled, unaware she had been thinking aloud.

"That's right. He'll be there along with Morgan Henry, the president of the company. Following lunch, more meetings and then a happy hour when everyone can mingle, and then it's back to the airport in time to catch the last flight home. You won't even need to pack a bag."

She studied the situation. She had to think. Karl had said the account managers like himself had been told to bring in all their major suppliers. She scowled. *Those other suppliers would undoubtedly use that opportunity to increase their share of the AJS purchases. If they did, their gains could be at my expense.* Exhaling forcefully, she knew she had no other choice. *I have to attend.* "I guess if you have the plane reservations, I'll come."

"Great! Glad to hear it," Karl responded. "The ticket will be waiting at your airport. All you have to do is show up. When you get to Spokane, grab the hotel shuttle. I'll have it waiting for you outside baggage claim."

With the call over, she let out a hearty whoop. "We've become a ranch to be reckoned with!" No longer hungry, she refilled her mug as her dad's pickup rolled past the window. With mug in hand, she went to the door.

On his way across the porch, her father smiled. "You look like one of the barn cats just after it caught a mouse." He glowed. "Good news, I hope."

"Fantastic news," she said. Grabbing his arm, she led the way to the kitchen. "I just received a call from Karl, my AJS buyer. AJS is holding a big meeting of all division managers tomorrow in Spokane, and their major cattle suppliers have been invited to attend, me included! Can you believe that? Little ol' us is now an important-enough supplier to that big company to be invited to their regional meeting. They're even paying my plane fare over and back."

Seth questioned, "They're holding the meeting tomorrow. Isn't their invite rather abrupt? A week-in-advance notice, I could understand, but the next day, what gives? They had to know about this further in advance than that."

"I don't know," Kate said. "Maybe I'm a fill-in for someone who couldn't make it." She smiled. "Who cares? All I know is that Karl, my AJS account manager, just got off the phone, and I have been invited to that meeting for the first time. We're now a big-enough supplier to be included in their quarterly meetings."

"I still say it sounds strange, but if that is what they have done, so be it." Seth beamed. "You probably want me out early to drive you to the airport."

She shook her head. "No, I'll need you here to watch over the cattle being moved. Gene is moving the last of the range fed beef to the high country, and I'll need you here in case any questions come up. I'll drive myself to the airport and leave my Suburban at the terminal."

Seth studied what she said and slowly shook his head. "No, take your pickup. That auto-feeder assembly Dan's been working on won't be ready until noon. I was going to bring it out tomorrow, but if I come out early, it won't be ready. You can pick it up when you come back from Spokane."

She shook her head. "No can do. Dan will be closed by the time that late flight gets in."

"That's right," he said. "On second thought, I'll tell Dan that when he finishes, he can put the feeder in the back of your truck by the airport." He laid down the mail he brought out and walked toward the door. "If I'm going to be here all day tomorrow, I need to get back to town. I have some banking I was planning to do tomorrow that I'll have to do today."

Darkness enveloped the ranch by the time Wylie called. "We got here okay," Wylie began. "Made it with time to spare. Patty and her father are with her mother now. She's doing better."

"That's good to hear," Kate replied.

"And you. Anything today?" Wylie asked.

"Yes. AJS Foods is holding a quarterly meeting tomorrow in Spokane, and all their major suppliers, me included, have been invited to attend. Isn't that something? I'm now considered one of their major suppliers." She related how Karl was paying her airfare over and back for the one-day meeting, and she wouldn't even have to pack a bag. Her enthusiasm came across in her voice.

Wylie was quick to respond, "Isn't that awful short notice? I'm sure they knew of that meeting for some time."

Kate shook her head. "I don't know about the short notice. Maybe someone couldn't attend, and I'm the next alternative," she said. "All I know is that I'm being invited for the first time, and that is good enough for me."

"So you're going?" Wylie asked.

"Darn tooting," Kate stated. "Karl said all their major suppliers would be there, and I have no other choice. If I'm not there, those big guys could grab more of the AJS purchases. I have to attend. I'm sure those guys will be pitching the AJS management for all they're worth."

Wylie was quick to reply, "Be sure to put in a good word for all the little ranchers like me and Patty and the Wilsons. We can't afford to lose any sales."

"Don't worry," she assured him. "I'll be speaking for all of us."

Wylie continued, "You'll have to be at your best tomorrow. If they've invited all the major operators, that means all our competition will be there and, like you said, trying to get more of AJS purchases. Whatever you do, you can't let that happen. Those big guys are tough." He hesitated. "Do you think you're up to that?"

Kate paused. Perspiration trickled down her sides. "I've been fretting over that all evening. It was all I could do to keep my dinner down."

"But do you think you can take on the big corporate ranchers face-to-face?"

She swallowed hard. "I don't have much choice, do I? I have to."

About to turn in, Kate took a late call from her father. "What's up, Dad, for you to be calling so late?"

"I just heard from an old friend in the State Planning and Land Use Department. According to him, they, the state, just received a land-use request from the development consulting group of Warren, Causwald, and Jordan. According to him, WCJ wants all the records of the water rights and utility designations for the three properties owned by Wylie, Patty, and you. According to him, these people are serious. They want the information now and are willing to pay whatever it takes."

Kate focused on the call. "Did they say what they planned to do with the property? Do they have a specific use for the three places?"

"No, and I asked," her father replied.

Kate continued, "Did they designate a specific buyer?"

"No. He didn't offer the name of a potential purchaser I know. I asked, and my friend said he only knew the name of the consulting group. He said the consultants wouldn't divulge the customer's name. They said it was confidential until the customer decided if they were going ahead with the project. If they were, the customer would make the announcement themselves."

Kate focused on the phone. "This is a major setback. I need the property grandfather sold off to Wylie's folks and Patty's dad and the Wilsons to restore the Clark family ranch. I need to know what these people planned to do."

"Yes, I know," Seth replied. "I'll call my friend and see what more I can find out."

The next morning, Kate parked her pickup a few feet from their small terminal building. She had that flight to catch to Spokane. With no luggage to fuss with, she grabbed her shoulder bag and headed for the lobby. At the counter, the attendant greeted her. Years before, he had worked a summer on her ranch. "Good morning, Kate Clark, I have been expecting you," he said. "I have your boarding pass, and I have checked you in. The plane will board as soon as it gets here."

Thanking him, she stepped over to the window to watch for her flight. Behind her, a man approached the counter. She couldn't help but hear the attendant explain to the man, "I'm sorry, sir, but there has been a computer hiccup in our reservation department. The morning flight is overbooked. You have been bumped, and I have moved you to a later flight."

"Bumped! A later flight!" the man exclaimed. "I have a standing reservation. I have an important sales presentation I have to make this morning. I have to be there. You can't bump me."

The attendant continued, "Sir, I'm sorry for the mix-up, but the plane is full. We have booked you on the flight that leaves at eleven-fifteen. As compensation, we are rebating you 25 percent of your ticket."

"You've what?" the man said. There was a pause, and then he continued, "Well, for 25 percent, I'll just have to take the later flight." He chuckled. "The meeting wasn't that important anyway. It's the same every Tuesday. Twenty-five percent, you say?"

The attendant agreed.

5

As Karl had promised, the hotel shuttle met her at the airport. Alone in the van, Kate gnawed anxiously on the inside of her cheek. *I have to be on my best today. Many of the big corporate ranches and feedlot operators ship more beef in a few days than I do in a month.* The idea of being compared to the big-time operators caused perspiration to trickle down her sides. Staring out, she mumbled to herself, "Considering the short notice, I'm probably an amusing afterthought. Invite the little blonde rancher and watch her squirm."

"You say something, ma'am?" the driver called out.

Glancing up, she checked his reflection in the driver's mirror. "Aaah, nothing. I was just thinking aloud." She looked past him as they exited the freeway. "How much farther?"

"Not much." He pointed at a hotel complex a few hundred yards ahead.

Kate took a breath as the perspiration continued to flow. She considered what she had to do. *Great-granddad fought hard to build our ranch, and it's my job now. I have to be strong. I have to be tough. I have to win.*

Stopping under the portico, she checked her reflection in the glass front of the building. Dressed in her best Western pants, Western dress shirt, cowhide blazer, and polished boots, she nodded. *I look as much like a successful rancher as I ever will.*

Inside, she had no trouble finding the room AJS had reserved. All she had to do was follow the AJS Foods signs posted on easels along the way. A few feet from the room, she stopped and looked at the door. "This is it," she whispered to herself. She considered what she was about to undertake. *You're as good as they are. You own a big ranch, and you're profitable. You don't have to take a backseat to anyone.* Strengthening her resolve, she stepped for the door. She blinked on seeing the room filled exclusively with men. Most were in business suits, but the more obvious ranch owners and feedlot operators were in twill pants, boots, and Western shirts.

"Katherine Clark," Karl announced loudly as he stepped up to greet her. "Glad you could make it. Did you have a good flight over?"

A bit taken aback by his abrupt greeting, she tossed off the first words that came to mind. "We didn't crash, if that's what you mean." Turning, she looked about quickly. She had to identify her competition, and she had to do it fast. Across the front of the room was a platform a couple of feet high. Atop the platform, two tables with AJS Foods banners as skirting flanked a lighted lectern. Six men in suits stood behind the tables. *Those have to be AJS managers*, she concluded and moved on.

Karl laughed. "Didn't crash. That's a good one. I'll have to remember to use it sometime." He motioned for her to follow. "Come, we'll get coffee."

As Karl led the way, Kate surveyed the men in the room. Picking up on one, her pulse quickened. *Oh my god, that's…yes, it has to be. That's Drogan Garrick. The feedlot giant of giants from Nebraska. Geez, is he here?* While she had never met the man, she was sure it was him from the pictures she'd seen. *What's he doing here?* She didn't have to think long, for she knew the answer. *He's out to get more business.* As Kate exhaled, the perspiration flowed. *Wow. I'll have to watch out for him.* Turning, she continued her search. Stopping, she focused hard. *Son of a bitch, is he here too?* She tried to think. *That's…Vernon… um, what's his name?* She searched her memory and came up with an answer. Her palms were damp. *Yes. Vernon Merlock, the biggest rancher in New Mexico. He's no pushover. He'll be after all the sales he can get as well.* He too she'd never met, but she could recognize him from trade publications. Turning, she looked past the men in suits with dress shirts and ties. *They're most likely AJS management.* She focused on another. *Yes. That has to be Spencer Nygard, the big-time operator from Wyoming.* Swallowing, she gulped in a breath. *Damn! Have they left anyone out? Karl said they were going to invite their biggest suppliers, and they've really done that.* She looked about. *Dang. They're all here to get more business. I'm going to have to be on my very best. I have to be strong.*

Karl stopped at the coffee table.

"Coffee, miss?" asked a man in waiter's whites behind the table.

"Yes, black," Kate said and continued her survey.

Karl directed her to a man in boots and a fringed cowhide jacket. "Kate, I'd like you to meet Howard Huxford."

A-ha, yes. She smiled. *One of my competition. He's not one of the giants, but all the same, he'll be out to make more sales.*

Howard's eyes sparkled. The lines that radiated from the corners of his eyes cut deep creases in his sunbaked face.

"Kate," Karl continued, "Howard used to be a rancher, but now he manages our Eastern Oregon processing plant."

"Pleased to…meet you," she said, reaching for his hand. She smiled when she realized her original assessment had been wrong. Howard was not one of her competition; he was a packing plant manager.

Howard shook her hand. "I'd like to thank you. Your records are the best I've seen. I wish all the cattle they bought came from you."

"I appreciate your support," Kate said. "But tell that to Karl. I need him to buy more beef."

Karl stepped to a front-row table a few feet from the platform. "We're here," he announced. "This is our table."

Kate looked about. "It is?" she asked and anxiously studied the location. Seated there, all the ranchers and feedlot operators out to get more sales would be behind her. *Not good.* Without turning, she could already feel them staring. *This isn't right. They should be in the front where I can keep track of them.* She turned to Karl. "Can't we move back a few rows? This is a bit close for my comfort."

Karl shook his head. "No. This is the table assigned to us."

"Oh," she said and reluctantly settled in.

The morning meeting went smoothly. Five of the men on the platform took turns reporting on their individual divisions. They spoke about the measures they were taking to assure the public, in spite of the mad cow publicity, that beef was safe to eat. When the fifth man concluded, he deferred to the president, Morgan Henry. From behind a door off to the left came the muted sounds of people whispering and dishes clinking as the hotel staff prepared to serve lunch.

Kate swung her gaze past Henry, who was taking a moment to thank each of the presenters, and stopped when Jarrett Sinclair stepped through a side door. She gasped softly and worked to catch her breath. Partially concealed in the shadows, he was dressed in a dark charcoal-gray suit that was a shade lighter than his glistening black hair. His shoulders were huge and his gaze intense. When their eyes momentarily met, her pulse quickened. *Oh my god, you're beautiful.*

Henry looked off to the side. "Good, you made it," he said when Sinclair moved out of the shadows. "I was afraid you might have gotten tied up and couldn't get here." He turned his attention to those in attendance. "Lady and gentlemen, it's with great pleasure I turn these proceedings over to the man whose forward thinking and tremendous energy have lifted this company from the throes of financial ruin to what it is today. We all know him, so let's give a big AJS welcome to our boss, Jarrett Sinclair."

Everyone stood, and Kate followed as applause filled the room. That suited her as she really felt conspicuous now after hearing Henry address those in attendance as lady, singular, and gentlemen, plural. Sinclair glided effortlessly up on the platform. Skirting around in front of the tables, he grabbed the microphone from the flexible stand. "Thank you, thank you, very much." Smiling, he motioned for everyone to be seated. That satisfied her.

Seated, Kate was forced to lean back to look up at Sinclair. She whistled softly to herself. The pictures in the magazine had not done him justice. He was taller that she expected. His suit coat was open, and his muscular chest made ridges under his shirt. She swallowed hard. Patty was right. *You are a hunk.*

Sinclair turned and thanked Henry. As expected, everyone applauded. When the applause abated, he stepped to the edge of the platform. "Let me begin by thanking all the ranchers and feedlot owners who were kind enough to come to our meeting today. We're most indebted to—"

Henry leaned across the table and tapped Sinclair.

"Yes?" Sinclair scoffed.

Morgan apologized. "Jarrett, you have to realize, in spite of our best efforts, only one rancher showed up."

"What!" Sinclair snapped back. Turning, he focused on Morgan. "I told you to get all our major suppliers here, and only one rancher showed up? Don't those people appreciate our business?"

Kate blinked. It took a moment for his remark to sink in, and then she froze. *What? I'm the only rancher here? No way. That's impossible. Where's everyone else?* Twisting slightly, she tried to scan the men in the room. *They can't all be AJS employees, can they?*

Still standing, Henry leaned farther across the table. "Jarrett, the invitation was on very short notice and conflicted with the new regulation certification seminars being given right now. Most of the big ranch owners and feedlot operators are off attending those seminars. Only one of our representatives was able to get a rancher to attend. A two-day notice wasn't enough."

Sinclair turned and scanned the audience. "Who is this person? Point him out to me."

Kate swallowed.

Henry pointed her way. "It's not a him but a her. Ms. Clark is seated right there."

She flinched.

Sinclair stared down at her and then turned back to Henry. "If those certification seminars are so important, why isn't she at one?"

Morgan smiled. "She didn't wait until the last minute to be certified. She's one of our best suppliers."

"Oh," Sinclair replied. Smiling, he turned her way.

When their eyes met, her body froze. His gaze was electric. She tried to catch her breath but couldn't. His smile was like nothing she had experienced looking at his picture. The hot flash she felt looking at his picture exploded within her. She tried to swallow but couldn't. *Oh god, what now?*

Sinclair made with a warm smile. "Ms. Clark, thank you for coming. I'm glad you could make it. I hope you've found the discussions so far interesting." That said, he turned to address those in attendance.

Kate tried to thank him, but the words wouldn't come out. *Wow, you're something else.* Getting a breath, she gritted her teeth and looked down at the table. *Get a grip. You've got a man, and we're about to be married.* Exhaling slowly, she settled back. *That's better,* she concluded as she regained her composure.

When Sinclair finished, the food was served. Kate glanced at Sinclair as he ate with Henry and the presenters on the platform. Not once did she catch him looking her way. At the end of the meal, he thanked everyone and left.

Relieved, she settled back. She wouldn't have to do battle with the giants in the industry. When the last speaker concluded, Henry stepped to the microphone. "Ms. Clark and gentlemen, I apologize. The afternoon session has run a little long. If you'll bear with us, the bar is being wheeled in and will be open momentarily."

Everyone sounded their approval. Standing, Kate checked the time, and the happy hour was going to impinge on her getting to the airport the requisite hour and a half early. She turned to Karl. "As much as I'd like to stay and visit, I can't. I have a plane to catch."

Karl glanced at his watch. "There's no rush. It's only a commuter flight. The hotel shuttle will get you there in plenty of time."

"I hope so. I don't want to miss my flight."

Between visits with those in attendance, she caught herself looking for Sinclair. *The least I would have liked to have done was shake your hand.* Momentarily alone, she stretched to her full height and looked about when from behind her came his voice.

"Ms. Clark," Sinclair said.

Warmed by the sound, she turned. "Mr. Sinclair," she said and extended a hand in greeting. "Thank you for inviting me."

"Thank you for coming. Your presence here was appreciated." Smiling, he took a step back. "I apologize I'm not able to visit longer. There are some people I have to see before they leave." He shook her hand again. "Have a nice flight home, and again, thank you for coming."

"Ah…um, yes." The rest of what she wanted to say died in her throat as she watched him leave. He was gone. *So much for meeting the owner of my biggest customer.*

Morgan Henry stepped up. "I see you had a chance to meet my boss. We appreciate that at least one of our major suppliers was able to make it to our meeting. I told Jarrett most of the big ranchers would be attending that last seminar and very few would be able to attend."

Kate agreed. Morgan was right. The owners of the big ranches collectively campaigned hard to get the new regulations rescinded and had boycotted the earlier certification seminars. As they said, more government intervention they did not need.

"We're most impressed with the quality of your range-fed beef. It brings a premium price. You can look forward to a banner year."

She checked the time. "Excuse me, Mr. Henry. I've enjoyed being here, but I have a plane to catch. I really must go."

Henry motioned for Karl. "Ms. Clark needs to get to the airport."

Karl led her to the van, and in no time, she was on her way. Being alone in the van gave her time to reflect. Turning, she looked back at the hotel. *I really need to get out more often, at least go to more cattlemen's conventions. Horse shows are not enough*, she told herself. *Then maybe I'll be able recognize my competition.*

In line at security, she pulled off her boots and put them along with her blazer and portfolio into the tubs. *As soon as I clear security, I'll have fifteen minutes to make my flight.*

The man ahead of her stepped into the detector shroud. The light flashed. He stepped back. She watched as he dug into his pocket and pulled out a handful of coins. "No kidding," she grumbled. The man stepped into the metal detector, and again, the light flashed. "Damn." She snorted. She craned around and tried to see past security. *My flight is about to board, and I'm stuck behind some idiot who can't read signs.* The man stepped back. The attendant pointed at a key fob hanging from his pocket and the silver clasp around the man's tie. Kate snarled. *At this rate, I'll miss my flight.*

This time, he passed. "Finally," she grunted and stepped into the detector tunnel. The light flashed. "Miss, you'll have to go back. Empty your pockets. Take out everything that's metal."

"What!" Kate questioned and looked down. "My pockets are empty."

The woman pointed at her waist. "Your belt buckle. Take off your belt."

She jerked off her belt and tossed it into a tub. She passed. With her belongings in hand, she dashed for the gate. Feet from the podium, she slid to a stop when the word DEPARTED leaped out at her. "What do you mean my flight's left?" she said to the attendant and pointed at the announcement board. "It's not supposed to leave for another ten minutes."

The person looked up. "A weather front moved into Eastern Montana that caused it to leave early." He checked his computer. "Are you Ms. Clack?"

"Yes," she said.

"We tried to call the number you left, and all we received was voice mail."

Kate pulled out her phone, and it was off. As requested at the door to the meeting, she had clicked it off when she entered. She sagged back on her heels. "How am I supposed to get home? You're the only airline that even comes close to my town."

"No problem. We have you confirmed on our first flight out tomorrow morning."

She blinked. "Tomorrow morning! Are you kidding? I have no luggage. What am I supposed to do tonight?"

He smiled. "Enjoy Spokane. There are a number of motels not far from here. I'm sure if you check, one will have a room, and we'll pick up the cost."

"Really!" Stomping her foot, she pondered what to do next. *I could rent a car. If I drive straight through, I'd get home about the same time as if I took the early flight. Not good.*

Turning, she looked toward the concourse. She tried to think. People were scurrying by. About to look away, she stopped. A person she recognized was weaving his way through the crowd and appeared oblivious to her being there. About to call his name, Sinclair glanced her way. Seeing her, he diverted.

"Well, hi there," he said with a broad smile. His eyes sparkled as he approached. Dressed in jeans, a polo shirt, and jodhpur boots, he looked past her toward the gate. "When does your flight leave? Soon, I presume."

She shook her head and pointed at the announcement board. "It's already gone. Now I'm stuck here with no luggage or a place to stay tonight."

"Really?" he said. He studied the board. "Maybe I can help. I'm on my way to Minneapolis in the company jet. I can drop you in your town if you'd like."

Kate's expression brightened. "Yes, thank you, Mr. Sinclair. I'd like that very much. If it wouldn't be out of your way, I'd appreciate the ride." Stepping back, she assessed him quickly. Even in her cowboy boots, she had to look up. When their eyes meet, she froze. A surge of excitement shot up within her. There was warmth in his expression she did not expect.

"My names is Jarrett, and please call me that," he said. "And your name is Katherine, right?"

She smiled. "Correct, though I prefer Kate."

"Then Kate it shall be." He pointed down the concourse. "My plane is parked down the way. Shall we go?" He led the way and, after a few hundred yards, stopped. "We're here."

She looked where he pointed and blinked. The plane parked at the gate was massive. The plane she'd flown over in might even have fit under the wing. "My god, what is it?"

"A Boeing 757." Taking her arm, he guided her down the tunnel. In the plane, he handed her off to the attendant. "Sheryl, this is Ms. Clark. Please make her comfortable." That said, he turned and disappeared out the door.

"Aren't you…coming along?" Kate's voice trailed off. Confused, she looked toward the exit and then back at the attendant. "Isn't he coming with us?"

"Yes, Ms. Clark, he is," the woman said. "When he flies, he likes to make sure everything is right with the plane before we take off." As she spoke, the woman directed her toward one of a many oversized seats. Upholstered in light-gray leather, they were large and appeared comfortably soft. Farther back was a Plexiglas partition etched with scenes of sailboats and speedboats crashing through waves. Visible through the partition was a conference table with chairs all around. Beyond that was a paneled wall with a door to the rear of the plane.

"What's back there?" Kate asked.

"Past the partition is a conference room. Beyond that is his stateroom and other sleeping accommodations. You're welcome to go back and take a look."

Kate shook her head. "No, that's okay. I was just curious."

The attendant asked, "Can I get you something to drink?"

"Coffee, black, will be fine." Alone, she settled in and ran her hands over the seat. *Wow. I could get used to flying around in this.*

Sheryl returned with a china cup and saucer on a silver tray. "Your coffee, miss."

Minutes later, Jarrett returned and came her way. "Unbuckle and follow me," he said and pointed toward the front of the plane. Passing through the galley, they stopped in the crew-section aft of the cockpit. To one side, curtains were pulled back, exposing an upper and lower bunk; opposite were two pairs of seats. "This is Janine, our other attendant, and that's Warren, my second pilot. On trips when

I'm busy in the back, he flies the plane. When Warren isn't helping me fly, he's my throttleman when I race my boat." He stopped at the cockpit door. "Normally, I let women go first, but it gets a little crowded up front, so I'll lead the way, and you follow."

Kate followed with Warren close behind. "Allow me, Ms. Clark," he said as he reached around and swung down the jump seat. He pulled down a small earphone and secured the band over her head. "You'll be able to hear the tower communications with that."

Buckled up, she looked at Jarrett seated forward and to her left. She tapped his arm. "Are you driving this thing?"

"Oh yeah," he said. "I've been flying these for years." With the checklist complete, he looked to the man with silver hair to his right. "Starting number one." From behind came the whine of one of the engines as it came up to speed. "Starting number two." He repeated the process. With the second engine running, the voice of the tower controller crackled in her earphone. They were cleared to go. Jarrett guided the plane toward the runway. The controller's voice crackled again. They were cleared for takeoff. Behind her, the engine noise grew as he swung the plane onto the long paved strip.

Kate smiled. She was going home.

6

A t her town's airport, Warren extended the built-in retractable boarding stairs housed beneath the main deck floor to the ground. She stopped in the plane's doorway and looked at her pickup parked next to their terminal building a hundred plus yards away. She shook her head. He didn't need to park that far from the building; after all, he was only going to be there long enough for her to thank him before he continued on to Minneapolis. Stepping back from the door, her expression brightened when Jarrett exited the cockpit. "I'd like to thank you. This was an unexpected conclusion to what I anticipated was going to be a very dull evening in some motel."

"My pleasure. I enjoyed having you aboard. We'll have to do this again sometime." Stopping in the plane's doorway, he looked about. "This is beautiful country."

She beamed. "Some of the best in the West."

"So I've heard." He looked at her. "If it isn't too much trouble, I'd like to see where we get all those great cattle." Stepping into the doorway, he leaned out and scanned about. "Is your place close by?"

"Ah…no," she said. "It's about an hour from here."

Jarrett looked at her. "If you have the time, that sounds okay to me. Can we go there?"

"Um," she mumbled. She hadn't planned on a trip out to her ranch. She looked at him. He was expecting an answer. "Well, I guess I can drive you out there. It's a good ways out of town. It'll be late by the time I can get you back here. It might make you late getting to Minneapolis."

"I'll get there in plenty of time," he said. "If you have the time, I'd really like to see your ranch. I don't know when I might be back through here again."

"Oh," she said and pointed at her dust-covered truck. "If you don't mind, my pickup is over there. If I had expected a guest, I'd have brought in my Suburban."

He looked where she pointed. "Your pickup looks fine to me. I've ridden in worse."

At the truck, she grabbed a rag and dispatched the ever-present dust from the passenger seat. "Go on. Climb in." Circling around the back, she muttered, "Rats," when she saw the truck box was empty.

"Is there something wrong?" he asked when she slid in behind the wheel.

"Sort of. The local implement dealer was supposed to put a piece of equipment he'd been repairing in the back while I was gone. It's not there, so Dad will have to bring it out tomorrow." She looked at him. "May as well settle back. My ranch is a good ways from here."

Driving the limit of what the two-lane county road would take, she made the unpaved drive leading into the ranch in forty minutes. With the paved part behind them, they passed the rusty mailbox on the weathered wood post. They rumbled over the cattle barrier and under the timber arch emblazoned with the ranch's brand. Behind them, two spirals of dust curled up as she raced across her land. "Not far now," she said.

Sliding forward, Jarrett looked about with interest. Not seeing any buildings, he turned her way. "How far is not far?"

She snickered. "Ten miles. It goes without saying I don't walk out to get the mail in the afternoon. In fact, the postman doesn't even drop it off there anymore. Dad brings it out from town."

One grassy knoll bled into the next as they raced across the expansive plains. Turning slightly, she glanced at Sinclair. *My god, you're handsome.* He was smiling and appeared interested in what was outside her truck. When he picked up on her looking his way, he turned and caught her eye. A spark of excitement welled up within her. Her pulse quickened. She felt warm all over. *Oh my, what now?* Looking away, she shook her head. This was not what she had expected. Exhaling slowly, she stared out the window. *Get a grip. He's not interested in you. He only wants to see where I raise the cattle.*

Cresting a rise, a collection of buildings resembling a small town emerged. "We're here," she announced. "This is where I live." Slowing, she parked behind her house.

"Wow," Jarrett exclaimed. Sliding out, he turned about to take it all in. "This is some place," he said as he slowly ascended the three steps to the porch. At the top, he stopped. Nodding admiringly, he pointed at the house. "The covered wraparound porch, the open balconies above, the columns, the symmetry of the windows to the door—it's so antebellum in design. It's definitely a page out of the Old South." Studying the all-white structure, he gazed knowingly as he turned and looked her way. Spreading his arms wide, he straightened up and began to recite slowly in deep oratorical tones. "There was a land of cavaliers and cotton fields called the Old South. Here in this pretty world, gallantry took its last bow. Here was the last ever to be seen of knights and their ladies fair, of master and of slave. Look for it only in books, for it is no more than a dream remembered, a civilization—gone with the wind." He grinned. "David O. Selznick. The opening of the movie *Gone with the Wind*, 1939." He stopped. "I'm a bit of a film buff." He sagged back on his heels. "Aw, the Old South, a great chivalric era of knights on gleaming white steads, grand manors, and courtly love. Quite the time." He exhaled slowly. "I was born a century and a half too late."

She watched as he stepped to the porch rail. *Gleaming white steads.* She sighed. What immediately came to mind was a shiny silver 757.

"How much of this land is yours?" he asked, looking about.

"All of what you can see and a lot more," she said proudly. "That ridge you're looking at is three miles from here. My south property line is ten miles south of that."

"Did you build all this?" he asked as he pointed at the white fenced corrals, the houses, barn, and the mixture of work buildings that made up the ranch compound.

Kate shook her head. "No. Great-Granddad built the barn, the bunkhouse, the foreman's house, and this great home. This was his signature piece of having amassed the largest ranch in the state." She pointed toward the newer building with the large domed roof. "I built the arena and stables and the white-painted horse corrals." Turning, she led the way through the vestibule and stopped in the kitchen. "All the counters and cabinets, I had redone a couple years back. I put in all new appliances then as well. The rest is pretty much as Great-Granddad built it. The little room over there that is now my office used to be the pantry." She pointed at the double-wide refrigerator. "There's beer and wine in there. Help yourself. There are glasses in the cupboard beside it. I'd serve you except I'm about to wilt. I have to change." She pointed toward the front of the house. "I'll be down in a minute."

Making her way around the table, she glanced at the mail her dad brought out from town. Neatly sorted, the magazine atop the third stack was *Today's Fashion*, a subscription her two sisters-in-law gave her every Christmas. It was their not-so-subtle hint she needed to dress and act more like a woman. *I'd like to see them rope a calf and run a ranch in a dress.*

Upstairs, she stared down toward the floor below. Her pulse quickened. About to let her mind run, she pulled back. *Forget it. You have a man.* She settled back. *This is only a business meeting. So he's handsome. So is Wylie.* Shaking her head, she stared off into nowhere. *You're not some giddy teenager. You're a woman.* Taking a breath, she thought, *You really need to get out more often.*

While hot enough for shorts and a tank top, she chose the more conservative jeans and a sleeveless blouse and headed for the floor below. At the base of the stairs, she stopped. He was in the living room examining a framed photograph and did not immediately look her way. When he did, he pointed at a picture. "Who are these people?"

"That is my great-grandfather Nathaniel and great-grandmother's wedding picture," she said. "He was quite the cattle baron. Unfortunately, shortly after he built this house, he was killed by a bull." Moving along, she pointed to an even older photograph. "Those were his parents. I think that picture was taken by the first photographer in the area in the late 1800s." She moved on to a picture of a small one-story house. "That was the house they lived in before Great-Granddad built this. The original ranch house was a log cabin. We don't have a picture of that."

Jarrett stopped and stared at the large oil painting of a man on a bucking horse that hung over the fireplace. The horse was off the ground and twisted in the air. Rays of sunlight streaked through the clouds of dust. The man had one hand on the reins, and with the other, he was slapping the flank of the tawny animal with his hat. "Where did you get that painting? It is fantastic. That's one of the most magnificent Western paintings I've ever seen."

"That's a painting of my father breaking a stallion when he was a young man. It was done by his father."

Jarrett blinked. "Your grandfather did that?" She nodded. "He was an incredible artist."

She rolled her eyes. "An artist maybe, a cattlemen no. Unfortunately, he sold off much of our inheritance to support his art hobby."

Jarrett pointed at a large trophy case. "Who won all those awards?"

She beamed. "The trophies on the top two shelves are all the first places I won with Ramrod. He's my cutting horse. We took first place in every competition that year. That more than doubled his stud fees. The trophies on the lower shelves, I won barrel racing and exhibition riding back when I was in high school and college." She motioned for him to follow. "Come on, let me show you my ranch." She grinned. "Well, not all of it as that would take a few days."

In the vestibule, she pulled on her boots and led the way to her pickup. Driving toward the barn, she pointed at the winter pasture. "The last of the range-fed beef you wanted to see have been moved. They were going to do it today, and it appears they have. There are calving sheds up past the barn. The stock there is young and not ready to market." She pointed to the south. "I have a couple of large feedlot operations an hour or so from here. If you want, we can drive over there, but it'll make you late getting back to your plane."

"Nah, the calving shed will be fine. I'll leave the feedlots for next time."

Next time? What next time? Kate questioned. Unable to come up with an answer, she stopped outside the barn. "This is the closest. This'll only take a minute. I'll show you my horse, and then we'll see what cattle we can find. Ramrod and I work stock together."

Ramrod whinnied and leaned out through the open top of the Dutch door to his stall.

Jarrett stopped when he saw the horse. "Wow! He's one beautiful animal."

"That, he is. When he gets on a cow or steer, he won't let up until it's where I want it to go."

Jarrett's stomach growled. "It's me," he said. "It's been a while since I've eaten."

"Likewise," Kate agreed. "With all the men at my table asking questions, I wasn't able to eat much."

"Same with me. Morgan and the rest wanted to talk."

She pointed toward her house. "I'm sure I can find a couple of steaks we can grill and potatoes I can microwave. There's lettuce and tomatoes to make a salad, and I think there's even apple pie for dessert."

"Sounds like a plan. Show me the barbecue. Steaks, I can do."

Both ate quickly. Only after they finished with the salad and were halfway through the steak did they begin to slow down. He chuckled. "I apologize. It must look like I haven't eaten in a month. I missed breakfast and was too busy talking at lunchtime."

"Me too," she agreed. She looked at him. His rich black hair brushed his collar and framed his face. Rugged and tanned, his skin was smooth and his complexion flawless. With a squared-off chiseled jaw line and pronounced cheekbones, his features were classically masculine. The warm feeling once again welled up within her.

Finished, Jarrett wiped his mouth and leaned back. "That was fantastic. One of the best meals I've ever had." He pointed at his plate. "The beef was grown right here on the ranch?" he asked.

"That, it was. So was the lettuce, tomatoes, and apples for the pie." She looked out, and the sun had already begun making long shadows across the yard. "After I clear the table, I can show you some of the cattle you want to see."

"Allow me," he said, getting to his feet. Picking up plates, he started toward the door. "Let me help you clean up. When we get inside, I'd sure like a tour of your house. As you can tell, I'm a big admirer of antebellum architecture, and this is a magnificent example."

"Ah…," she hesitated. *Showing you cattle is one thing. Making dinner and then showing you the inside of my house, well, that's something else.* She looked at her house and then at him. Short of an outright refusal, there was no polite way she could say no. Nodding, she hesitantly offered, "I guess so."

7

With the dishwasher loaded, he looked toward the front of the house. "Now, that tour."

She hesitated and looked where he pointed. *What should I do?* Her stomach knotted. *Wylie's not here.* She tried to think. She looked at him and then quickly away. *Forget it,* she concluded. *This is just a brief diversion before looking at cattle.* Leading the way, she stopped at the first room beyond the kitchen. "This is the dining room. You'll have to pardon the dust. We don't use this room much. Meals, formal or otherwise, are usually served in the kitchen." She sighed. "When Mom had cancer, we converted this into a makeshift hospital room. She died in this room."

After the dining room, she directed him past the living room to two tall doors near the entrance. She stepped aside. "This was Great-Grandfather's office." Floor-to-ceiling bookshelves lined two walls. A massive desk dominated the center of the room. A cowhide-covered sofa and two very masculine matching chairs were off to the side. "I tried using this room, but it was too dark and too far from the kitchen. After I had the kitchen redone, we weren't using the pantry, so I converted that into my office." Pausing at the base of the grand staircase, she looked toward the floor above. She hadn't planned on a bedroom tour. *But if this is what he wants, so be it.* "You'll have to pardon the way it looks upstairs," she said as she reached for the first step. "I wasn't planning on company."

At the top, she turned him away from the direction of her bed-room and toward the front of the house. She stopped at the room farthest from hers. "This is the guest suite. It has its own bath and access to the wraparound porch. When Great-Grandfather built this place, getting here was quite an ordeal, and guests needed someplace to stay." Stepping aside, she allowed him to check the room. As in the office below, the bedstead and nightstands were hand-carved, mas-sive, and masculine.

Moving back, she pointed at the next rooms. "These were our rooms. This was where my brothers and I grew up." Swinging open the first door they came to, she pointed inside. Smiling proudly, she stepped aside. Two walls were covered with ribbons. "This was my room," she said as he stepped in and looked around. "Those are ribbons I've won with my horses. I stayed here until Mom died. After that, Dad moved into town, and I moved into the master suite." Stepping back, she directed his attention to the doors across the hall. "Those rooms belonged to my brothers. They lived here until they went to college."

Jarrett pointed down the hall. "What's down there?"

"The next door is the nursery, which mom used as a sewing room, and the double doors beyond that lead to the master suite."

He took a step in that direction. Grabbing his shirt, she pulled him back. "Let's not go there," she said. "That's my room, and it's not made up." While the room was made up, there was no way she was going to take him close to her bedroom. Associate or not, being alone with him created enough anxiety without showing him where she slept.

"Hey, no problem." He looked up and down the hall with its arched ceiling, grand chandeliers, and wainscoting. "This is quite a house. A true classic." He pointed at another door across from the nursery. "Where does that door go?"

"That goes to the attic," she replied.

"Really? What's up there?" he asked.

She shrugged. "Nothing much. Mostly stuff we've accumulated over the years. Granddad Jacob did his painting up there."

Moving back, Jarrett ducked down and looked out a window in her old bedroom. "If we hurry, we can catch the sun from the porch as it sets behind those mountains." Turning, he was down the stairs.

"Um," she mumbled. *Looking at the sunset will get us further from checking out the cattle you want to see.* She threw up her hands. *Whatever you say. You're my biggest customer.*

In the kitchen, he had the wine bottle from dinner and was busy refilling their glasses. "I saw a bench swing out on the porch. It looks like a great place to watch the sunset." With glasses in hand, he nudged her along. Outside, he led the way to a swing. Close to eight feet in length, it would easily handle two people. "Go on. Sit down. Let's enjoy the view."

With Kate seated at one end, Jarrett settled in at the other and pointed toward the west. "Now, that's a sight, those mountains. Those rugged peaks bathed in all those colors and the sun's rays piercing through the clouds. That's absolutely magnificent. People in the cities would pay big money to look at something like that. I imagine you never get tired of the view." Giving the swing a push, he looked her way. "Tell me, do you own this ranch or manage it for the family?"

She hesitated. He was settled in and did not appear anxious to go look at cattle. *I guess if this is what you want to talk about, so be it.* "Aside from the 5 percent I still have to buy from Dad, this place is all mine."

"And your brothers? You said you had two brothers."

"Both of them are younger. In the past, the oldest male child would inherit the ranch even if he had older sisters. I was the first to break that tradition."

"Interesting. How did you accomplish that? Did your parents have a change of mind?"

She shook her head. "No, nothing like that. Everyone in the family was dead set to stay with tradition, and then I came along." She grinned. Even in the dim light streaming from the kitchen, it was obvious she was proud. "When I was growing up, I hung on my dad's every word. I was his biggest fan, and still am. To me, he is the greatest cowboy who has ever lived." She glowed. "Anyway, he went out of his way to teach me everything he knew about ranching, cattle, and horses. I was his star pupil." She settled back. "When my brothers were growing up, Dad treated them as if they should have known how to be good cattlemen because, after all, they were Clarks, and Clark men were always good ranchers. As expected, without training, they weren't, and he came down on them hard. He wouldn't teach them a thing. They turned against him and have been at odds with him ever since. Neither wants anything to do with Dad and the ranch and gladly sold their interests to me."

Jarrett studied what she said. "Sounds to me like your dad wanted you to inherit the ranch."

"Maybe so."

"And where are your brothers now?" he asked.

She looked toward the west. "The oldest is a dentist in Oregon, and the youngest is a football coach at a high school in Washington."

Turning slightly, he focused on her. "And what will you do with this place once it's all yours?"

Smiling, she was quick to answer. "I'll give it to my kids when I have some. This is a family ranch, and I plan to pass it down to the next generation."

"I take it you and this Wylie fellow are planning on starting a family?"

"Well…yes," she hesitated. He just referred to Wylie by name. *How is that possible?* She couldn't recall mentioning the name of the man who lived with her. *I must have, though, for how else could he have known his name?* "How do you know about Wylie?"

"I make a point to know the names of my suppliers," he replied.

"Oh," she said. She studied him. "We'll start a family as soon as we marry." Squirming a bit, she adjusted her position and swallowed hard. She had talked too much. "You've heard my story, so what about you? How did you happen to start AJS Foods? Were you in the meatpacking business?"

"No," he said. "They were a tenant in one of my properties, and I acquired them in a bankruptcy proceeding. I put in a new sales force and stressed customer service. As the saying goes, the rest is history. AJS Foods is now a multibillion-dollar company."

With curiosity piqued, she focused on him. "If you weren't in the meatpacking business, what business were you in?"

His expression brightened. "My father was in the construction business. He built single-family housing developments."

"Oh," she said. "Then you did construction work with your father while growing up?"

He chuckled and shook his head. "No, I'm no carpenter. If anything, I'm what you might call spoiled. When my parents married, Mother wasn't able to conceive, so they adopted a boy. Carter was his name. When he was seventeen, either by accident or miracle, Mom got pregnant, and I came along. By then, my folks were forty. The business was booming, and they didn't have time to fuss with a little one. I was brought up by nannies and, later, Dad's trusted assistant. During my teenage years, in lieu of love, they smothered me with money. They paid for my college and flying lessons and my hobbies of racing boats both power and sail." Pride showed in his expression. "I'm not complaining. I've had a great life. My folks are fantastic, and I love them dearly."

Straightening up, she focused on him. "If you were off playing around, how did you get involved with your dad's company?"

Sitting up, Jarrett's expression turned serious. "One day, nine years ago, I received a call from Mom. Dad had had a heart attack. I flew home. Mom was beside herself. Their company was broke. They had over a hundred unsold homes. They were bankrupt. Mom asked if I could do something, and I told her I'd try. I went into their company, and the creditors were minutes away from pulling the plug. I met with the creditors and asked them to give me six months to turn the company around. They gave me three and as much as laughed at me and told me it couldn't be done." Taking a breath, he continued, "I began by convincing the newspapers to give me more credit. I ran full-page ads and said if you had a job and good credit and were renting an apartment, give me your next month's rent, and with that, you can buy a house. Right then, banks and mortgage companies weren't parting with a dime. I decided if the banks wouldn't lend money, I would. In less than twenty-four hours, I had to have people take numbers. I sold all 122 homes in less than two weeks."

Her brow furrowed. "I'm confused. If you were bankrupt, what good was it to sell the houses if you did the financing?"

He laughed. "Ah, the method to my madness. Being a private lender, I could charge higher interest rates. Insurance companies and retirement funds paid cash for the high-interest real estate contracts as fast as I could write them. Flush with cash, I paid off the creditors and never looked back."

Twisting about, she had to ask, "And your brother and your dad?"

Exhaling, he continued. "Carter passed away a few years ago. He never got over the near-bankruptcy experience. And Dad, he's retired. He and Mom are in the South Pacific. Last I heard, they were island hopping. He's going on eighty-one and is taking up SCUBA diving."

Taking a breath, Kate studied him slowly. She had to ask, "Has there ever been a Mrs. Sinclair?"

Jarrett shook his head. "Other than Mother, no. Rachel and I were close a number of years back. That ended amicably four years ago. Prior to that, she moved into my house. She liked my Beverly Hills address and has stayed." When he saw Kate's questioning look, he shook his head. "It's not what it sounds like. I have a very big house. She has her bedroom and office in the wing at the far end of the building, and the rest is mine. I'm on the road a lot. She probably spends more nights there in a couple months than I do in a year. She looks after the place while I'm gone." Getting up, he went toward the kitchen. "She used to be a model. I'll be right back."

Moments later, he returned with the copy of *Today's Fashion* folded open. "I saw this on the table. This is one of her layouts, and that's Rachel right there." Settled in, he pointed at the lead picture in an article. "She doesn't normally work in front of the camera anymore, but her model got sick, so she had no choice."

Kate looked at the page in the light streaming out from the house. Rachel was gorgeous. Her figure was stunning. Her legs were long and straight, her complexion perfect. "My, she's very attractive."

He shrugged. "She's a professional model."

Kate set the magazine aside. "So are there any little Sinclairs running around?"

Again, Jarrett shook his head. "No. Since Rachel and I broke up, I've been too busy for a relationship. Between the real estate projects I develop and the movies I produce, I'm constantly on the go." His expression turned serious. "But don't get me wrong. I want children. I'm not building my business to leave it to a bunch of thieving investors who can run it into the ground. No, sir. I want a son I can bring up in the business and pass it on to. Much like you, I want what I've built to go on."

"Oh." Stifling a yawn, she looked toward the mountains. The sky was dark. "Wow! It's late. It's too dark to look at the cattle." She pointed toward her truck. "I better get you back to your plane."

Standing, Jarrett looked into the black that enveloped the ranch. "I didn't realize we had talked this long." Turning, he looked in the direction toward town. "This presents a problem. If I leave now, I'd be taking off on an unfamiliar runway in the dark. And then there are those mountains south of your airport that I'd have to climb over. Dodging them in the dark is a risk I'd prefer not to take."

"Oh," she replied. "Your flight attendant said you had a stateroom aboard your plane. I guess I'll take you back there."

Jarrett shook his head. "If you drove me to town now, it would be after midnight by the time you got back here. You've had a long day and appear tired. I'd feel better if you didn't have to make that drive so late, as tired as you are."

She looked at him. He had a point. Getting to her feet, she looked at her house. She had the space. "If you'd like, you're welcome to spend the night. The guest room is made up, and if you give me a minute, I'm sure I can find a new toothbrush for you."

"If you can find that toothbrush, I'm ready to call it a day."

8

Kate led the way to the stairs. This was not what she planned when she agreed to bring him out to the ranch. She tried to think. They were alone in the house. He was going to spend the night. Just the thought gave her a rush. Her cheeks flushed. She looked at him. *Forget it. This is business.*

At the top of the stairs, she led the way into one of her brother's bedrooms. "You'll need something to sleep in," she said and opened the closet door. "This was my youngest brother's room. He was close to your size. A few of his clothes are still here," she said and pointed at a dresser.

Jarrett searched through the drawers and found cutoff sweatpants. "This should do."

Back in the hall, she dug around in the linen cupboard drawer. "Here's that toothbrush." She pointed toward the guest suite. "There are clean towels in the guest bathroom and fresh linens on the bed. If you need anything, call. I'll be down at the other end of the house."

Stepping into her room, she pulled the door closed. She took a breath and touched her face. Her cheeks were flushed. She felt warm all over. Turning, she looked toward the front of the house. *What now?* she asked herself as she slipped into bed.

An hour later, she snapped upright in bed. The room was dark. The night air was still. Swinging around, she sat on the edge of the bed. She listened. There wasn't a sound. Still, she sensed something wasn't right. Easing to her feet, she tiptoed in the dark to the screen door to the porch. The screen in the door was there only to keep out the bugs. *Reek*, a porch board creaked. She jumped. Her heart felt like it skipped a beat. *Reek*, the board squeaked again. She grabbed for the switch. The porch light flashed on.

"What the hell?" Jarrett called out as he threw up his arm. Collecting himself, he took a step back. "Boy, did you give me a scare."

Kate switched off the light. "What did you give me? If I'd known it was you, I wouldn't have switched on the light." Stepping back, she looked through the screen. "What were you doing sneaking around in the dark?"

"I'm not sneaking around, and I didn't mean to scare you." He stepped to the door. "The sound of the crickets and frogs and the moonlight was too much. This air is so fresh and clean. I was coming here to see if you were awake. If you were, I was going to ask you to join me. I need someone to share this with." He opened the door and reached for her hand. "Now that you're up, please."

She hesitated. Dressed in a sleep shirt that extended barely to her knees, she had nothing else on. She looked at him. She should say no, except the word wouldn't come out. *What am I doing?* she asked as she accepted his hand.

Without speaking, he started around the house toward his bedroom at the opposite end. Away from the yard lights, the far side was dark. What light there was came from the moon. Near the guest bedroom door, he set her down on a small bench with restrictive armrests along each side. "Pardon me," he said. Nudging her over, he wiggled in beside her. "Isn't this something?" He leaned back and looked at the sky. "The night air. The view."

His leg and hip were pressing hard against hers. She could feel the heat of his body through her shirt. Their shoulders too were tight together. This was the closest they'd been since they met. She looked his way. The moon's bluish glow outlined his profile. His chin was distinct, as were his deep-set eyes. Their shoulders were pressed together as well. A surge of excitement welled up within her. She couldn't help herself. A cool breeze rolled down from the Rockies. She shivered.

Standing, he reached for her hand. "That's enough," he said. "You're getting cold. I better get you inside." Helping her up, he walked her toward his room. About to the door, he turned and followed the wall back to her room. Taking both hands, he held her out. "I had a wonderful evening. Thank you. It's been a joy sharing this with you."

Kate blinked. She took a step back. *And that's it? No friendly embrace, or anything?* She shook his hand and stepped back into her room. *What more should I expect?* She asked herself. *Nothing. This is only business,* she concluded. "Thank you," she said. "It's been a wonderful evening." Taking a breath, she watched him disappear around the corner. *So much for that.*

Sunrise came early in June. Out past the bunkhouse, a dog barked. Crows squawked their greeting to the new day. Pulling the blanket up under her chin, she tingled all over. She'd never felt so alive. *Oh, what a day this is going to be.*

A rooster crowed from somewhere down in the yard. It was time to get up. She didn't know when she had fallen asleep and knew she should be tired, except she wasn't. Dressing in a hurry, she eased open the door and peered down the hall. The door to the guest room was closed. Smiling, she tiptoed toward the stairs. *City folk aren't accustomed to getting up so early.*

At the base of the stairs, she turned toward the kitchen. The aroma of coffee flavored the air. There was only one person who could have made it, and he was nowhere in sight. She looked out, and Jarrett was at the porch rail, with his back toward her. His polo shirt followed the distinct lines of his muscular shoulders. *For a busy executive, you're hardly out of shape.* She splashed coffee in a mug and went outside. "Good morning. You're up early."

"The alarm clock woke me."

Stopping beside him, she rested a hip against the railing. "The alarm clock?" she questioned. "I can't recall one in the guest room."

He shook his head. "Not in the room. Out there." Just then, a rooster flapped his wings and crowed. "Yes. There he goes again. He woke me a little after four-thirty. I could have sworn he was standing outside my door."

She chuckled. "I don't hear him unless I'm listening for him."

Smiling, his expression glowed. "Well, I heard him, and it wasn't all that bad. In fact, it was a pleasant way to wake up. Folks in the city have nothing like that." He pointed at the sky. "The sunrise was beautiful." He looked at her mug. "As you discovered, I made coffee. I hope it's to your liking. My kitchen skills aren't the sharpest at four-forty-five in the morning."

"No, it's fine," she said and licked her lips. "So what have you been doing since four-forty-five?"

He pointed at the mountains. "Admiring the view. Everything here is so fresh and clean. The mountains are rugged and bold."

"We like it," she said and glanced at his empty mug. "If you're not in a hurry, I can make breakfast, and then we can drive up so you can see some of the cattle you'll be getting. By the time we get back, my dad should be here. I know he'll want to meet you. After that, I'll drive you to your plane. Do you have time for that?"

He smiled. "Sounds good to me."

With breakfast over, they headed out in her truck. After a hundred or so yards, she stopped. "Foreman's house," she said.

Gene bounded out. "Morning, boss."

"Morning, Gene." She leaned back so Jarrett could see past her. "Jarrett, this is Gene Delain. He's my foreman." Jarrett reached across and shook the man's hand. "Gene, this is Mr. Sinclair. He's the head of AJS Foods. He's here to see some of the great range-fed beef we produce. Speaking of which, did you get the last of the cattle up to the high range yesterday?"

"No, we stopped them in the meadow last night. We'll be moving them the rest of the way this morning."

"Good. That's where we're going." She slipped the truck into gear. As she drove, she pointed out the calving sheds where she produced the dairy cow stock and the stables where she kept her championship horses.

"Looks like you are into a little bit of everything," Jarrett commented. "Beef cattle, dairy cows, horses."

"No, a lot of everything." She grinned proudly. "All of what you see here is my handiwork. The stables and the sheds are all my doing. I'm diversified. When beef prices are down or feed prices are up, I don't suffer like the other ranches around me. I have other products and markets to take up the slack." Farther on, she slowed as she approached one of many small corrals.

Jarrett looked where she pointed. "Now, that's quite a bull," he said. As he spoke, the animal glared between the rungs and gave out a snort. "He looks dangerous. How do you handle an animal like that?"

"Very carefully. Actually, I don't handle him. I leave him to Gene and the hired help."

Miles farther along, she stopped in the meadow where the cattle had been held overnight. Her wranglers had them moving, and they were coming their way. She grabbed the door on her side and motioned for him to do the same on his side. "Swing out and up into the box in the back. We can stand up there and get a better view."

Jarrett followed her lead and was quickly up in the pickup truck box. "*Wow*," he said. "You're right. This is an incredible sight."

Her expression brightened as the sea of animals swarmed around them. "Quite something, huh?" The mooing and bellowing of the passing stock forced her to yell. "Some of the best cattle in the state, and this is only part of my stock."

"This is quite something," Jarrett said, fanning his hand before him. "The dust, the smell, The noise is incredible. I wouldn't have been able to picture this unless I saw it." He leaned close and called into her ear. "I guess this is what cattle ranching is all about."

She grinned. "You got that right."

He pointed across the meadow at the rugged hills and mountains beyond. "What does your ranch look like farther up?"

Her grin grew. "It's fantastic. There's unspoiled wilderness with ponds and streams and waterfalls. Beyond that is my high-range summer grazing area. That's where those cattle are going."

He reached around and started to swing back down into the cab. "Let's drive up there. I'd like to see your mountain wilderness. I bet it's beautiful."

She shook her head. "It is, but not today. A mile or so past those trees, the road is nearly impassable. It's only good enough to get the cattle through," she said. "Anyway, you have to get to Minneapolis, and I have a day's worth of office work to catch up on."

On the way down toward the compound, the dirt road turned bad. Swinging the steering wheel sharply, she tried to miss the biggest potholes. Negotiating a curve, she had no choice and hit a deep one straight on. "Hold on," she called out as her pickup dropped and then bounced high into the air. Thrown about violently, she caught sight of Jarrett as his head snapped forward and then back abruptly. Struggling to hold on, his eyelids drooped shut. Slumping forward, his chin fell to his chest. For a few seconds, he just sat there. His eyes were closed. Perspiration formed on his brow. Seconds passed, and he slowly sat up.

Startled, Kate slowed the truck. "Are you okay?" she asked as he carefully opened his eyes and settled back to an upright position.

Blinking, it took him a few seconds to respond, "Yeah. I'm good."

She focused on him. He appeared to have momentarily blacked out. "What was that all about?"

Wiping his brow, he adjusted his position. "An old sports injury," he mumbled. "Nothing to get excited about." Turning, he looked back to where they had been. "That was a hell of a hole. I felt like my teeth were going to fall out."

"Sorry about that," she said. "I tried to miss it but couldn't." She settled back. "Good news. We're past the worst ones. From here down, the road will be better."

Rolling up to the house, she parked next to her father's pickup. "Dad's here," she said warmly when her father appeared in the doorway. "He's limping," she whispered to Jarrett when he stepped out. "He has a bad hip and needs to get it replaced." She swung down from her truck. "Dad, I'd like you to meet Jarrett Sinclair, CEO of AJS Foods."

Jarrett bounded past her and up the stairs. "Morning, Mr. Clark," he said, reaching for her father's hand. "Pleasure to meet you."

Kate stopped. "What does the *A* stand for in AJS Foods?"

Turning, he looked at her.

She continued, "I guessed the *J* and the *S* in AJS are probably for Jarrett Sinclair. And the *A* stands for?"

"My first name is Albert," he said. "I was named after my father. Everyone wanted to call us Big Al and Little Al. Mother wouldn't hear of it, so she took to calling me by my middle name."

"Oh."

Jarrett turned to her father. "Mr. Clark. You've quite a rancher here in your daughter."

"She is," Seth said. "But please call me Seth."

Kate looked at her father. "I see your limp is bad today." She glared. "You got on a horse yesterday and helped the boys move the cattle?" She didn't blink until he slowly agreed. "Just as I suspected." She pointed toward the kitchen. "Let's go inside. I need coffee, and you need to get off your feet."

Seated at the table, Seth addressed Jarrett, "What do you think of our country?"

"Fantastic," Jarrett said. "From what little I've seen, it's spectacular. I can only imagine what the rest of your place must look like toward the mountains."

The telephone rang. Kate held up her hand. "Kate Clark here." She listened and turned toward the men. "It's Sheriff Rawlins," she said and returned to the call. "Yes, Sheriff, the plane belongs to AJS Foods. The chairman of the board flew me home and came out to the house to discuss business." She listened and then turned back to Jarrett. "It seems your plane has drawn quite a crowd. He's had to call in off-duty help to cover the increased activity. The sheriff's wondering when you plan to leave."

"I'm ready to go whenever you are," Jarrett replied.

She returned to the call. "Sheriff, we'll be leaving here in a few minutes. We should be there in under an hour." Finished, she pointed at her father. "While I'm away, I don't want you to move." Taking a prescription bottle down from the cupboard, she shook out two pills. "Take these and see if they'll ease the pain."

"Yes, boss," Seth said.

Jarrett pointed at an ibuprofen bottle he saw when Kate opened the cupboard door. "Could I get a couple ibuprofen? I have a beast of a headache."

"By all means." Kate shook out two. "That old sports injury or too many potholes?"

"Both. Mostly the potholes."

"Oh," she remarked. Having grown up on the ranch, ruts and holes in the roads were an everyday part of life. The fact he said they gave him a headache passed by her. Turning, she checked her father seated at the table. Satisfied he would be okay, she grabbed her grocery list, and they were off.

Neither said much as they drove down the long unpaved drive. Swinging onto the county road, they ran down the windows and left the dust cloud behind. Jarrett turned toward her. "Have you ever considered doing something other than ranching? Have you ever considered moving to the city?"

Kate blinked. "And do what? I'm not a city person," she said. "Hell," she chortled, "I'm a cowpuncher. I breed and train championship horses. That's what I do for a living." Turning, she looked at him. "Anyway, what can I do in the city?"

"There's a lot you can do in a city," he said. "You're college-educated and bright. You graduated with honors. You're—"

Kate threw up a hand. "Whoa there," she called out. "How do you know I graduated with honors? I never mentioned that. What have you been doing, checking up on me?"

"Yes," Jarrett acknowledged. "I have thorough background checks done on all my major suppliers. I have too much to lose if they go broke."

"Oh." Sitting up, she was about to vent her ire when she settled back. What he'd done was only good business. *If I'd been in his place, I probably would have done the same.* She settled back. "Okay, so you checked up on me. What else have you learned?"

"We know you're profitable. Your credit is excellent. You're an astute businessperson and could do well in Los Angeles. You should be in the city with people. That's where you belong."

Shaking her head, her expression turned cold. "You're wrong," she stated. "That's not where I belong. I belong right here." She focused on him. "Sounds like you're trying to get me to move off my ranch? Why? What's in it for you?" Pulling herself up straight, her expression cooled. "More importantly, what's in it for me?"

Leaning back, Jarrett waved his hand. "Hey, don't get me wrong. I was just suggesting that you might want to look at being with people in the city, that's all."

"Oh." She paused. *Maybe I have overreacted. Maybe he wasn't trying to get me to move.* She shrugged. *After all, what could he hope to gain by having me leave my ranch?*

Shaking slightly, the idea of moving to Los Angeles gave her the chills. She had to change the subject. "What do you think of my cattle operation?"

"Very impressive," he said. "Standing in the back of your truck while the cattle swarmed by is something I'll never forget. It would've been nice if we could've gone up to your high country. The lakes and streams up there must be something to behold."

"They are. They're beautiful, but getting there right now, with the road washed out, would have been tough. In fact, near impossible." She slowed on her way down the long straight stretch of road toward town. In a few minutes, he'd be gone. "After your meeting in Minneapolis, are you going back to Beverly Hills?"

"What?" he asked and slowly agreed. "Yes, I'll be flying back home."

"Where to after that?" she asked. Taking a breath, she looked at him. She was coming on to him but couldn't help herself.

Staring ahead, he appeared to think. "Lillian has me scheduled to go to Las Vegas and then to Phoenix. We have a couple projects there I have to attend to."

"Lillian?" Kate asked.

"My faithful assistant," he said. "She's been with the company forever. She more or less raised me. She was Dad's right-hand gal, and when he cut back, she was Carter's. Now she's mine. She watches over me and schedules everything I do. I'd be lost without her."

Kate slowed. The airport was just ahead. She had to think of something. "I'll be attending a software training seminar in LA in a couple of weeks. Maybe I can swing by your office and discuss selling AJS more beef."

"When's your trip?"

Her expression brightened. "Two weeks from Monday. I'll be in town a week."

Thinking, he shook his head. "Nope, I won't be there. Lillian has me in Florida that week."

"Oh," she replied and settled back.

A crowd lined the fence where his plane was parked. "I can see why the sheriff had to call in more help," she said. "Looks like everyone in town is curious about the largest plane ever to land at our little airport."

Some distance back, she slowed to a crawl. "We may as well say good-bye here. It's too crowded to do it up near the fence."

He pointed at his plane. "If you have a minute, I have a beef marketing report in the plane I'd like you to have. We can say good-bye up there."

People stepped aside as she and Jarrett made their way to the break in the chain-link barrier. He directed her up the stairs to his plane and around the partition to the conference area.

Following him, she watched as he dug through drawers. "I'd like to thank you again. I enjoyed the flight home and our visit. It's a shame you're going to be out of town when I'm there."

"Where and when is that seminar you're attending?" he asked. Without looking up, he continued his search.

"Logan Software in their building in downtown LA. Two weeks from Monday. I'll be staying at the Crown Royal Hotel." Her cheeks flushed. She was coming on to him. She couldn't help herself.

"Ah yes, I know both places, Logan Software and the Crown Royal. Neither are far from my office tower." He handed her the folder he pulled from the drawer. "Here's the report. It's proprietary, so please don't go showing it around."

"I won't," she said.

Jarrett took her face in his hands. His palms were hot. With a hold of her cheeks, his mouth came down on hers, smothering her with a kiss. His tongue darted out and swirled about in her mouth. The sensation of his tongue touching hers caused her body to arch. Her pulse quickened. She could feel her heart pound. A surge of excitement coursed through her. Immersed in his passion, she forgot what she was doing. She slid her hands up his chest and stroked his powerful neck. He pulled her tighter to his body. She responded. Her fingers dug in. She held him. Not thinking, she kissed him back. She answered his passion with her tongue. He was excited. She could feel his erection against her. She gasped. *What am I doing?* Crimson-faced, she struggled to break away. Her skin felt like it was on fire. She ran her tongue over her lips, and the taste of him sent a shock wave through her body. She had kissed him back. *What have I done? What'll I tell Wylie?* She tried to push away. "I have to go."

Holding her shoulders, he looked into her eyes. "I'm sorry. I've insulted you." His expression was sincere. "I shouldn't have done that. Please accept my apology. If I offended you in any way, I didn't mean to. My actions were impetuous and brash." He studied her face. "You're very special, and I've overstepped my bounds. Will you be okay?"

Taking a breath, she tried to think. Her pulse pounded. She didn't know what to do. She felt all jumbled inside. She wanted him like she had never wanted any man before, but that was wrong. Very wrong. She slowly spoke, "Yeah. I'll be okay," she replied, forcing a thin smile. She didn't want to leave but knew she had to. At the door, she stopped and pushed some hair from her face. "Have a nice trip to Minneapolis," she mumbled. Without looking back, she left the plane.

People watched as she stopped at the airport side of the chain-link barrier. Clutching the report, she looked back as the far engine came up to speed. Moments later, the stairway tilted up and disappeared into a cavity below the main cabin floor. Kate watched as the near engine came up to speed. Shaking, everything was tumbling out of control. She didn't want him to leave. The engine noise grew. *What now?* she asked herself. The wheels rolled, and the plane turned toward the runway. Dust and gravel flew back. She held up the report, but not quickly enough. Dirt peppered her face and got into her eyes.

With eyes watering, she dashed to her Suburban. She had to get out of there. Dust boiled up as she raced away. At the end of the airport, she ground to a stop. Shaking, she didn't know what to think. She gasped. She had kissed him back. *What can I tell Wylie?*

Stepping out, she looked down the length of the runway as the plane turned onto the paved strip. The engine noise built as the aircraft grew in size. Moments later, the nosewheels came up and the plane lifted off. Kate covered her ears as the big jet thundered overhead. She watched as he climbed straight toward the noonday sun and disappeared into a wall of clouds. Her whole body ached. She had kissed him back, which was wrong. Very wrong. *Oh, what do I do now?*

9

Motoring away, Kate stared at the road ahead. Ever since she could remember, she had her life neatly laid out. She'd rebuild the family ranch. She'd marry Wylie. They'd have children. She'd teach them how to be good ranchers. The Clark ranch would go on.

Confused, she slapped the steering wheel. Jarrett had entered her life. His kissing her had brought out feelings she had never experienced before. *What am I going to do?* She trembled. *Why didn't I push him away?* she asked herself. She knew the answer. During those few seconds, he had excited her like no man had ever done before. During those same seconds, she wanted him like she had never wanted any man ever. She sighed. She couldn't help herself.

Staring out at the road, she pulled herself up straight. *What am I thinking? Erase Jarrett from your mind. Wylie'll be back in a few days. Life will go on. I'll buy the Wilsons' ranch, along with Wylie's and Patty's. The Clark ranch will be back together.*

Miles later, she approached the entrance to the Wilsons' ranch. Looking over, she slammed on the brake. "Rats!" she called out when she saw her grocery list had fallen out of her pocket and lay on the seat beside her. *I've got to go back. If I forget the groceries, Dad'll want to know why.*

In town, she found everything on her list. The customer ahead of her was checking out. "I heard a developer was in town," she said to the cashier. "Do you know anything about it?"

Kate blinked. *A developer was in town?*

"Not much," the cashier replied. "I heard the same from Jim at the feed store."

"I hope the rumor is true," the woman replied. "We could use the economic help. Most of us are going broke."

Maybe that's your problem, honey, but it sure isn't mine, Kate retorted.

"Do you know who it was?" the woman asked.

Kate perked up.

"No," the cashier replied.

Kate sighed. The only developer she knew was Jarrett Sinclair. She considered their discussion on her side porch. *He's into commercial development, shopping malls and office buildings.* Straightening up, she strengthened her resolve. *All the same, I'll have to keep on alert. I don't want to be caught off guard.*

With the groceries loaded, she headed for the ranch. *Whoever was here was pretty transparent.* She thumped on the steering wheel. *At least they weren't near my ranch. If they were, I sure would have seen them.*

Parked behind the house, she grabbed a couple of bags and dashed for the door. When she saw her father, she relaxed. "Good. You haven't moved."

Seth grabbed a chair back and prepared to get up. "Is there any left out there for me to carry in?"

"Not on your life," she said. "You stay put. I'll bring in the rest." She put down the bags and waited until he was back in his chair. Confident he would stay there, she retrieved the last of the groceries.

Seth watched. "That Jarrett fellow appears like a nice sort."

"Yes, he is," she sputtered. The mention of his name brought back the last moments aboard his plane. Her pulse quickened. A hot rush swept over her. She squirmed. *I kissed him back. How can I explain what I've done? I can't.* She studied her father. *He would never understand.*

Seth watched as she worked. "When I came out this morning, his plane was the talk of the town. I hope he got off okay."

"He took off just fine," she said without turning. She couldn't. Her cheeks were flushed, and her hands trembled. "He even had room to spare."

Seth continued, "So he spent the night here?"

Spinning around, she glared at her father. "Yes, Dad, he spent the night here." About to say more, she stopped. She had overreacted. Pulling back, she turned away. Collecting herself, she continued while unloading the groceries. "After he flew me back from Spokane, I brought him out because he was interested in seeing the cattle. I showed him Ramrod, and we were both hungry, so we had dinner out on the porch, and after that, we sat and talked business. By the time we finished, it was late. He didn't want to take off in the dark, so I suggested he stay, and he accepted. He slept in the guest room. End of story." She picked up a can. *Oh my, what now?*

"Do you plan on seeing him again?"

She pulled the last item from the bag and slowly put it away. Folding the bag, she set it aside. A bit more composed, she grabbed the chair across from her father. "No immediate plans," she said. "I'm sure I will again someday. I'm going to LA in two weeks for that software class. I was hoping to meet with him then and discuss beef purchases except he's going to be in Florida that week."

Seth's gaze narrowed. "It looks like you two hit it off pretty good. Is there anything going on between you two?"

"No," she sputtered.

Tapping on the table, Seth studied his daughter. "It didn't look that way to me."

Her eyes narrowed, and she focused on her father. "Well, your look is wrong."

"Whatever you say." Settling back, Seth continued to tap on the table. "How are things with you and Wylie? Is marriage in the works?"

"Yes!" she quickly replied. "We'll get married as soon as he gets his ranch turned around." Taking a breath, she eased back in the chair. "You know he doesn't want people accusing him of marrying me simply to bailout his operation."

"Whatever." Getting to his feet, Seth stroked his backside. "I've been sitting too long. My butt's gone to sleep." With a hold of the chair backs, he worked his way around toward the sink. "I've seen the reasons he's in over his head. That new diesel pickup is costing him a bundle, not to mention the payments on that Kenworth truck and custom aluminum trailer he purchased and his payments on that tractor with the air-conditioned cab. The boy is a walking financial disaster. Show him a new toy, and he has to have it." He let go of the chair and took a step without assistance. "My hip feels a lot better. I was getting pretty stiff sitting there."

<hr />

Later, alone with the day's work done and dinner over, Kate typed Jarrett's name into her computer. *You've checked into my background without asking. Now it's my turn.* She studied the screen. *He's the head of Sinclair Enterprises. That much I already know.* "Um." *The corporation is privately held. There are no annual reports available to review.* "Rats."

Focused on the screen, she continued to read. Sinclair Enterprises: a multinational company, developer of strip malls, office buildings, business complexes, and condominiums. Below it was a list of properties held. She scanned the list. All were listed as this building LLC or that mall LLC. A click on any revealed each was privately held. Nowhere did she see any mention of luxury resorts. "Darn. Another dead end." She searched further and stopped. "A-ha, this is something," she mumbled when AJS Foods appeared on the screen. Through Mr. Sinclair's hands-on management style, the company has grown to be one of the foremost wholesalers of premium meat in the United States. "Huh! That I already know," she said, thinking aloud. Reading on, nothing new was revealed about AJS Foods. *Isn't there anything about this guy? There has to be something. He can't be a total mystery.* "Or can he?"

She clicked her mouse, and a new screen appeared. Her expression brightened. "Okay!" she remarked on seeing Jarrett being interviewed at a movie premier. She studied the picture. "God! You're good-looking." He was smiling. His eyes were aglow, and it held her for a moment. A fancy-dressed female with ample breasts clung to his arm. She scanned from screen to screen. He was pictured at the premier of one movie after another. "A producer with the magic touch," read the caption at the top of the screen. The interviewer said, "Three box-office blockbusters back-to-back must be some kind of record."

"I don't know about records," Jarrett replied. "When I see a good script, I find the best talent and put them together. I enjoy making movies." As in the other pictures, an attractive female was at his side.

Kate continued her search. Aside from him pictured at one opening after another, there was little else she could learn. Business-holding companies and LLCs were listed and seemed to run on forever. Yawning, she reached out and shut down her computer. *So much for online searches.* The telephone rang. It was Wylie. She swallowed hard. *How can I ever tell him what I did? I can't.* She took a breath and tried to sound upbeat. "Hi, honey, how was your day?"

"Mine was okay. Patty's mother's wasn't so good. She had another small stroke. Nothing too serious. All the same, the doctor wants to keep her in the hospital at least an extra day. Instead of her going home the morning after my class is over, it's going to be the next day."

Kate was quick to step in, "You're staying until she's home? If you don't, you'll leave Patty stranded in Billings."

"Yeah, I'll stay and give her a ride back." He cleared his throat. "Did you make it to Spokane okay?"

"What? Oh yes," she replied.

"How was it? Did we lose any sales to the big guys? I'm sure they were working the AJS people for all they were worth."

She looked at the phone. She had to tell him what happened. "Actually, I was the only rancher there."

"Really?" Wylie questioned. "I find that hard to believe."

"I thought so too, but as it turned out, the meeting had been scheduled on short notice, and all the big operators were hung up attending seminars like you are right now. I really lucked out."

"No kidding. So we might see more sales. That's great." Pleased, it came across in his voice. "So you got over and back okay. How was your flight?"

She hesitated. She had to tell him how Jarrett had flown her home and stayed overnight. If she didn't, the town gossips would. "Yeah, I made it over okay, but when I was ready to come home, our little airline had scheduling problems and left early."

Wylie laughed. "The pilot probably had a hot bowling date in Bismarck. So how'd you get home? Drive?"

Kate carefully selected her words. "No. The AJS Foods' chairman flew me home in their company jet. He was going to Minneapolis, and we were on his way."

"No kidding. A jet? A big plane?"

"A Boeing 757." Beads of perspiration trickled down her sides. Her palms were damp. She looked at the phone. She had to tell Wylie about his staying overnight. But how? She paused. "When we landed, it was early, and he wanted to see the cattle, so I brought him out. I showed him around and served him dinner. We talked business, and by the time we finished, it was late, so I let him use the guest suite. After I showed him the cattle this morning, I took him back to his plane." Her hands shook. She stared at the phone. She had lied to the man she had known all her life.

10

Come Saturday with her office work done, Kate gazed out the window. Wylie was due home shortly. Her palms were damp. She'd made a mistake on Jarrett's plane. Her only excuse had been she'd briefly lost control of her emotions. She knew that was hardly a good excuse. She recalled their embrace. Her pulse quickened. With her eyes closed, she could feel his tongue in her mouth. She was excited. She tried to push the memory of Jarrett's erection from her mind, but it wouldn't go away.

Exhaling forcefully, she straightened up. *So I made a mistake. Everyone is allowed one or two little mistakes.* She shook her head. *But this was no little mistake. I kissed him back. I really kissed him back.*

Her shoulders drooped. *What can I do?* Stomping her foot, she stared off into space. "Get a grip," she grumbled and turned back to the present. *You're not a flighty schoolgirl. You're a woman. You're a cowpuncher, a breeder of horses. You're not in love with Jarrett. Put him out of your mind. You're committed to the man due here momentarily.*

Rolling up, Wylie parked behind the house. Gripping his head with both hands, he entered the kitchen. "I'm here, but my brain is so crammed with stuff. My head feels like it's about to explode."

She snickered. "Your head looks fine to me." A warm feeling surged within her. Her friend was back. "Obviously, you learned a lot." Kate held out her arms. "I need a kiss. You've been gone a week, and I missed you."

"I missed you too," he said and gave her a peck on the cheek. Setting her aside, he stepped toward the refrigerator. "I'm starved. What's for dinner?"

Kate pulled him back. There was no electricity. No racing heartbeat. Nothing like what she experienced aboard Jarrett's plane. She looked at Wylie. "Dinner can wait. Give me a real kiss."

Taking her, he kissed her hard on the mouth. He held her tight and then let her go.

She licked her lips. Again, there was nothing. *Could we have been friends so long all the sparks have gone out of our relationship? Is this what I have to look forward to?* Straightening up, she stopped. *That has to be it. After all, we've been friends since we were little kids.*

She reached for him to pull him back, but he was already on his way to the refrigerator.

"The development company called," Wylie said as he reached for a beer. His expression brightened. "And they might be interested in the area around our ranches."

"Our ranches?" she questioned.

"Yes. Yours, mine, and Patty's."

Kate's expression chilled. "My ranch is not for sale, and neither should yours and Patty's be. We've got this dream, and we're not far from putting this place back together. If they want wilderness land, let them look somewhere else. There's plenty between us and Glacier Park."

Wylie held up his hand. "Whoa there. Don't get so excited. So far, it's only talk. The man said he'll be calling the owners of the ranches they might be interested in. If he calls, I'll see what he has to say."

"You do that, but from what Monty heard, they're only interested in paying bargain prices."

Wylie's expression chilled. "If that's the case, we're not interested in selling."

"Damn right, you're not interested in selling. Together we're going to rebuild this place. That's the goal, and we're going to make it come true."

Days later and less than a week before she was to fly to Los Angeles, Kate scrolled through the orders from AJS Foods. Compared to the previous month, the numbers were up. She studied the totals. *Could this be a result of his visit and the kiss aboard his plane or just a coincidence?* Unable to decide which, she pushed back from her desk. Dinnertime was approaching, and Wylie would soon be there.

She pulled out a couple of steaks as Wylie roared up. Bursting in, he grabbed her and planted a kiss on her mouth. Warmed by his greeting, she hugged him back. "You're in a particularly good mood. What's up?"

He grinned. "The developer phoned, and they're interested in our wilderness area and want to meet us in Missoula tomorrow."

Kate's expression chilled. "I said my ranch was not for sale, and I meant it. I'm not selling."

Wylie stepped forward. "Come on, Kate." His brow furrowed. "Going there to meet with them won't mean anything other than we're interested in seeing what they have planned. Will you come with me and Patty tomorrow?"

"No," she announced. "I'm not interested in their plans. I'm not selling, and that's that."

Wylie's shoulders sagged. "I know you're not up to selling, but Patty and I would like to know what they are planning and how big a resort they are proposing. Wouldn't you?"

Kate shook her head. "No."

11

The next evening, it was after seven when Wylie returned from the meeting in Missoula. He had phoned ahead and told her not to hold dinner. When he entered, he was carrying a sheaf of papers along with a large rolled-up print. When he saw her, he said, "You look comfortable in shorts and a tank top." Still dressed in his best Western pants, white Western dress shirt, and polished boots, he shoved the salt and pepper shakers and ketchup bottle aside and unrolled the print.

"It hit ninety-one here today," she said and pointed at what he was unrolling. "What's all that?"

Wylie's expression brightened. "This is the development they're planning, and I, for one, think their ideas are exciting. And let me tell you, he was disappointed you weren't there."

"He was, was he? Why?" Kate demanded.

"Because he wanted to show you what they've planned." As Wylie spoke, he unrolled the combined aerial photos of their three ranches. Beside that, he spread out the artist renderings they had given him. He pointed at an outline area on the overall aerial print. "This is where they want to put the main village." As he spoke, he picked out the colored sketches of the shopping mall and hotels with their rustic Western facades. "Their village would look like this, and it would take in most of Patty's lowland and my lower fields. They plan to put in a lake and stock it with fish. Initially, there'll be three golf courses and miles of riding trails and a half-dozen major ski runs."

Kate ignored what he had spread out. "Who's he?"

"Huh?" Wylie grunted. "Oh. The headman himself met with me and Patty. We were the only ranchers there. He's only interested in our properties, and he wished you had come along."

Kate's expression didn't soften. "Who's he? What's his name?"

"Roger Gillie. He heads up property acquisition for Wilderness Pines Development. He struck me as the type of guy who gets what he goes after. And like I said, he was disappointed you weren't there."

"Tough."

Wylie ignored her chilled response. "I told him your ranch wasn't for sale, and he honored your wish. Everything from the meadow down all the way out to county road is untouched. They are only interested in your range area from the meadow on up. That's where they planned the ski runs and the Swiss-type village with condos and little stone lodges."

Kate's expression didn't change. "I said my ranch was not for sale, and I meant not any of it."

Wylie eased back. "Come on, Kate, be reasonable." He bowed his head, and after many seconds, he looked her way. "They're not after everything your grandfather sold off. They're not after Wilsons' place. Buck is close to retirement. I'm sure you can work out a deal with him."

"And why aren't they interested in Buck's place?"

"According to Gillie, it's too far from what they've planned." He looked down at the table. "I think they have fantastic ideas, and unlike what Monty said, they're offering a premium price. He told me if you say yes, the deal can be closed by the time you get back from Los Angeles."

Kate's brow furrowed. "How does he know I am going to Los Angeles?"

"I don't know," Wylie said. "I didn't tell him, at least I don't think I did. Anyway, with beef prices down, Patty's ranch and my place are worth a fraction of what they were a decade ago. Nobody wants small stand-alone ranches anymore, and these people are willing to pay full price of a few years back, and you're turning them down. Why?"

Kate hit the table. "You know damn well why I don't want to sell."

"Yes, I know," he said. "Clarks have been on this land for five generations."

"That's right!" She snorted. "That means more than money can buy." She pointed at what he laid out. "Tell them to refigure their plan."

"But Kate—"

"But Kate nothing. I'm not selling. Period," she said and took a step back.

Gone was all life in Wylie's expression as he slowly tucked the rolled print under his arm. "I'll talk to them and see what they have to say. Your saying no has probably killed the deal."

"That's my plan," she replied.

With drawings in hand, he moved toward the door. "I need to think this over. I'm going home to see what I can come up with."

Kate glanced about. "This is home."

Wylie shook his head. "No, I'm going to my house."

Kate stopped. Short of agreeing to sell, she knew of no other way to change his mind. "I'll be going to that seminar on Monday and will need a ride to the airport. I guess I better ask Dad?"

Wylie shook his head. "No, I'm taking you. I have to check on a piece of equipment at Dan's anyway."

<hr />

Dressed in her best Western clothes, including polished boots, Kate grabbed her carry-on bag and her suitcase when Wylie drove up. She was pleased to see he had dusted off the front seat and cleared away the gear that customarily cluttered the passenger-side floor. With a clean place to sit and a clear area to put her feet, she tossed her suitcase and carry-on onto the backseat and climbed up into the cab. "What have you decided?"

He eased back in the seat. "I've given this a lot of thought. You've worked hard to rebuild this place, and I can understand where you're coming from. Nat had a dream, and so do you. I know your reason for not selling. When you get back, we'll see what you, me, and Patty can work out."

Parking at the terminal, he watched as she retrieved her suitcase and slung the straps of her carry-on over her shoulder. "What do you have in that carry-on? It looks heavy."

"It is," she said. "I have my laptop, my purse, and all my course materials." At the ticket counter, she addressed the attendant, "I have a reservation to Salt Lake and on to Los Angeles."

"Yes, Ms. Clark, I've been expecting you." He printed the luggage tag and attached it to her suitcase. "The plane will be here shortly."

Clear of the runway, the small commuter plane flew south. After changing planes in Salt Lake, she was off to Los Angeles. *I wonder what I would do if Jarrett were there?* "Nothing," she mumbled. *It's best he'll be in Florida. The last thing I need is another encounter like aboard his plane.*

At LAX, the first hitch occurred. All the luggage from her flight had been unloaded, and still her suitcase had yet to appear. Having had enough, she addressed the woman at the service counter. "I came in over a half hour ago and no suitcase yet."

The woman took her ticket. "I'm sure I can get this straightened out. It was probably sent to a different baggage claim."

Kate watched as she punched her ticket information into a computer. The woman scanned the screen. "There's been a problem. I need to call the West Central Air office." She grabbed a telephone and read off the ticket numbers. "Ah-huh, ah-huh, uh-huh, okay. I'll tell her." She put the phone down. "It seems there was a bit of a mix-up in Salt Lake. Rather than your bag being transferred to come here to LAX, West Central Air mistakenly put it on a flight heading east that connected to a flight to LUX, Luxembourg."

Kate's jaw dropped. "Luxembourg! Why, that's in Europe. How can that be?" She looked down at what she had on. "What am I supposed to do without clothes? When will I get my suitcase back?"

"West Central Air has caught their mistake, and while the plane to Europe can't be turned around, they've assured me your bag will be coming back as soon as that flight lands in Amsterdam," she explained. "That's where that flight connects to Luxembourg." She smiled. "With luck, you should have your suitcase sometime tomorrow. In the meantime, you need to go to the WCA office and put in a claim."

"Great!" Kate stepped back and looked down the concourse. The West Central Air office had to be there somewhere.

The woman motioned for her to come back. "They don't fly into LAX, so they have no office here, but their main office is in downtown LA. If you hurry, you can catch the shuttle and be there before they close."

It was after five-thirty when the van let her off in front of an office tower downtown. The bold letters above the entrance caused Kate to stop. "Sinclair Tower," she mumbled. *So this is where you work.* Stepping back, she looked toward the top. His office had to be up there somewhere. Momentarily distracted, she wondered what she'd do if she saw him. She shook her head. *Nothing,* she resolved. *He's in Florida. What's important is getting my suitcase back.*

In the lobby, she stopped at the information desk. "I need to file a lost-luggage claim with West Central Air. Can you tell me where I'm supposed to go?"

"Yes, ma'am," the uniformed man said and pointed off to the side. "Their service office is on the mezzanine. Take the open staircase to your left." As he spoke, he directed her attention to the glass-fronted office on the open balcony above. "It's right up there."

"Thank you," she said and proceeded to the floor above. At the WCA office, she addressed the woman behind the counter. "All my clothes are in a suitcase your people in Salt Lake mistakenly sent to Europe. When do you think I might get them back?"

The woman slid a form in her direction. "Fill this out, and I'll get things started. With luck, you'll have your suitcase tomorrow. Do you have a hotel tonight?"

Kate affirmed, "Yes, I have a room." She completed the form and slid it back.

The woman looked at the form. "This'll take me a few minutes. If you'd like a coffee, we have an employee coffee shop a few doors down. The food service is closed, but there's coffee there, and the remaining doughnuts are free for the taking."

Kate considered the woman's offer. She was tired and couldn't wait to get to the hotel, but right then, a cup of coffee and anything that resembled food sounded good. "May as well."

The woman pointed at Kate's carry-on bag. "That looks heavy. If you'd like, you can leave it here. When you get back, I'll have the vouchers waiting."

The woman was right. The bag was heavy, and she had lugged it around enough that day. Pulling her wallet from the case, she stuffed it in her hip pocket and went to the employee coffee shop.

Minutes later, after downing a cup of coffee and two glazed donuts, she returned to the airline office. The door was closed. She gave it a shove. It didn't move. She tried it again. *It's not stuck. It's locked. What's going on?* She checked the time, and the office was supposed to be open another twenty minutes. About to step back, she saw the note taped to the glass. "Ms. Clark. Excuse the inconvenience. I had to rush off. A family emergency. Your handbag and vouchers are inside and safe. I've notified maintenance. They'll be here shortly to unlock the door."

"Really," Kate grumbled and sagged back on her heels. With nothing to do, she took a seat on a marble bench next to the open railing that overlooked the lobby. Below her, people dashed from the elevators toward the doors to the street. She snickered. *Quitting time. Almost like a stampede of cattle heading to a watering hole after a long drought.*

Caught up in watching the people, she lost track of the time. Now after six, the flow of people dwindled, and still no person from maintenance. Getting to her feet, she made one last check for someone with a key. *Where is that person?*

"Are you the one who needs to get something out of the WCA office?" came a voice from behind her.

Kate gasped. She recognized the sound immediately. He was supposed to be in Florida. She turned, and not ten feet away stood the man she'd last seen moments after they had kissed aboard his plane. He was dressed in jeans, a golf shirt, and yachting shoes, spattered with paint. She grinned. "We seem to keep bumping into each other."

"That, we do," Jarrett replied.

Undecided what to say, she checked how he was dressed. "This is either casual-dress Monday, or you do the maintenance here as well."

"Neither. Opening doors for forgetful females, yes, maintenance, no."

"Forgetful. Ha!" She responded. "I didn't lock my bag in there. The woman who worked there did that." She pointed at the note. "She had to leave early." She turned back to Jarrett. "You're hardly wearing what I expected of a chairman of a big company."

"I've been moving stuff to an apartment this afternoon." As he spoke, he pulled out a ring of keys. "I was on my way to my car when someone from maintenance asked if I'd go up and get some woman's bag and vouchers out of this office. I take it you're the person and that's your bag on the counter?"

"Correct on all accounts." Warmed by his presence, her expression eased. "I understood you were to be in Florida this week."

"I was," he replied, "but the meeting was canceled. Weather. Lillian's busy redoing the balance of my week. I won't know until tomorrow what my next move will be." As he spoke, Kate took a step toward the airline office door. "Relax. I'll get your bag," he said. Unlocking the door, he was in and out before she had taken more than a couple of steps.

She checked over the vouchers, and seeing everything was correct, she shoved them and her wallet in her carry-on bag.

"Everything okay?" he asked.

"Yeah, fine," she said and slung the straps over her shoulder.

Frowning, he looked at her. "What are you doing here? Aren't you supposed to be at a training seminar?"

"Yes. Someone in Salt Lake misrouted my suitcase. It's now on its way to Luxembourg. Without it, I've nothing to wear. I came here to put in a lost-luggage report. The woman in there assured me my bag would be back tomorrow."

Jarrett took her arm and started toward the elevator. "Sounds to me like we need to take you shopping," he said and moved her along. "When they say they'll get your suitcase here by tomorrow, don't count on it for a couple days, maybe even a week or more."

Kate pulled free. "Do you really think it can take that long?"

"Probably," he said and continued toward the elevator. "Which is more reason we need to go and find you something to wear."

Down in the garage, he helped her into his car. She glowed. Her day was finally looking up. "Where are we going?" she asked as they roared from the building. "Hopefully somewhere not too expensive."

Focused on the traffic, his response was little more than a grunt. After a couple of miles, he turned sharply into a lot surrounding a large brightly lighted mall. She looked up and balked as he screeched to a stop. "No way," she said. "We're not going to Nordstrom's. I doubt that little airline will believe I had a suitcase filled with clothes from Nordstrom's."

"Sure, they will." Jumping out, he dashed around to her side. "You're the owner of a big ranch, and they would be surprised if you came to town dressed in anything less." He pointed at her carry-on bag. "You don't need to carry that heavy thing around right now. I'll lock it in the trunk. Your hands will be full enough shopping."

She took a step back. "I'm not replacing my whole wardrobe. All I need is something to tide me over a couple days."

"Whatever." Reaching out, he slid her carry-on off her shoulder and set it in the trunk. Taking her arm, they entered the store. "It's going on seven-thirty. We have to get moving." Inside, he pointed

89

toward a designer section. "I think a good place to start would be over there."

She looked where he indicated and shook her head. "I don't need anything that expensive," she said and stepped into sportswear. She chose a shirt and stepped up to a mirror to see how it went with her Western pants. Jarrett frowned. Catching that out of the corner of her eye, she asked, "What's the problem? You said I needed to buy some clothes."

"Mind you, I'm not trying to tell you how to dress, but...," he said and pointed at what she had on. "Now, I'm only suggesting, but down here, it would be more appropriate to wear something a little less ranch-like and a little more businesslike. Twill pants and cowboy boots are a little..."

She made with a raised eyebrow. "Rustic? Is that what you were about to say?"

He nodded. "Professional women attending business conferences here usually wear skirts and blouses and business suits." His expression brightened. "You're a beautiful woman, and you might as well show it off."

"Oh." Her cheeks flushed. She hadn't expected a compliment. He was smiling, and not just a little. "Aaaah," she mumbled and looked down at what she had on. "Do businesswomen here attending an educational meeting really dress like that?" Smiling, he nodded. "Well then, I guess I better get with the program."

In the next department over, a young sales clerk was quick to approach. "Can I be of assistance?"

"I'm in need of something to wear to a business conference," Kate said.

The young woman surveyed Kate's Western attire. "This way, miss." Leading the way, she started back toward the sportswear section.

An older woman from some distance away closed on them quickly. "Ms. Collins," she said to the young clerk. "You have a phone call in the back. I'll tend to your customer." She motioned with a flick of her eyes for the younger woman to move. When the clerk stepped away, she smiled. "Did I hear you say you were in need of something to wear to a conference?"

Kate looked in the direction from where the woman had come. She was not aware her voice had carried that far. "Yes. I flew in this afternoon, and the airline misrouted my luggage. I'm attending a business seminar, and I have nothing to wear."

"Sorry to hear that," the woman stated and led the way toward the store's designer section. "Attending a business seminar?" she questioned, and Kate affirmed. "I know just what you need."

Kate followed her into the neighboring department. When she saw the woman's name badge, Kate discovered she was no ordinary sales clerk but rather the head of the women's wear department. One by one, the woman presented a selection of skirts, blouses, and jackets. With each combination Kate tried on, Jarrett's eyes appeared to shine brighter.

"Do you like this one, or do you prefer the first one or the second outfit?" Kate asked of Jarrett.

He studied the three outfits she had already tried on and the final outfit she was wearing. "I like all four. You look wonderful in each. Let's get all four."

"Really, Jarrett, I don't need that many clothes. I can wear an outfit more than once. Anyway, I can mix and match the jackets."

"Forget it." Jarrett turned toward the woman. "We're getting all four. And while you're at it, she'll need cocktail dresses for the evening."

"Yes, sir. I have just the dresses for her."

"Really, Jarrett," Kate said. "I don't need..." Her voice trailed off.

"Yes, you do," Jarrett interrupted. "You and your group will be going out in the evening, and then there is the formal celebration at the end. Trust me, you'll wear them all."

"If you insist." Tired, she sagged back on her heels. "I no longer have the energy to argue."

Kate modeled the three cocktail dresses the saleswoman brought out. The first two were identical midknee sheath style, one white and one blue. The third was a black very formal off-the-shoulder creation. Kate stopped and held it out. "Jarrett, this is really not me. This is far too fancy and formal. Our farewell dinner will probably be just that, a casual get-together at the end."

Jarrett held up his hand. "You're wrong. Trust me, that black dress is you." When she tried to interrupt, he continued, "Up north, that's your country. You call the shots. Down here, this is my country. You'll have to trust me. I know what works."

"If you say so." Kate laid the black dress on the counter.

"That should cover all your needs," the saleswoman said.

Kate looked at the skirts, blouses, dresses, shoes, and even underwear the woman had collected. "I should hope so," Kate said without checking over each piece individually. "I can't picture I'll need all that."

"Yes, you will," the woman insisted.

"If you say so," Kate said and reached for her wallet. She patted her hip pocket and discovered her wallet was in her purse locked in Jarrett's trunk. "Jarrett, I need the keys to your trunk. My credit card is in my purse." She looked at the woman. "How much does all of this come to, or should I not ask?"

Jarrett pulled out his charge card and stepped to the counter. "I'm getting this."

Kate stepped forward, blocking his way. "No, you're not! Helping me pick them out is one thing, paying for them? No way."

"Suit yourself," Jarrett replied. "If you pay, it'll take you months to get reimbursed. If I pay, I'll take the receipt into their accounting department tomorrow, and they will cut me a check."

"Just like that, they'll write you a check? Why won't they do that if I pay?"

"Because you don't own the building they're in, and I do."

"Oh."

12

L oaded down, Jarrett led the way to his car. "The keys are in my right side pocket," he said and motioned in that direction. When she hesitated, he motioned again. "Go on, pull them out. We don't want to stand here all night."

Stepping behind him, she shoved her hand deep into his pocket. His jeans were tight, and she had to use force to get to the bottom. Digging around, she could feel the heat of his body and more as she searched for the keys. Licking her lips, her pulse raced. She dug even farther. Finding them, she popped the trunk. With her purchases loaded, Jarrett led the way to the passenger side. "I'm starved. I know a great place to eat. They have fabulous Polynesian atmosphere, and the food's great. What do you say? This'll be our only opportunity to have dinner together. I'm sure Lillian will have me out of town the rest of the week."

Kate quickly agreed. This was hardly what she had planned. *Why not? Come tomorrow, I'll be on my own.* "Let's do it," she said. "I'm hungry. The hotel can wait."

Seated in the restaurant, she looked back toward the entrance. "There was a sign back there that read reservations required."

"So?"

"We walked right past everyone in line. Did you call for reservations?"

Jarrett shook his head. "No. The owner and I are good friends." He grinned. "Of course, it doesn't hurt that I have flown him to restaurant tradeshows in the company jet and have taken him tuna fishing miles offshore."

"And for that he lets you walk right in?"

"That's right," he said. "He's left orders I'm to be seated immediately upon arrival."

Across the way, two couples stood and started toward the door. When one of the men saw Jarrett, he diverted the group in their direction. Shaking a finger, he glared at Jarrett. "Remember. You promised me you'll be my captain. I've too much invested in this race not to have you at the helm."

Jarrett held up his hand. "Kate, this is Andrew Fletcher. He's one of those dot-com guys with more money and free time than he knows what to do with. He's heading up a group to be the next America's Cup challenger for the United States."

Focused, the man continued, "I'll win the damn thing hands down too if I can get you to skipper my boat."

The woman with the other man in the group stepped forward. "You're Jarrett Sinclair," she said. "Our friends Mandy and Earl never stop talking about you. You saved their son's life when you flew him off Everest. I can hardly wait to tell them I met you."

Fletcher nudged her aside. "Remember, Jarrett, you promised me. I need you to race my boat."

Kate watched as the couples departed. "What was that all about?"

"I've raced sailboats for years. It's a passion of mine," he said.

"No," she said. "Not that. That woman said you saved her friend's son on Everest, the mountain I presume? What were you doing over there?"

"A company I own developed a high-altitude helicopter. We picked the government of Nepal as our first customer and were there doing a demonstration. When that kid fell, I flew him out." He smiled. "It made for a convincing sales presentation."

She recalled the pictures of him in the *Nation's Meat* magazine with spray flashing by. "As I recall, you also race speedboats."

"We prefer to call them powerboats," he said. "But yes, I race them every chance I get. Next time I go racing, you'll have to come along."

Kate drew back. She couldn't picture herself in a bikini hanging over his shoulder as he bounded from wave to wave. "I don't think I'd be much good on a boat. Anyway, it looks like you already have a couple helpers."

Studying what she said, he slowly laughed. "Oh, you mean the picture in that magazine?"

"Yes," she said.

"That was the editor's idea. He thought it would sell more copies." He shook his head. "What I meant was, you should come and watch the race from the shore."

With dinner over, she stifled a yawn. "Jarrett, it's late, and I need to get to the hotel and get some sleep. It's been a long day, and I have to be alert tomorrow."

Jarrett agreed. A mile from the restaurant, he stopped at an all-night megapharmacy. She looked at the store. "Why are we stopping? You need something?" She could only imagine what it might be. Was he planning a big evening and had forgotten protection? Sliding away, she widened the space between them. She glowered. *I'm really not into quickies.*

He pointed at the store. "You'll need a toothbrush and toothpaste and whatever. You better stock up here. The hotel gift shop is probably closed."

"Oh," she replied and slowly agreed. "Good idea."

Minutes later at the hotel, she discovered her decision that the hotel could wait was flawed. "I'm sorry, Ms. Clark," the manager explained, "we're full."

She stared at the man. She was tired and needed a place to sleep, and this was not what she wanted to hear. "I don't understand. I have a reservation. I made it weeks ago. It was an all-inclusive package program."

"Yes," the man said. "I know you're part of the Logan Software group. You were also the only one not sharing a room. When twelve hours passed and you hadn't checked in, as per instructions, we assumed you weren't coming and let the room to someone else."

She couldn't recall reading anything about checking in twelve hours in advance, but it sounded logical.

Jarrett stepped forward. "She needs a place to stay tonight. Can you get her into another hotel nearby?"

Shaking his head, the manager cast a critical eye. "The hotels that have rooms available around here at this late hour are, well, shall I say, not exactly respectable. To find anything respectable, she'll have to go north to San Fernando or south of Anaheim. This being summer, every decent hotel nearby is booked solid until September."

Kate looked at the manager. With no knowledge by which to validate his statement, she assumed what he said was true. "What am I supposed to do? I need a place to sleep."

"If you have friends in town, you might give them a call."

She looked at the man. The only person she knew in Los Angeles to ask that kind of favor was standing a couple feet away.

Jarrett pointed toward the door. "I guess you're going to bunk with me tonight. My place is not far. You can sleep there. It's only minutes from your meeting."

"If it isn't too much trouble, borrowing a room in your house would be appreciated."

He shook his head. "A room in my house is out. Rachel and her gang are working to meet a deadline. The place is a hellhole. I even moved out myself. Until they're finished, I'm staying in the apartment I keep in my office tower downtown. It's comfortable and not far from your class."

Nothing more was said as he drove to his building. Too tired to comment, Kate followed. The elevator stopped one floor from the top. "Where's your office?"

"One floor up," he said and led the way down the hall. Pushing the door open, he hit a switch, and lights came on at each end of a long sofa.

Surveying the room, Kate's spirits lifted. "Wow, this is nice," she said. "A cute living room." She smiled agreeably on seeing the large sofa and end tables. Turning, she looked toward the kitchenette. "Now, that's handy. A stove, little refrig, a sink," she said. Next to that was a table with two chairs. Beyond that were floor-to-ceiling windows with a commanding view of the city. Next to the glass was a bar with two tall stools. Satisfied, she nodded agreeably. *I'll be comfortable here*, she concluded and stepped toward the sofa. "Don't even offer me a bed. If you have a spare blanket, I'll be quite comfortable on the sofa."

"I doubt that," he said and set her packages down in front of some bifold doors. Stepping over to the sofa, he pressed a panel, and the sofa lowered, and a wall section swung down, revealing a fully made-up king-sized bed. He pointed at the bed. "Pick your side," he said and motioned toward the closed door. "The bathroom is there. If you want, you can have the side closest to it. It's your choice."

Kate shuddered and took a step back. "Sorry, Jarrett, when you said bunk with you, I thought you meant in the same house, but not in the same room, and especially not in the same bed." With jaw muscles set, she backed toward the hall. "I'm sorry, I'm not into one-night stands."

Jarrett pulled his shirt from his pants. "Who said anything about that?" he grumbled. "I'm exhausted. I need a good night's sleep. Now, if you have some funny ideas, you can keep them to yourself." Yawning, he pointed at the bed. "Make up your mind. That bed is wide enough for you, me, and your horse. So pick your side and let's call it a night. We're both exhausted."

Looking at the bed, she studied the situation. *What choice do I have? Where else can I go?* She looked at him and then at the bed. *Put that way, I guess it'll be okay.* She yawned. *He's not coming on to me. He's just offering me a place to sleep.* She pointed at the bed. "I'll take the side closest to the bath."

"It's yours," he said and motioned toward the bifold doors. "There's the closet. Push my stuff to the side and use whatever space you need. You can change in the bathroom, and I'll change out here."

She pulled a sleep shirt from one of the sacks and, with the bag of toiletries went to the bathroom. Changed, she studied her reflection in the mirror. *What am I doing? How will I ever explain this to Wylie?* She stared at herself. *I won't. Tomorrow he'll be gone.* She cracked the door open. "Okay to come out?"

"Yes."

He had turned off the lights with the exception of the one on the small stand on her side of the bed. Seated at the bar, he was silhouetted in the light coming up from the street. She hung up what she had taken off and looked his way. "What are you drinking?"

"Wine. I opened a bottle." He pointed toward the kitchenette. "Have some if you want. Glasses are in the cupboard above the sink."

She studied the situation. Alcohol, she didn't need right then. Empty-handed, she hoisted herself up on the other stool. She looked down at the street a couple hundred feet below and on to downtown Los Angeles silhouetted against the night sky. "Quite a sight."

"Nothing like what you have up north." He drained his glass and set it on the counter. Dressed in cutoff sweatpants, he set his glass in the sink. "Morning is going to come soon enough. I hung up your dresses. The loose stuff you can put in the drawers tomorrow. I could put on a nightlight except there's so much light coming up from the street I don't think you'll need it. When you're finished, pull the curtains closed. I've set the alarm for seven. In the morning, stop by the security desk, and they'll get you transportation to your class."

"Thanks. I'll grab breakfast down on the street and take a cab to the conference." She closed the curtains and made her way around to her side of the bed. Across the way, he was already in bed. His breathing was slow. *Unbelievable. He's already nearly asleep.* She sighed. *Thank goodness for that.*

The morning light shone bright against the closed curtains. The space beside her was empty. The door to the bathroom was open. She checked his side of the bed—cold. *Huh. The least you could have done was say good-bye and have a nice stay.* She stopped. *On second thought, maybe leaving unannounced was for the best.*

After showering, she reached into one of the bags and dug around for clean underwear. Her sturdy chest-flattening sports bra and comfortable cotton panties from the day before were soiled. She raised an eyebrow when the first thing she came up with was a sheer lace bra and matching low-cut briefs. She checked each quickly and laid them aside. "These are definitely not me," she mumbled with a measure of resolve. "What could that woman have been thinking to pick these? Didn't she see what I was wearing?" She continued her search and found only more of the same. Laying them out, she made with a negative groan. "Black, white, neutral, and more white and another black," she said, thinking aloud. "I guess I don't have much choice." Picking a bra, she slipped it on and the panties that matched. She looked down. "Oh god, this is really not me," she whispered and adjusted the fit.

Moments later, her expression eased. To her amazement, they were comfortable, so comfortable in fact she was nearly unaware she was wearing anything at all. "Wow," she whispered. Turning, she checked herself in the full-length mirror. She took a breath. Unlike with the everyday, chest-flattening, industrial-strength bras she wore in Montana that kept her all trussed up so things wouldn't flop and jiggle when she worked horses and cattle, she felt free. She could breathe comfortably and move unrestrained. Running her hands over her breasts, she glowed. *Unbelievable. Almost like when I float naked in my mountain lake.* The lace bra shaped her like no bra had ever done before. *My god, I look like a woman.* Blushing, she studied her reflection and slowly smiled. *Yes, this is better.*

Picking out the first skirt-and-blouse combination Jarrett had helped her select, she dressed and stepped into the bath to check in the mirror. She stared at her reflection. "Yes, this is something," she whispered and studied the finished product. "Maybe this is what the big city is all about."

Exhaling, she grabbed her brush. Behind her, the door to the hall inched open. "Are you decent?" Jarrett called. "Can I come in?"

Spinning around, the brush flew from her hand. Fumbling about, she caught it before it hit the floor. "Yes," she replied and stepped out into the room. *Oh my.* She gasped. Dressed in a dark suit, he was more handsome then she remembered him from Spokane. Studying him, a smile graced her lips. "Weren't you supposed to be out of town today?"

He set a sack on the kitchenette counter. "I am. I'll be leaving in an hour."

She pointed. "What's in the bag?"

"Breakfast. There was nothing here in the apartment, so I went down to the cafeteria. I found orange juice and breakfast rolls and some eggs, bacon, milk, and butter. There are mugs in the cupboard, and the coffeepot is over there." He glanced at the time. "Either you got up early or dress really fast. The alarm must've just gone off."

"I was up early. I even had time to shower."

He snapped his fingers and dug in his pocket. "I almost forgot. Here's a key to the apartment. You're free to come and go as you please." He handed her the key and a laminated plastic card. "This is your ID card to get in the building after hours. Show it to the night guard, or if he's not there, run it through the reader beside the front door. That'll get you in the building."

Kate studied what he handed her. He was either going to be out of town or too busy to see her. *Be thankful you had that time together last night.*

At Logan Software, she was directed to the classroom. With the introductions completed, the instructor began. Before long, she discovered the instructor was lecturing directly from the course material they had supplied. She had studied that and could easily follow along. Halfway focused on the instructor, she scanned the others in attendance. Aside from herself, there was one other woman who was with her husband. She grinned subtly when she caught many of the men more than casually glancing in her direction. *How about that?* She nodded warmly. *I don't know if underwear makes the woman, but it sure appears to make a difference.*

13

Following class, Kate returned to the apartment. The room had been neatly made up. The kitchenette was cleaned. The door to the bath was open, and she could see a note had been taped to the mirror.

> *Hi, Kate. Had to fly to Flagstaff. Should be back by seven. I'd like to show you some of LA and then take you to dinner.*
>
> *See you. Jarrett.*

Kate glowed. "Great, I won't be eating alone." She checked the time, and in fifteen minutes, Jarrett would be coming through the door. Looking away, she caught sight of the telephone. "Oh my god, Wylie. I've forgotten to call him." Grabbing her cell phone, she flipped it open. She started to call, and the screen went blank. "Damn! The battery is dead," she said. Turning, she grabbed the apartment phone. She punched in her home number and listened to it ring until her answering machine clicked in. "Wylie. I'm not at the hotel. My reservation got fouled up. I'm staying in an apartment. My cell phone battery died. I'll charge it tonight. The phone number here is…" She looked down to get the number off the phone, and there was nothing there. "Forget it. I'll try you at your place."

Using the same phone, she dialed his house. Wylie answered in one ring. "Where are you? Where've you been? Are you okay? I called

102

the hotel, and they told me you weren't registered. I telephoned the software company, and they didn't know where you were staying. I tried your cell phone and no answer. What are you doing? Where are you?"

"Yes. I'm okay. I'm sorry. I'll charge my phone tonight. What are you doing at your house? I tried our place, and you weren't there."

"Your dad has everything under control. He's running things from his pickup. I had work to do at my place, so I'm staying here. So where are you?"

No matter how she described last night's sleeping arrangement, she knew it wouldn't sound good. "The airline lost my luggage, and I had to go downtown to put in a claim. I bumped into...." She caught herself when she realized it would sound less personal if she used Jarrett's last name. "Sinclair. He took me shopping. We went to dinner, and by the time I got to the hotel, they were full. He's letting me use an apartment they have in their office tower downtown."

"Is that Sinclair fellow around?"

She looked toward the door. "No. Last I heard, he was off east someplace."

"You watch out. There are a lot of hoodlums in LA. I see it all the time on TV. You take care and make sure you keep the door locked at night."

"Don't worry, I will," she said. Turning, she checked the door. Jarrett would be there shortly. She needed to conclude the call.

Wylie continued, "I talked to the development company today, and I can't believe it, but even without your upper range, they're still interested."

"Is that a fact?" Kate questioned. The door opened, and Jarrett stepped in. She glanced at him and back at the telephone. The developer's ideas were not something she could discuss right then. "Let's talk about this tomorrow? I have to go to dinner."

"Don't you have a minute to hear what the developer had to say?"

Kate shook her head. Jarrett was but feet away. "No, I'm late. Please let's talk tomorrow." As she spoke, Jarrett stepped over to the kitchenette and pointed at the bottle of wine. She mouthed yes and returned to the call. "Wylie, I have to go. People are waiting. I'll call tomorrow. Okay?"

With the call concluded, Kate stepped over to the bar. "I didn't get a chance to call Wylie last night." With the wineglass in hand, she climbed up on the other stool. "I guess you're not going to be out of town the rest of the week."

Seated sideways, he rested an arm on the bar and the other on the back of the stool. "Lillian juggled things around and has everything straightened out."

"I bet you're glad of that," she said. "By the way, thanks. I appreciate the note. How was your trip to Flagstaff? Everything went well, I hope?"

"Yes." He held up his watch. "I told you I was going to show you some of the city and then buy you dinner." He pointed toward the closet. "You need to change. We're going upscale."

She glanced down at her dark suit jacket with the matching skirt and formal white blouse. "This won't work?"

"Nah. It's a little too buttoned up. You have those cocktail dresses. You might as well wear one."

"Whatever," she said. Stepping over to the closet, she pulled out the three dresses. "Which one, blue, white, or black?"

He studied the three. "The black is too formal, and the white to sterile." He continued, "Wear the blue one. It'll fit the occasion."

A few miles from the apartment, he pointed off to the side. "Our symphony performs there. I'm a major contributor and know the conductor well. They're off this week. Otherwise, I'd introduce you."

She looked where he pointed. "You go there often?"

He shook his head. "Not as often as I'd like. I'm on the road a lot."

Further on, he made a sweeping gesture. "This is infamous Hollywood. If we turn at the next corner, we would go past the Hollywood Bowl." Further on, he slowed and pointed at the street ahead. "This is Hollywood and the Walk of Fame." Minutes later, he turned into a narrow street and stopped in front of a theater.

Kate looked out. "Are we going to a show? I thought we were going to dinner?"

"We are. I'm making a quick stop." Jumping out, he dashed around to her side and reached for the door as the valet stepped up. "I'll take it from here, Eddie." He pointed at the car. "You don't need to park it. We're only going to be a couple minutes."

"Yes, sir, Mr. Sinclair."

Jarrett led the way past the entrance and down the alley off to the side. She looked back. "The valet knew you. You must come here often."

"He better know me. I own the theater and the production company producing the play." The attendant at the side door let them in. Jarrett pulled her close. "We'll have to keep our voices down. It's not yet intermission."

Just inside, a man greeted them. Speaking softly, he little more than mouthed his words. "Evening, Jarrett."

Kate looked around. She was backstage in a dark wing off to the side. Women stood ready with racks of clothes to help the actors change. Performers stood in the shadows, waiting for their cues.

The man who greeted them whispered to Jarrett, "The numbers are in. We're sold out through September. You have another big hit."

"Excellent," Jarrett replied. Leaning close, he whispered to Kate, "Calvin is the manager. You two talk. I'll be right back. I'm going to the office."

Minutes later, the houselights came up, and the curtain was drawn. "Intermission," Calvin said in a normal voice. He waved to one of the actors exiting the stage. "Kate, this is our lead, Phillip Claymore. You've probably seen him in a number of Westerns." He turned toward the slender actor with graying hair. "Phil, this is Katherine Clark. Jarrett's rancher friend from Montana."

"Ah yes, Westerns. I used to do a lot of them when I was younger. I was a pretty good rider, if I say so myself."

She studied him. "Yes, I remember you. You were one of my mother's favorites. Mom used to say your voice sounded like it came out of a canyon. She loved listening to you, and Dad enjoyed watching you ride."

The actor beamed. "Your mother has good taste. I'd love to meet her someday."

Kate quickly explained her mother had passed away, but her smile put him at ease. "I can hardly wait to tell my dad I met you."

Jarrett returned. "Calvin, the numbers look great. There's no way we can shut down at the end of this run."

"You'll have to get that other theater finished so the new show can open there."

"I'm working on it," Jarrett said and turned toward the actor. "Phillip, your performance is, as usual, magnificent. I'd swear I could hear that great voice of yours two blocks away."

The actor grinned. "Only two blocks away, Mr. Sinclair? I must be losing my touch."

Everyone chuckled. "We'd talk longer, but you need your break, and we're heading for dinner," Jarrett said. Taking Kate's arm, he led the way to the car.

She glowed as they pulled away. There was so much to do in Los Angeles—the theater, the symphony, the Hollywood Bowl. Every day would be different. Her pulse quickened. *Montana is nothing like this.*

Jarrett pointed at another theater. "That's where most of the movie premiers are held. You'd love going. The list of celebrities is endless."

She looked where he pointed. *Seeing all the celebrities would be quite an experience, but then again maybe not. Would I be just another one of the many photographed with him, hanging onto his arm?*

"We're here," Sinclair announced. Stopping in front of a restaurant, the attendant was quick to offer assistance. As at the theater, Jarrett was around to her side. He reached to help her out. "You look fabulous."

"Thank you," she replied. "You don't look so bad yourself."

The uniformed doorman bowed as he opened the door. "Good evening, Ms. Clark. Good evening, Mr. Sinclair."

"Evening, Jimmy."

Inside, she whispered, "They know you here too. Don't tell me you own this place as well?"

"Yes. I called and told them I was bringing a guest and gave them your name." He moved past the people waiting to be seated and around the red rope across the entrance. "Hello, Charles."

The maître d' said, "Good evening, Mr. Sinclair. Good evening, Ms. Clark. Your table is ready."

"Amazing," Kate whispered. "You own a theater and a restaurant."

"Actually, I own three theaters and five restaurants. If I like them, I buy them."

She took note of the surroundings as the maître d' led the way. She suspected many of the people at the tables were persons of note. Some might even be celebrities she'd recognize, but she chose not to stare. They stopped at a table set off by itself. The maître d' assisted with her chair. "Thank you." Seated and with the man gone, she looked at Jarrett. "Do you come here often?"

"Mostly with business contacts."

She studied the menu. Everything looked to be in French or some language she could not read, and she set it aside. "This is your restaurant. What do you suggest?"

"If you would like, I can do the ordering."

She agreed.

He motioned to the waiter, who was quickly table side. "Robert, this is my guest, Katherine Clark." He handed the menus to the waiter. "Robert, what muse does Antwain have this evening?"

"Sir, the amuse-bouche is magnificent. Antwain has personally prepared his special salmon mousse. It is on a cucumber slice with his own signature Dijon vinaigrette."

"Excellent." Jarrett winked at Kate. "Antwain is my chef. He's an artist, one of the best in the country." Mentally reviewing the menu, he looked at the waiter. "We'll have the amuse-bouche with a small glass of Cristal. Then we'll have the caviar with Stolichnaya and the foie gras with Chateau d'Yquem 1959. For fish, we'll have the abalone with Fiano di Avellino Campania 2003." Kate watched as Jarrett rattled off item after item. He looked at the waiter. "How is the ostrich tonight?"

"Sir, the tenderloins are some of the best I've seen."

"Excellent. We'll have the ostrich tenderloins with Chateau Latour A Pomerol '61. After that, bring a selection of cheeses with some Rémy Martin cognac. And dessert, hmm." He looked at Kate and then back at the waiter. "We'll have the vanilla bean crème brûlée...on second thought, make that the Grand Marnier soufflé. After that, we'll finish with Torrefazione Italia coffee."

The waiter left. Kate's brow arched. "Wow. That sounds like a lot of food. I don't know if I'm up to eating all that."

Jarrett grinned. "Don't worry. Antwain makes the portions small."

When the first course arrived, she studied it. "This is beautiful. I'm almost afraid to eat it."

"It is, except Antwain would feel slighted if you didn't," Jarrett said.

Finishing the fish course, she leaned back. The service had been as it was supposed to be: nearly invisible. "This food is without equal. The best I've ever had." She took a bite of ostrich and savored the taste. "Mmmm," she murmured. "This is magnificent, and that's something coming from a person who makes her living raising beef."

After dessert, she looked to Jarrett. "You said Lillian has everything straightened out. Where are you off to tomorrow? Florida?"

"No. Florida has been delayed. Tomorrow morning, I have a project dedication in San Diego, followed by two meetings here and then a dinner session at the state capital, which is expected to run quite late. From there, I'll fly to an early meeting in Dallas, and then up to Denver to check on a possible development, and then back here."

"Then you'll be in town day after tomorrow?"

"Yes. It'll be our last chance for dinner before your farewell celebration on Friday. I hope you don't mind, but I've planned something special for our last night together. The medical research foundation I started is having a cocktail reception to celebrate their fifth anniversary. It's going to be quite the formal affair. That black dress you have will be just the ticket. I'd like it if you'd accompany me."

A warm feeling swelled up within her. They would be together again. "I'd love to."

"Then it's settled. I'll pick up you at the apartment at seven on Thursday."

On his feet, Jarrett extended his hand, when the music started. "May I have this dance?"

She hesitated. *Whew, I don't know if I'm up to this. The only dancing I've done has been square.* Getting to her feet, she drew back. "Jarrett, it's late. I have class tomorrow, and I have to get some rest."

Back at his office tower, he opened the door to the apartment and stepped aside. She stopped in the doorway. "Thank you. It's been an enjoyable evening, and one I'll never forget. I'd invite you in, but it's late, and I need to get to bed, and I imagine you want to get home as well."

He looked past her and pointed at the bed. "While I could have you toss out a pillow and blanket so I can sleep here in the hall, I'd prefer to sleep in my bed."

"What?" She looked at the bed and then back at him. "Your friend and her crew are still working in your house?"

"Yes," he said.

Taking a step back, she gnawed on her lip. Turning, she looked at the bed and then back at him. "You're not going home?"

"Correct."

She looked at the bed and swallowed hard. "Then you want to sleep here?" Again, he affirmed. She hesitated. "I guess if your house is still a mess, it's not my place to say no."

Grabbing what she needed, she disappeared into the bathroom. Changing slowly, she studied her reflection in the mirror as she tried to sort out what to do next. For the second night, she would be sharing the bed with a man, and not just any man, Jarrett Sinclair. *What'll I do? How will I explain this to Wylie? I can't.* She inched the door open. "Okay to come out?"

She waited, and there was no response. About to repeat her request, she heard a faint, mumbled, "Yes."

Kate stepped out. The room was dark. To her relief, Jarrett was already in bed. He was on the side he used the night before, facing away. "Thankfully," she whispered. Sliding in, she pulled the covers up and looked his way. His breathing was slow. *It can't be. He's already asleep?*

14

When the alarm rang, Kate was quick to sit up. The room was empty. Jarrett was gone. "Thank goodness," she mumbled. Showered, dressed, and having downed a couple cups of coffee, she went to class. With her mind on Jarrett, she heard little of the instructor's lecture. Fortunately, she had studied the text and followed along easily. By the end of class, she was ready to collapse.

Exhausted, she trudged into the apartment and shoved the door closed. As before, everything had been put in order. She deposited her course materials on the bed and looked toward the bathroom. Once again, a note had been taped to the mirror.

> *Hi. Sorry I missed you. I flew to San Diego and then back here for those meetings. I'm leaving now for Sacramento. I'll be back tomorrow night. I'm looking forward to our last night together. I'll be by at seven to get you. If you want to eat in, I had the cafeteria stock the refrigerator. Jarrett.*

Settling in at the table, she kicked off her shoes and reached for the phone. She owed Wylie a call. After yesterday, she needed to let him finish. "You'd met with the developer and were going to tell me what they had to say."

"I told the representative from Wilderness Pines your position. He was surprised but didn't seem too bothered. He said he was meeting with the owner of the company tomorrow and would get back to me after that. Even without your property, they're interested. Don't you find that exciting?"

"No, I don't find that exciting," Kate snapped back. "Without my upper range, they'll have nothing. So they'll have yours and Patty's places, where'll they build their ski runs? And that Swiss village? What about that?"

"I don't know. I just know he's still interested in our ranches. He said he'd get back to me shortly with an offer."

Kate pulled back. "Are you telling me you'd consider selling to them?"

There was a pause. When he continued, his voice had taken on a conciliatory tone. "I don't know. I'd at least like to hear what they have to say."

She glared at the phone. "Need I remind you it has been our goal to rebuild the ranch to what Nat had envisioned?"

"No, I haven't forgotten," Wylie replied. "I know that has always been your goal, but still I'd like to hear what they are thinking."

Kate slumped back in the chair. *Arguing with you right now is pointless.* "Wylie, I'm exhausted. Let's talk about this when I get home."

"You're right. We don't have to discuss this now. You sound beat. Call me tomorrow."

"I…" She caught herself. Jarrett had that special evening planned that probably wouldn't be over until late. "Tomorrow we'll be going out to dinner and an evening on the town. If you don't hear from me, that's why. And Friday is the farewell dinner. If I call, it'll be early."

⁂

At Logan Software, it was late when the instructor looked at his watch. "It's after six, and we can finish tomorrow." He closed his laptop. "Remember, our farewell dinner tomorrow night at the Crown Royal. Neat casual is the dress code. What you have on today will be fine."

Kate grabbed her materials and was out the door. At the apartment, the message light was flashing on the answering machine. It was Jarrett. "Hi. Tonight will be special, so I had Lillian get something extra to go with that black dress. See you at seven."

Kate found the Cartier bag and pulled out the small box. Inside were earrings each with a single diamond a good couple karats in size. "Wow." *This indeed is going to be a special evening.*

Dressed in the black dress, she stepped to the bathroom mirror. The folds of the material draped smoothly from her shoulders. "Ooooh," she whispered as she ran her hands down the dress. The soft fabric against her skin made her feel warm and feminine inside. "Yes," she said and turned from side to side. *This is definitely better than jeans and a Western shirt.*

The hall door opened. It was Jarrett. "Are you ready?"

"I am," she said. He was dressed in a black tuxedo. The white fluted shirt was in stark contrast to his golden tan and flowing black hair. "My, aren't you handsome."

Jarrett motioned for her to turn around. "I have something for you." When she did, he slipped a necklace under her chin.

"What's this?" she asked and ran her fingers over what he had hung around her neck.

"It goes with the earrings."

"It does?" she said and stepped into the bathroom to look in the mirror. When she did, she gasped. He had hung around her neck a string of diamonds in a white-gold setting, which matched the earrings for both size and brilliance. "Incredible. What are these for?"

"They're a little something to complement the dress."

She returned to the main room. "This must have cost a fortune."

"A couple hundred, but I can afford it," Sinclair replied.

She blinked and ran her fingers over the necklace again. "A couple hundred, thousand, dollars?"

He nodded.

She looked at him. *What could have possessed him to spend that kind of money on such a frivolous gift? What could he expect in return?*

Downstairs, the doorman opened the door to the awaiting Rolls Royce limousine. "Good evening, Mr. Sinclair. Good evening, Ms. Clark."

Kate looked at the car. *This indeed is going to be very special.*

Across the city, the car eased to a stop in front of a large Moorish-style building set on the breast of a hill. The building's white marble exterior picked up the colors of the setting sun. Positioned overlooking the city, the Los Angeles Basin was spread out below. The valet reached for the door. "Good evening, Mr. Sinclair."

"Evening, Robert," Jarrett said and reached in for Kate. "Allow me."

The gold letters above the entrance read "The Albert and Amelia Sinclair Medical Research Center." Beneath that, the tall doors were open. Beyond the foyer was a large central hall filled with people, formally dressed. Holding her arm, Jarrett led the way to an older couple, standing apart from the rest.

"Kate, I'd like you to meet my mother and father. Dad, Mom, this is Kate Clark. She's one of AJS Foods' major beef suppliers."

Jarrett's father stepped forward. "Hi, I'm Albert, and this beauty is Amelia." His eyes shone as he reached for Kate's hand. "We've heard he had a beef supplier here from Montana. He didn't tell us how beautiful you are."

Kate blushed. "Thank you. Jarrett said you were in the South Pacific SCUBA diving."

"We were, until he sent a jet for us." His handshake was firm and his smile friendly. "So you're here to sell him more beef?"

Jarrett stepped forward. "No, Dad. She's here attending a software conference."

Jarrett's mother nudged the two men aside. "You two go talk business. It's my turn to visit with this lovely person." With her arm hooked around Kate's, she started toward the center of the room. A shorter woman with a pronounced matronly figure, she motioned to a waiter and got them each a champagne. "Let's go outside where it's cool. It's too stuffy in here." Not until they were on the terrace overlooking the city did his mother let go.

The lights of the city were coming on and twinkled in the waning light. To the west, the sun appeared to have momentarily stopped at the edge of the horizon, reluctant to let go of the day. "Quite a sight," Amelia said. Below them, headlights beamed, and turn signals flashed. Turning smartly, she looked at Kate. "What do you think of my son?"

Kate blinked. Studying Amelia's expression, she sensed the woman was expecting an answer. "He's very determined and has accomplished quite a bit. I'm pleased to be one of his major suppliers."

Amelia's gaze narrowed. "You're right he's done far more than his father and I ever considered possible." As Amelia spoke, she pointed at the building. "This is all his doing. He's built the businesses way beyond anything we could have imagined, and at the same time, he's done all this. Oh, sure, our name is on the front, but that's just his way of showing everyone what he thinks of his mom and dad. The money behind this foundation and the driving force is all Jarrett."

Amelia's expression turned serious. "Nine years ago, when Jarrett came home after Al's heart attack, we were dead broke. The banks were ready to take what little we had left." Her expression brightened. "And then Jarrett took over. He grabbed the company by the seat of the pants and took control. In two months, he'd pulled the company away from the brink of disaster. He'd found his calling. He's aggressive and plays to win. He's an incredible businessman. When he sets his mind to do something, he doesn't stop until he gets it. Those who have gotten in his way have lived to regret it. That's the Jarrett who built this building and funded this foundation." She sighed. "I guess you have to be ruthless to build an empire." Easing back, she continued, "He has a softer side, though, and it's that side that his father and I love dearly. I'm sure that's the side of him that attracted him to you."

Kate sipped champagne and half-listened as Amelia rambled on about what she and Albert were doing. *What do you mean that's the side that's attracted him to me? Yes. He's handsome and exciting, but I didn't seek him out. Circumstances have put us together.*

Amelia tugged on her arm. She motioned in the direction of the slender man with thinning hair and rimless glasses walked their way. "Kate, I'd like you to meet the director of the foundation, Dr. Condon Norman. A brilliant man. Jarrett was lucky to get him." Amelia reached out and accepted his hand. "Condon, this is Jarrett's friend from Montana, Kate Clark."

"Good evening, Ms. Clark. Amelia is most flattering. Jarrett has given me free rein to focus on what I've always wanted, Alzheimer's research."

Amelia patted Kate's arm. "It's been a pleasure. I'm looking forward to us getting together. I'll give you a call Monday. We can have lunch before Pappy and I head back to the South Pacific. I have to get to know you better."

Norman drew Kate away. "Amelia, I'm sure she'll be in touch, but it's my turn to visit with our guest of honor and then introduce her to some people she needs to meet."

About to tell Amelia she wouldn't be in town next week, she snapped around to focus on Norman. *What do you mean guest of honor? Jarrett's parents are the guests of honor. After all, the foundation is named after them.* She studied the man. *And what people do I need to meet? Are these people you think I should know, or is Jarrett behind that as well?* Half-focused on the man, she looked for Jarrett. *If there are people I need to meet, why aren't you doing the introductions?*

Dr. Norman guided her back to the main room. "Ms. Clark, I'm pleased you could honor us with your presence. This is our fifth anniversary, and with Jarrett's connections and financial support, we've done remarkably well in a very short period of time." Kate worked on the champagne while he told her about the great strides he was making in his research. "We're so looking forward to your addition to our board of directors. Here's my card. Call me next week. I'll introduce you to our board, and we can have lunch together. You're the kind of person we need."

Kate blinked. "You're offering me a position on the board of directors? Why? We've only met. You don't know anything about me."

"Oh, I know quite a bit about you," he said. "I've studied the dossier Jarrett sent over, and I'm as impressed as he is with your qualifications and your understanding of business. I realize you live in Montana, but if you can see your way clear to join us here, you can be an asset to our organization."

Momentarily speechless, Kate stared at the man. "Really?" she questioned. "You've studied my dossier?"

"Yes," Norman replied.

She looked for Jarrett. *You have a lot of explaining to do. You shared what you learned about me without my permission. Where do you get off doing that?* Her brow furrowed. *Where is that man?*

Dr. Norman tugged on her arm and directed her attention toward an unshaven man in jeans, a wrinkled white shirt, and a battered black leather sports coat. "That's Stanley Rolstadler." When Kate made no response, he continued, "You know, the two-time Academy Award-winning movie producer/director. He's the hottest thing in Hollywood right now. Whatever he touches turns to gold. The last three films he and Jarrett have done together were box-office sensations." Getting them each a fresh champagne, he made their way to the man. "Stan, this is Ms. Clark. Kate, this is—"

Before he could finish, Stanley took her hand and pulled her away.

"So this is the celebrated cattle rancher from Montana I've heard so much about. How marvelous."

You've heard about me from whom? Jarrett? About to ask Rolstadler that, she couldn't as Dr. Norman continued, "Kate, I'll leave you to Stan. You have my card, so give me a call Monday, and we can have lunch next week. I have so much I want to share with you."

Kate looked from one man to the other. She was about to tell Norman she'd be leaving in two days, but Rolstadler was tugging on her hand, and Norman had faded into the crowd.

Rolstadler spoke up, "When AJ wanted to get into the movie business, I got him started."

Kate's brow furrowed.

"AJ, Jarrett," he repeated. "That's what I call him. Anyway, when he wanted to get into the picture business, I gave him his big break when all the other directors in this town turned him down. No one took this brash young man with a pile of money seriously. Now, don't get me wrong. People in this business are always in need of funding, but still no one would let him in because he demanded a significant say in each movie. Jarrett is a controller. He'll look at what I've shot and say he wants this scene or that reshot, and to keep him happy, I'll do it. If that keeps the money flowing in, who am I to complain?" He chuckled. "Did he tell you we're doing another movie together?"

Kate shook her head.

Not letting up, Rolstadler continued to describe their current project. He pulled out a business card and wrote a number on the back. "Here's my private number. Give me a call next week. I'll give you a tour of the studio."

"I'd enjoy that," she replied.

He checked her over. "I'll do even better. I'll put you in a scene or two as an extra. You'll be right up front, where all your friends can see you."

As Stanley continued, Kate's attention was drawn away by a man with graying hair who stepped up and reached in for her hand. "Hello, Ms. Clark, I'm Dr. Kenneth Carswell, dean of obstetrics and gynecology at the University Medical School." He turned to Stan. "It's my turn now. You've had her long enough," he said and tried to draw her away.

Stan held firm. "Kate, call me the first of the week. When you do, I'll slip you into a small speaking part. It'll only be in a couple of scenes but noticeable all the same." He winked. "You'll have a ball, and it'll give you something to show off to the people back home."

"I'll do that," she said. *What am I saying? My class is over tomorrow. I'll be going home this weekend.*

Dean Carswell tugged on her arm and drew her away. "I'll give Stanley credit. He at least had the decency to wear a black jacket to this formal affair. I'm sure Stanley has told you how he let Jarrett invest in his movies."

Kate nodded.

"The truth is, Jarrett is a great judge of talent and scripts. When Jarrett says a scene needs to be reshot, Stan does it. Stan is an okay director, but the real force behind his movies is Jarrett," he said knowingly. "Stan gets to play the big-shot director while Jarrett stands in the background and collects all the money." As he spoke, he pulled out his card. "Give me a call next week. I've reviewed what Jarrett sent over, and I'm impressed. Come next week, and I'll give you a tour of the hospital and introduce you to the selection board. We'd like to have you on the scholarship selection committee."

About to counter, *I can't because I'll be gone,* she eased back. A pattern had formed. *This is the second person who is offering me a position. I have my ranch to run. I can't move down here to do what these men are asking.* She looked for Jarrett. *Where are you? You have a lot of explaining to do. Are you trying to get me to move off my ranch and why? What do you hope to gain by doing that?*

Dean Carswell nudged her and directed her attention to a young woman across the room. "Recognize her?"

Kate looked where he pointed and blinked. "Is that who I think it is?"

"That's Erica Heath," he said. "Academy Award-winning actress. She's been in a couple of their movies." He leaned in close. "Keep your eye on her. Rumor has it at one time she was after Jarrett. She still might be."

"Really?" Kate asked.

Carswell stepped up to the actress. "Erica, this is Kate Clark, Jarrett's friend from Montana. I'll leave you two to visit." He turned to Kate. "Now, remember, call me next week, and we'll get together. I'm looking forward to showing you our program."

"I will," she said. Turning, she was drawn to the actress. Her figure was slight, her facial features striking, and her smile inviting. *Oh my, you're beautiful.* Sipping on a fresh champagne, she studied the woman and tried to think. *What do you say to someone who has won an Academy Award? Da. I raise cattle, and they eat hay.*

Erica looked in the direction of Dean Carswell. "Let me guess, he said I have eyes for Jarrett."

Kate slowly responded, "Something like that."

"Yes," Erica said. "I find him fun and exciting. He's gorgeous and rich. Half the actresses in Hollywood have dreamt of going to bed with him. But hey, there's no law against that. I've enjoyed accompanying him to premiers, but get seriously involved? No way. If I can't get ahead on my acting ability, I'll give this up and go back to teaching school." As she spoke, the waiter tried to hand her a fresh champagne.

Kate shook her head. "No. I've had two already," she said with slurred speech, unaware she was about to finish her third glass.

Erica studied her. "I'm in awe of what you do. I heard you also raise champion horses."

Kate affirmed.

"I have great admiration for anyone who can barrel race and do tricks."

Kate's brow furrowed. "Where did you hear all that?"

"From Jarrett," she said. "He called last Friday and invited me to this celebration. He said you'd be here and that I'd enjoy meeting you." Erica paused. "You do raise cattle and horses and have won all those trophies and ribbons racing and competing?"

"Yes," Kate replied and glanced about for Jarrett. *So he planned this before I even left Montana. You scoundrel. What are you trying to do?* She looked around. *Where are you?*

"Please tell me more," Erica continued. "Your ranch backs up to the Rocky Mountains? That must be beautiful country."

"It is," she replied. "You'll have to come and visit sometime."

Erica pulled out her phone. "Give me your phone number and address."

With numbers exchanged, Erica pointed at a large buxom woman dressed in a brilliant orange sack-like dress with a scarlet cape draped over one shoulder. "That's Isabel Howard, the head of the Tramonte Galleries. They specialize in exhibiting paintings done by people in motion pictures and the theater. I'll introduce you sometime. The fellow she's talking to is Forrest Pendleton. He was in my last movie."

As Erica spoke, Kate picked up on Jarrett coming their way. Erica saw him too and took a step back. "Kate, I'll give you a call. We need to get together next week. I'll give you a tour of the studio, and we'll do lunch." Turning, she melted into the crowd.

"Let's," Kate started to say, but her voice trailed off as Erica disappeared. She considered Erica's offer. *I could stay an extra week and hear everyone out.* She slowly decided, *Yes. I've earned a vacation. Wylie and Gene can run the ranch a few more days.* Turning, she steadied herself. *So Jarrett's behind all this. Who cares? I doubt these people are his puppets. Money has power, but even that has limits.*

Collecting herself, she watched Jarrett make his way in her direction. *You've got a lot of explaining to do. You've gone to great lengths to orchestrate this evening. Why? Dr. Norman, Dean Carswell, and Stanley Rolstadler are all successful, so what motivated them to make me those offers? Do they really think I'm that qualified, or are you behind this as well?* About to confront him, she lost that thought when their eyes met. Smiling, she could feel the warmth of his expression explode within her.

Taking her arm, he pulled her close and nuzzled her cheek. "I'm hungry. Let's go to dinner."

15

I n the limousine, Jarrett pulled her close. "You made yourself a number of new friends." His eyes sparkled. "You were the hit of the reception, the most beautiful woman there."

Dulled by the champagne, Kate was slow to responded. "There were a lot of—"

Jarrett interrupted, "No. You were the most beautiful woman." He ran the black isolation panel up that shut off the driver's section from the back. Stroking her hands, he continued, "Do you mind if I kiss you?"

She slowly shook her head.

"I'm sorry. Yes, you mind if I kissed you?"

"No," she said and reached for his jacket. "You don't have to ask." Pulling him close, she kissed him gently. When their lips met, they melted together. Their tongues touched. Her pulse pounded. She could taste him. Grabbing him, she jerked him close. His tongue swirled about in her mouth. *Oh God.* She swooned and kissed him back. She couldn't get enough of his passion. The limousine slowed. The restaurant entrance was feet away. Letting go, she straightened her dress.

"We're here," Jarrett mumbled and reached for the door. "Shall we?" he asked as the valet approached the car. "This is a great place. The food is outstanding."

Kate looked out and shook her head. "No, I'm not hungry. Let's go to the apartment."

Minutes later in the dark apartment, the door to the hall clicked shut. She looked into his eyes. They appeared to sparkle in the light coming up from the street. He reached for the switch. "No lights," she whispered. Smothering him with a kiss, he responded. He was excited. She could feel his arousal against her. Grabbing his jacket, she all but tore it from his body. He groped for her zipper but couldn't find the pull. "I'll do it," she mumbled. Seconds later, her dress was off and everything under it. He too was out of his clothes, almost ripping them from his body.

Entwined together, they tumbled onto the bed. He was on her. His strong hands ran over her body. Gripping her chest, he slid his hands over her breasts. She quivered. Her nipples felt like they were about to explode. She pulled his mouth to hers. She wanted him. She had to have him. He reared up and slid down her body, kissing her neck, then her shoulders and her breasts. Stopping first at one breast, his tongue circled her nipple. It was hard. It stood up. He slid over to her other breast and did the same. Sliding between her breasts, he kissed her as he worked his way down and stopped at her waist. Pulling back, he looked up. Even in the dim light, she could see into his eyes. Right then, she felt she was looking into his soul. Jarrett was her man. They had connected. Her mother was right. *When you see Mr. Right, you'll know. You'll see it in his eyes. You'll feel it in your heart.* "Make love to me. Make love to me now," she called out.

Tilting his head back, he looked at her. "Stay with me. Don't go home. Stay down here. Go with me in two weeks to Florida. I have a boat to race. After that, we can go to the Bahamas. I own an island. We can make love and lie in the sun. Stay here with me. You don't have to be isolated up there anymore. Sell off some of your land with your neighbors. Come and join me here."

Kate gasped. "Sell off some of my land?" she exclaimed, almost choking on the words. "How do you know my neighbors want to sell their ranches?"

"I own Wilderness Pines Development Company. We're preparing to make you and your friends a generous offer. Don't turn us down."

"WHAT!" Kate exploded. Flinging him aside, she sprang from the bed. "Sell off some of my land! Is that what this getting me drunk has been all about? You've been doing all this to get me to sell? You've been playing me for a fool?" Grabbing her dress, she jerked it on. "You own that development company, and you want my land."

"Yes, Wilderness Pines is my company. And yes, with the addition of your upper range, my proposed development would be a colossal project. It would be the ultimate in luxury North American resorts. You're a businessperson. You can see the value in that. What we can build together would make us a pile of money." He slid from the bed and collected his trousers.

She glared at him. "Is that all you're interested in, money? Doesn't my goal to rebuild my ranch mean anything to you? Great-Granddad had a dream, and so do I. It's some of the last unspoiled wilderness in the state, and I plan to keep it that way."

"Fine," Jarrett said. "Except a ranch is just so much land."

"WHAT!" Clenching a fist, she prepared to slug him. "You miserable son of a bitch. You're nothing but a goddamn money-grubbing piranha! A vulture in a fancy suit." Stomping her foot, she pulled away. "I've met some crooked people in my day, but you're the worst. You've been manipulating me all along. You've done all this to get me to sell. You told all those people tonight to be nice so you can get what you wanted. Jesus, you're slime."

He shook his head. "I did nothing of the kind."

"Oh, really? Just on their own, those men asked for my dossier so they can offer some nobody they've never met those positions? God, you're deceitful. Stop treating me like a fool."

He reached for her, but she jerked away. "Before you go spouting off any more, you're not some nobody. You're a very sharp business-woman. I've millions sunk into both the foundation and the scholarships. I have no idea what they're doing with my money. I need someone I can trust on those boards to watch over my interests. You have a place down here. You don't belong up there with some character head over heels in debt. He's a loser. He needs us to buy him out."

Kate's nostrils flared. "I have a half a mind to punch you in the face." She glared at him. "That 'loser,' as you call him, is honest and trustworthy, which is more than I can say about you." She pointed at the door. "Out! I know this is your apartment and this is your building. By rights, I should be the one to leave. If I knew where to go, I would, except I don't, so please find somewhere else to stay. I'm very tired, and I want to be alone. Tomorrow I'll get a motel by the airport."

Jarrett stepped toward her. "You don't understand. We can make a good team. We think alike."

Enraged, she snarled. "No, we don't think alike, and don't ever accuse me of that again."

Stepping back, Jarrett collected his clothes and reached for the door. "You don't have to get a motel. Your farewell dinner is tomorrow night. A car will be standing by to drive you to dinner. It'll take you to the airport when you're ready."

The door latch clicked. Jarrett was gone. The lights from the city filled the room with an eerie glow. Down below, an aid car raced by. Its emergency lights flashed off the buildings, making red streaks across the empty street. The wail of its siren pierced the quiet of the night. Drained of all emotion, she stepped over to the kitchenette and dropped the necklace on the counter. The ear studs were next, which she put in the little box. That done, she collected the clothes she'd torn from her body and stopped. The message light was flashing on the telephone. She pressed the replay button, and Wylie's voice burst forth. "Hi, babe. It's me. When you called the other night, this number came up on my caller ID, so I gave it a try. If it's yours, I want you to know I checked on your dad. He's doing okay. He had a little pain in his chest. The doc assured me it was only a bit of angina. But don't worry, he'll be fine. I'm running things until you get back. I've sent him to town to rest. I checked your flight, and unless I hear otherwise, I'll be at the airport Saturday to meet you. Call me if there's a change."

The sound of Wylie's voice caused her to stop. Dropping her clothes, she collapsed into a chair. *What have I done? I've come within seconds of violating the trust placed in me by the man I've known all my life. What a fool I've been.*

Tap, tap, tap—burrowed in, Kate was awakened the next morning by a knocking on the door. Bleary-eyed, she struggled to a sitting position. "Who is it?" she tried to say, but the words wouldn't come out. Her mouth was dry and wouldn't work. *Oh God, I've never drunk that much champagne before, and especially not on an empty stomach.*

Rap—there was another knock on the door, this time harder. About to call out, Kate gasped when she heard the lock tumblers click. Whoever was out there was using a key. The handle moved. Kate jumped to her feet. A two-hundred-thousand-dollar necklace lay within easy reach on the kitchenette counter. She tried to think. She had to do something. The door inched open. Kate grabbed for a chair.

A woman's face appeared. "Hello. Are you awake?" the woman called out.

"Yes. Go away," Kate managed to say.

The door swung farther open. "Ms. Clark, can I come in?" asked the woman with silver hair.

"What?" Kate replied. She watched as an older woman in what was obviously an expensive suit appeared in the opening. She surveyed her quickly. *If you're a burglar, you're extremely well-dressed.* Rubbing her eyes, she ran her tongue around in her mouth until she felt she could talk. "Can I help you?" Kate asked.

The woman stepped into the room. Many inches shorter than Kate, she had to look up when she spoke. "Good morning, Ms. Clark. I'm Lillian Linenthaller, Mr. Sinclair's assistant. Security advised me they had not seen you, and it was getting late. They think you might have overslept, so I came down to check."

"Oh," Kate mumbled. She looked back at the clock beside the bed. The woman was right. "Thanks. I guess I forgot to set the alarm." She looked at Lillian still in the doorway. She did not appear anxious to leave. "Is there something else? Right now I'm in no mood to talk."

Lillian looked toward the kitchen counter. "If you'd like, I can make coffee while you get ready."

"Ah." Kate looked toward the empty coffeepot and then at the woman. "What the heck," she mumbled. *She's not a burglar. She's his personal assistant.* "Thank you. That'd be appreciated."

Grabbing the necklace and what she was going to wear, Kate disappeared into the bathroom. When she stepped out, she zeroed in on the aroma of freshly brewed coffee. Lillian was seated at the table and appeared settled in. Kate poured herself a cup. Stepping forward, she handed the necklace to Lillian. "I'd like you to return this to him."

The woman handed it back. "You keep it. It was meant as a gift."

Kate glared. "I know what it was meant as, but he can forget it. I don't want it." As she spoke, she retrieved the small box with the diamond ear studs. "And give these earrings back to him as well."

Lillian pushed them away too. "Those are yours. They go with the dress."

"I don't want anything that reminds me of him." She studied Lillian. When she sensed the woman was not ready to do what she was asking, she looked at the necklace and little box. "These are mine. I can do with them as I see fit. Is that right?"

Nodding, the woman agreed. "Correct."

Kate handed the two items to her. "Then here's a gift." When it appeared Lillian was about to speak, Kate held up her hand. "They're yours. Period."

Lillian studied them and slowly shook her head. "He's not going to like this."

Kate glared. "I don't give a damn what he likes or dislikes. If he gives you any trouble, tell me. I've handled tough angry bulls and spirited horses. I can handle him too." That said, she picked up her cup. "I'm keeping this apartment tonight. I'll be leaving tomorrow morning. I've an early flight. I'll leave the clothes we purchased in the closet. What I haven't worn can be returned. The other stuff, you can do with as you see fit. When my suitcase eventually gets here from Europe, send it to me up north."

Lillian stood. "Your bag's here. I'll have it brought up right away. Regarding the things you purchased, I've ordered a large suitcase so you can take all those clothes back home. The airline has paid for them, so they are yours to keep."

"Forget it. I don't want them. They were a part of a fantasy, and it's time to get back to reality." She opened the door. "If you'll excuse me, I have to get on with the rest of my life."

16

True to her word, Kate left the clothes Jarrett purchased in the apartment. Approaching her town, she gazed down at their airport. Reality in the form of a trusted friend was standing next to the terminal building. Warmed at seeing Wylie, she smiled.

Tired as she was, she dashed from the plane. She gave him a hug and a welcoming kiss. Red-faced, Wylie pulled back. "Not in public," he whispered and glanced nervously about.

She shook her head. "Forget it. I missed you, and I'm glad to be home."

Seated in his crew cab, they headed for her ranch. It didn't take long for her to sense something was awry. He was not known to be overly chatty, but right then, he was inordinately quiet. A mile from the airport, he pulled off to the side.

"Why are we stopping?"

Shifting into neutral, he looked her way. "We need to talk."

A chill swept over her. He must have sensed something had happened in Los Angeles. *How am I going to tell him? He probably already knows, but how am I going to explain what I've done?* She looked at him. She still liked the man seated next to her; she just didn't love him. "Yes. You're right. There is something we need to discuss."

"Me first," Wylie said. He hesitated. After many seconds, he continued, "I'm in love with Patty," he said. "At first, I didn't want to admit it. It happened so fast. I didn't plan it that way. I guess that's the way love is." Resting his head on the steering wheel, he rolled it to the side and looked at her. "First off, we've done nothing to embarrass you. I mean, no sex or anything like that. She hasn't slept at my place. Second, I still like you. I like you very much and will always respect you. You're a wonderful person. This isn't a result of anything you've done."

Settling back, he slowly shook his head. "That's not totally true. You paired us up on that trip to Billings. We discovered we had a lot in common. She doesn't want children, and neither do I. She's tired of ranching, and so am I. She loves to eat, and so do I," he said. "So I guess you had something to do with getting us together." He turned her way. "I'll be moving my stuff out this weekend. I didn't move anything yet. I figured that would only be right."

Kate stared out at the distant snowcapped peaks. "I don't know what to say except I wish you two all the best."

A minute passed, and Wylie gave her a nudge. "You don't look too upset." He waited for a reply and, when none came, continued, "Has that Sinclair fellow won you over? You spoke of him quite a bit after his visit."

Kate shook her head. "No. He's out of my life. True, I was briefly infatuated, but that's over. Once I learned all the fancy dinners and cocktail receptions were a trick to get me to sell part of my ranch, I saw him for who he really was. He's a conniving, manipulative, money-hungry, miserable son of a bitch. A bastard." Reaching over, she stroked his shoulder. "You set the standard for honesty, and I wish you and Patty all the best." Exhaling, she slowly said, "I'll be okay. I just need some time alone to sort things out."

⁂

The sun had just broken over the horizon when she rolled from the bed. Dressing to work cattle, she made her way to the kitchen. Wylie would soon be there to collect his things, and she didn't want to be around when he arrived. The mail had piled up, but she'd get to that later. With coffee mug in hand, Kate went to the barn. Ramrod

whinnied and pranced anxiously in his stall. "Yes, big boy, I'm back."
Leading him out, she saddled him and pulled the cinch tight. She
grabbed her Winchester and hung it from the saddle. She smiled.
She was home.

Monday, she buried herself in office work. She told herself it
was to catch up on the week she'd been gone, but deep down, she
knew it was to keep her mind off Jarrett.

The first couple of days home, her father stayed in town. On
the morning of the third, she lay aside what she had been working
on when his truck drove up. Stepping to the door, she watched when
he climbed the steps to the porch. He was limping, but only a little.
"Your hip must be better."

"It is."

"And your chest?" she said as he approached. "How are you
feeling? Do you have any pain?"

He shook his head and made with a comforting smile. "Nah. It
was simply a warning. I know now when to cut back. The doc says
I'm fine. I now know my limits." He gave her a hug. "I have a bunch
of things I have to go over with you. Do you have any coffee left?"

"Plenty," she replied.

With ranch matters covered and lunch completed, Seth leaned
back in his chair. Draining the last of the coffee from his mug, he set
it aside. "That development company has made Wylie and Patty a
very attractive offer."

"So I've heard. I figured without my upper range, I killed the
deal." She slowly circled the rim of her mug with her finger. "I guess
I was wrong."

"Have you considered selling any of the high range to them?
According to Wylie, that's what they're after."

She shook her head. "And break up this ranch? No way. You and
Mom worked your backsides off rebuilding this place. This is our
heritage, and I'm not giving any of it up."

"I'm glad to hear that," he said and looked toward her. "It would have been nice if you could have put the old place back together, but if you can't, at least you've kept the main part." Turning, he adjusted his leg. "Wylie said your bag was misrouted and Sinclair took you shopping. Did you get some nice clothes?"

"Yes," she said.

His expression brightened. "Well, Let's see 'em."

"They were city clothes, so I left them down there."

Seth shook his head. "Too bad. I would have liked to have seen you all dolled up." Leaning forward, he rested his elbows on the table. "Did you get a chance to spend much time with Jarrett?"

She told of their shopping and going backstage at the theater and the fancy restaurants they visited. She rambled on about the people she'd met at the medical foundation reception and of the offers she'd received. She left out the part about the champagne she'd drunk and her near major lapse in judgment back at the apartment.

Seth looked at her. "Just like that, those men offered you those positions? I find that hard to believe. They knew nothing of you."

"Oh, they knew plenty about me. It seems Jarrett ran an extensive background check on me and provided those in attendance with my dossier. Jarrett had arranged the whole evening, those offers included."

Seth got up and divided what was left in the pot between their two mugs. "Yes, I can see you on that board and on that selection committee. So Jarrett arranged it. Who cares, if the offers were real? You're smart. You're sharp. You've built this into one of the most profitable operations in the state. If you can do that in these tough times, I'm sure you can do wonders with those organizations as well. Sounds to me like you should have stayed down there and at least heard them out. Listening to them wouldn't have hurt. So why didn't you?"

Turning in the chair, she flopped her arm over the back. "When I figured out all those offers were a put-on to get me to sell, I didn't know what was real and what wasn't, so I said to hell with it and took the first flight home."

Seth studied his daughter. "Do you love him?"

"Jarrett?" she asked.

He nodded.

"I might have been briefly infatuated, but once I found out what he was like, I broke it off. He's a heartless developer out to get as much as he can no matter who he hurts, and I don't live like that."

"Does he love you?" Seth asked.

Taking a breath, she shook her head. "I doubt it. He's a scheming, heartless businessman whose only interest is money. That's his true love, dollars." Getting up, she looked down at what was left in her mug. "Cold," she muttered and left.

17

It had been nearly a week since Kate returned from Los Angeles. Alone in her office, she looked out at her ranch. Her fields were dry. Until the fall rains, the threat of fire was an ever-present danger. Turning back, she focused on what she had to do. Now that Wylie and Patty had sold to the developer, that left only Buck Wilson's place next door.

The telephone rang. "Hello, Kate Clark here."

"Hi, Kate. Remember me, Billy Brady, from down around Cheyenne?"

She beamed. "Yes, I remember you. We served on that tristate ranch owner's committee. So what has you calling?"

"I've heard that your friend Wylie and next-door neighbor sold out to that development company."

"Yes," Kate replied.

Billy continued, "Shortly after we were on that committee, Wilderness Pines made an offer for my place. It was nowhere as big as yours, but it was still my place. Anyway, I told them to get lost. A month later, my orders from AJS increased. They were paying top dollar and then boom. It was right at the start of the mad cow thing. A charge surfaced that my cows were diseased. AJS made a big stink and dropped me. I couldn't give my cows away. I had to destroy my herd. I was broke. I couldn't pay the bank. Wilderness came back and offered me pennies on the dollar for my land. I had no choice but to sell to pay off my loans. I suspected AJS started the mad cow rumor, but I could never prove it. Only a month ago, I learned AJS and Wilderness Pines were owned by the same people."

"Sinclair Enterprises," Kate said, thinking aloud.

"You're right," Bill said. "Take my advice. You need to contact your other customers and arrange for them to pick up the slack when AJS cuts back. I know the people who manage what wilderness built on my old place. According to them, you pissed off their acquisition guy, Roger Gillie. He was livid. According to them, he's going to be coming after you and won't stop until he teaches you a lesson."

"Really?" Kate said. She glared. "He's going to be surprised to see who's the teacher and who's the pupil."

With the call over, she pulled up beef sales and was surprised to see over three quarters of her cattle went to AJS Foods.

⁎⁎⁎

The next few days, Kate spent contacting her other customers. Checking off the last name, she set the list aside. She had successfully shifted the majority of her sales away from AJS Foods. Jarrett's company was now her smallest account.

The phone rang. It was Karl Schneider. "You're turning down my orders. Have I done something wrong?"

"No, you've done nothing wrong," Kate replied. "I decided I needed a change in business philosophy. Too much of my sales were going to one customer, so I decided to balance things out."

"You didn't have to do that," Karl came back. "We pay promptly."

"Yes, I know you pay well, but when Wilderness Pines tried to buy Billy Brady's place and he said no, they used AJS to put him out of business. I have too much vested in my place to risk letting anything like that happening to me. Your boss has tried to bribe me into selling him part of my ranch, and I too turned him down."

"Are you sure you won't reconsider?" Karl asked. "I have a quota to meet. What can I tell them?"

"Tell them I don't have any cows to sell right now," Kate concluded. About to get up, she stopped when the telephone rang. "Hello. Kate here."

"Hello, Kate. It's me, Erica," said the actress she had met at the research foundation reception. "Did I catch you at a bad moment?"

"Ah…hi, Erica, no. What's up?" Kate asked.

"I was wondering if I could come visit and hang out with you for a couple days."

"Of course, you can." Kate glowed. "You can stay as long as you want." As she spoke, she made a quick assessment of what she and Dolores would have to do to get the house presentable. A generous layer of dust had collected on everything. *That will have to be dealt with.* If she and Dolores worked at it, they could get the place cleaned up in a couple days. "How soon will you be here?"

"I'm in Missoula right now."

"Missoula," Kate exclaimed, almost choking on the word. At most, Missoula was an hour plane ride or a four-hour car ride away.

"Yes, Missoula. I'm driving, and my GPS says to take Highway 12. Is that a good way?"

Kate stared at the phone. "You drove all the way from Los Angeles?"

"I had to," Erica said. "If I had taken a plane, the paparazzi could have checked and been here ahead of me. So I drove. I see Highway 12 and Highway 208—208 looks shorter. What do you recommend?"

Even if she and Delores went all out, they couldn't get the place cleaned in four hours. "Ah, 12." Kate paused. "But if you have a GPS, take 208. It's crooked, and there're a number of turnoffs that foul people up, but it's more scenic, and if you have GPS, you won't get lost. I'll see you when you get here."

With the call over, Kate gasped. *We need all the time we can get, and I told her to take the shortcut. What was I thinking?* She punched in Dolores's phone number. Together, they would have to work fast. The telephone rang and rang. "Where is that woman?" Kate mumbled aloud.

136

About to go look for her, the screen door banged open, and Dolores flew in. "Ms. Kate come quick!"

Dropping the phone, Kate dashed for the door. It was summer and dry. One of her fields had to be on fire? She looked about. There was no smoke. There were no flames.

Dolores pointed past the barn. "The breeding bull you just bought broke out. He's heading toward the high range. Gene and everyone are over at the far feedlot. I tried to reach them but couldn't. Dusty saddled up his horse. He was going to go after the bull. I told him no. He's too small. He could get killed. I'm having him saddle Ramrod."

"Yes, he could get killed!" Kate replied. Grabbing her boots, she jerked them on. She called back as she bolted from the house. "I have an important guest coming. She's due here in three hours and is going to stay a few days. Do what you can to make the house presentable."

Kate ran to the barn. The bull cost her big money, and she had to get him back. It could take hours for Gene and the men to get there. By then, the bull could be halfway to Idaho. She should not be going, but what choice did she have? *None.* The fact her great-grandfather had been killed by a bull, she chose to ignore. Running into the barn, she grabbed her chaps and buckled them on as Dusty finished saddling her horse.

"I'm sorry, Ms. Kate. The bull broke out on its own. It wasn't my fault."

"I'm sure it wasn't," she said. Pulling on the cinch, she made sure the saddle was tight. She tied on her rifle and swung up onto her horse. On the way from the barn, she grabbed a coiled whip from a peg. Dusty followed. "Show me which way he went," she said. "When we get close, I want you to stay back, way back. I don't want you anywhere near that animal."

Three plus hours later, soaked with sweat and caked with dust, Kate had the bull back and locked in a pipe rail corral. Ramrod had come through. Although the bull was young and aggressive, Ramrod was more than its match. She turned toward the barn. "Whoops!" she said when she saw someone outside the large barn door. Dressed in shorts and a blouse with a baseball cap shoved back on her head, Erica sparkled when their eyes met. Kate took a breath. *One adventure is over, and another is about to begin.*

Kate trotted Ramrod toward the barn. Over by the house, what had to be Erica's car was parked near the steps to the porch. A coating of dust obscured all view through the windows on the side and back. Swinging down, Kate pulled off a glove and reached to greet Erica. "Welcome. I'm sorry I'm such a mess. I had to get a bull back in a corral."

"Thanks for letting me come on short notice. The public and press are constantly in my face." Erica pointed toward her car. "I hope you don't mind, but I brought along a friend. If two of us are too many, say so, and my friend will leave."

Erica waved. Kate took a breath. Erica knew Jarrett. Could she have brought him along? It would be just like Jarrett to come up with a scheme like this. Kate took a step back and watched as legs ending in spiked heels swung out. Erica continued as the woman approached. "When a friend of mine heard I was driving up to visit you, she insisted on coming along. I hope you don't mind," Erica asked as the woman approached. "I'd like you to meet Rachel."

Kate swallowed hard. "Ah…no, I don't mind." *What could have possessed Jarrett's friend to insist on coming along? I've never met the woman.* Straightening up, Kate studied her as the model approached. She was gorgeous and walked purposefully as models do. One hand, she extended in greeting; in the other, she held a large camera. Her eyes sparkled when she approached.

"Hi, I'm Rachel," she said. There was a disarming warmth in her friendly expression. "I know this is an imposition. When Erica told me she was going up to visit you, I insisted on coming along."

Kate looked at the woman. *Why did you insist on coming along? I don't even know you,* she thought as she accepted Rachel's hand in greeting. "I'm sorry. I'm such a mess," Kate said.

Rachel beamed. "You look wonderful." She held out her camera. "Can you do me a favor? I'd like to get some pictures of you, just as you are in your working clothes before you go clean up. Could you go back and come riding up like you did a minute ago? This time, though, can you ride up real fast and sort of slide to a stop in a cloud of dust?" She pointed. "Ever since I saw the pictures of you and heard you owned a big ranch, I knew I had to meet you in person."

Kate gasped. *What does she mean, ever since she'd seen the pictures of me she had to meet me in person? What pictures of me? The ones of me floating naked in the lake?* She would have demanded an answer except Rachel was motioning purposefully for her to get moving. *Who is this woman? Where does she get off telling me what to do?* About to go on the attack, she eased back. *She didn't tell me what to do. She asked if I could do her a favor.* Kate countered. "But I'm a mess. At least give me a moment to run a brush through my hair and put on something clean."

Rachel shook her head. "No, you're perfect. Go on. Come riding up so I can get some action pictures." She held up her camera and prepared to shoot.

Kate reluctantly swung up onto Ramrod. Seated, she looked down at Rachel. "What pictures did you see of me?"

"I'll tell you in a minute. Go on." She waved. "Let me get my pictures first."

If you insist. Kate tapped Ramrod, and they galloped off. Some distance out, she wheeled him around and let out a commanding *click, click.* Ramrod lunged forward. His long legs reached out as he raced toward the barn and feed. Kate pulled back on the reins. Ramrod's head reared back. His hind hooves dug in. He slid in the dirt. Kate leaped off and hit the ground running. "Is that the kind of action you wanted?"

Rachel beamed. "Fantastic!" she said. "That's exactly what I wanted. Thank you. Thank you very much."

Kate turned toward the woman. "What pictures? You mentioned some pictures you saw of me." With a grip on his bridle, she held Ramrod back from his desire to lunge into the barn for a helping of grain.

"The ones of you on horseback standing waving your hat and in the pond," Rachel replied. "The instant I saw your face—"

"WHAT!" Kate exploded. "You saw my face?" She stumbled. Her legs felt like rubber. Her worst fears had been realized. *For anyone to have seen such detail as my face, they had to have seen everything else.* "The pictures of me in the pond? In the pond, I was naked." Red-faced, she jerked Ramrod to a stop. "Jarrett showed those pictures to you? Who else has he shown them to? Everyone at the cocktail party? GODDAMN!" she called out. "No wonder everyone wanted to meet me." She slapped Ramrod's reins around a post and turned to stomp off.

Erica caught her. "No, nothing like that," she said. "Hear her out."

Rachel stepped forward. "The truth is, Jarrett didn't show the pictures to me. He doesn't even know I've seen them. As far as I know, from what Lillian has told me, he hasn't shared the pictures with anyone."

Kate glared. "So what has Jarrett done? Kept the pictures of me naked for himself? It would be just like him." She snorted. "God, what a sleaze."

Rachel shook her head. "No. The pictures Lillian got me in to see of you in the lake were blowups only of your face."

Kate blinked. She took a step back. "Only of my face? What happened to rest? Did Jarrett keep that to ogle over by himself?"

"No. According to Lillian, he was embarrassed when he went through the original survey file and saw the pictures of you in the pond. According to the report Lillian got back from the gal in their graphics department, there were ripples on the water that obscured most of the detail, but all the same, he wanted the images edited, and she agreed. Following his direction, she deleted everything from your bustline down. And that's what Jarrett had her blow up to near full size."

"He did? Why?" Kate asked.

"Who knows?" Rachel replied. "Lillian has told me that from the moment he saw your pictures, he had the images of your face enlarged. According to her, he's fixated on those pictures."

"Really?" Kate questioned.

"Yes," Rachel continued. "Since he's had those pictures, Lillian says he pulls them out every chance he gets."

"Oh," Kate replied.

Rachel continued, "That's when everything started. He had those pictures of you on your horse and the edited ones of you in the pond sent to all the AJS Food representatives who dealt with ranchers and people on the east side of the Rockies. He wanted to know who you were. He kept after them until one of their representatives said he knew you and gave him your name. Jarrett had that AJS rep call you and verify that you had been in the lake that day. Jarrett asked him to find out if you were married, and the representative verified you weren't. When Jarrett learned that and the man who lived with you was going to that seminar, all hell broke loose. Every office person was called in to put together that special company meeting in Spokane." She chuckled. "That was a real nightmare to pull off overnight. They had to get all those management people there in less than twenty-four hours. Not an easy task."

"I don't understand. If this was done overnight, how did they get the reservation for me on the commuter flight from my town? At best, that flight needs to be booked days in advance."

Rachel laughed. "Not if you own the airline." She grinned. "He told them to bump someone and replace the person with you."

"Really?" Kate questioned. "He owns the airline?"

"Yes," Rachel replied. "When we were going together I used to tell people I was going with a guy who owned an airline. True, he wasn't Howard Hughes or Juan Trippe and the airline wasn't TWA or Pan Am, but an airline is an airline and he owned one," she said. "Anyway, for your flight home from Spokane, he had the commuter plane leave early so you had no choice but to accept his offer for a ride. He arranged the whole thing, even his stay at your place overnight."

Kate shook her head. "No," she said firmly. "I take exception to that. His staying overnight was not of his doing. We had talked too long. He had to stay on. He didn't want to take off from a strange runway in the dark. It was too dangerous."

"A strange runway?" Rachel laughed. "Are you kidding? He was their chief pilot for three years before he bought the airline. He probably flew in and out of that airport more times than he wanted to count. He could have taken off in the dark and probably frequently had."

Momentarily silenced, Kate settled back. Right then, she had heard enough. Jarrett had manipulated everything. She looked at the woman whom she was just getting to know. *She appears to be telling the truth. I wonder if she knows about our kissing before I left his plane.* She considered asking but didn't know how without letting on that they had kissed, so she let it pass, at least for now.

Ramrod whinnied and stomped anxiously about. Guests or no guests, she had to care for her horse. "Give me a minute," Kate said. "He worked hard today and needs a reward." Putting a scoop of grain in his trough, she pulled the saddle from his back. As she did, Rachel clicked away with her camera. Hanging the saddle on a peg, Kate went after Ramrod with a brush. After a few strokes, she stopped and looked at Jarrett's friend. "You are a fashion editor for *Today's Fashion*, so what's with the picture taking? Do you do that as well?"

"When my photographer gets tied up on other assignments, I grab the old Nikon and go to it."

"Oh," Kate replied. She looked at the woman. That did not answer her question, but she was exhausted, sweat soaked, and caked with dust and wanted nothing more than to get cleaned up. She sighed. She'd press the woman for her need for pictures later. Laying the brush aside, Kate pulled off her chaps and pointed toward the house. "Right now, all I want is to get a shower and into clean clothes." She looked at them. "I imagine you two would like to see where you're going to sleep tonight."

The two women agreed, and they followed Kate to the house.

18

Showered and changed, Kate went down stairs. *What now?* she asked herself as she breezed through the kitchen and out to the porch. She looked about. Erica was there, but Rachel wasn't. "Where's your friend?" she asked.

"Upstairs," Erica replied. "I suspect she's busy uploading all the pictures she's taken." She paused. "I hope bringing her along wasn't an imposition."

Kate shook her head.

Erica continued, "I'm sorry I didn't call further in advance. I left on a whim. I had to get away. I figured if I waited until I was a few hours away, you would be more inclined to say yes."

"That's okay," Kate said. "Come anytime." She grinned. "Come during roundup, and I'll put you to work. I'll have you clipping on tags and branding in no time." Kate rolled her eyes. "The smell of calf hair burning is something you'll never forget. It gets in your nostrils. You'll smell it for days."

The screen door banged open, and Rachel approached in perfect runway form. "Me, I'd prefer to do the castrating. There are a number of self-centered bastards in the fashion world I'd give my eyeteeth to practice that procedure on."

Kate laughed.

Rachel continued, "I admit inviting myself along was selfish. When Lillian showed me the pictures of you and told me you owned a large ranch, I couldn't believe it. A young woman with your looks succeeding in the macho world of cattle ranching piqued my interest. While the main focus of *Today's Fashion* is current fashion trends, the magazine covers health and beauty issues as well. In addition to my fashion responsibilities, I write a popular segment on how women succeed. When Lillian told me you were in LA, I snuck over and watched as you arrived for your software class. I had to see if you were as feminine as you appeared in those pictures. When I saw that you weren't some tobacco-chewing, hard-bitten cowboy in a woman's body, I knew Lillian's idea was right. I had to do a feature on you. When Erica told me she was going to come up here, I invited myself along."

Rachel held out her camera. "I know I've been pushy and in your face with this beastly contraption. I apologize. Once you see the story I'm doing, I think you'll understand." As she spoke, she pointed at what Kate had on. "As contrast to pictures of you working cattle, I'd like to get some of you dressed like you are right now, doing ordinary, everyday, around-the-house kinds of things. Is that okay?"

Surprised that anyone would be interested in writing an article about her, Kate continued, "Fine, but let me warn you, life on a cattle ranch is pretty dull. Aside from a bunch of cows eating grass, not much else happens. I can't see your readers being interested in that."

"They will be when I finish the article," Rachel replied.

Hours later, after touring the ranch and with dinner over, the table was cleared. Rachel folded the towel she had been using at the sink. "Let me bring down my laptop, and I'll show you what I've done so far. That'll give you an idea of the article I'm putting together. I hope you'll give me the okay to continue."

With Kate to one side and Erica to the other, Rachel set her laptop on the kitchen table. The first picture she brought up was a full-screen image of Kate riding up to the barn.

Erica gasped. "That has to be your cover shot."

"My thoughts exactly," Rachel agreed. "The horse's hooves are dug in. Kate's flying out of the saddle. Those beat-up cowboy boots, the spurs, those weathered chaps, and the bullwhip in her hand—it's fantastic."

Rachel clicked her mouse, and two more pictures came up. The first was of Kate as she pulled the saddle from Ramrod's back. The next was of her on the way out of the barn. With hat in hand, she was wiping her brow with her sleeve.

"What's so special about that?" Kate asked. "It's just me at work."

"Exactly," Rachel replied. "Those three pictures define a hard-working woman in a business dominated by men. Every other magazine does articles on women who graduated from some famous university and are now a CEO of a Fortune 500 company. Fine. It's great that so many women are accomplishing great things. As contrast, I want to show my readers that not everyone has to work in an office. You're a hands-on, physically hardworking woman that I believe our readers will be interested in." Rachel clicked and pulled up the final picture. "Now the pièce de résistance."

Kate's eyes widened. "Where did you get that?" In the picture taken of her at the research foundation reception in her elegant black dress, she appeared deep in discussion with the dean of the university medical school.

"I have my sources," Rachel said. Leaning back, she looked at Kate. "What do you think? Can I do this article on you?"

Kate studied what Rachel presented. "Go for it," she said. "If you think that'll sell magazines, who am I to get in your way?"

<hr/>

Later, after everyone had turned in, Kate lay awake on her bed. Jarrett had gone to great lengths to orchestrate everything: the flight over, the meeting, the flight back, and his staying overnight. *Why?* she questioned. *What did he hope to accomplish?*

<hr/>

Next morning, Kate was up early and went to the kitchen. The first thing that struck her was the aroma of coffee. Not only had the coffee been made, but the pot was half empty. Neither of her guests was there. She looked out and found them seated at the patio table. Deep in conversation, they didn't notice her looking their way.

With coffee mug in hand, Kate walked outside. "My, you two are up early."

Erica was the first to respond, "Your crazy alarm clock," she sleepily replied and pointed at the chickens in the yard. The rooster crowed. Erica cringed.

Rachel spoke up, "To stay here another night, I'll need to have him for dinner." She glared as the rooster stretched to his full height and flapped his wings. "Come on now, 4:00 a.m., give me a break. Couldn't he have at least waited until five-thirty? I don't do well on three hours of sleep."

Kate settled into a chair. "I'll have Dusty catch the roosters and put them in a shed miles from here. I promise tomorrow you won't hear a peep out of them."

After breakfast, Rachel adjourned to the covered side porch with a giant mug of coffee and her computer. Erica whispered to Kate, "She has her coffee, laptop, and notes. She's done with her interview and is now writing the article. She'll be good for hours."

Kate studied Rachel. "I'm okay with that. We can go riding after lunch." She grabbed her grocery list. "What say we head to town? I have to get some groceries and check on my dad."

Erica ran her fingers through her hair and gave it a shake.

Kate blinked. "Wow. Without makeup and your hair done up, I barely recognize you."

"That's my plan. Up here, I don't want to be the celebrity everyone knows. I'd like to be an ordinary person."

With errands completed, Kate and Erica returned to the ranch. Kate grinned as they rolled up to the back porch. Patty's convertible was parked next to the steps. The fact that Wylie was no longer with her bore little on her relationship with Patty. "My neighbor, the one I told you about who eats and breathes fashion is here. It appears she has discovered Rachel." Kate grinned. "If we don't rescue her, Patty will talk her ears off." Kate grabbed the mail and a sack of groceries and started toward the house. Erica followed with the remaining bag.

Patty looked up and called to Kate. "You didn't tell me you had Erica Heath and Rachel here. What gives?" she asked. "Have you forgotten my phone number?"

Kate shook her head. "Follow us into the kitchen, and I'll explain while we make lunch."

Patty jumped up and ran to catch up. "Rachel showed me the article she's doing on you. It's going to be fabulous." She glared at Kate. "You didn't tell me about that cocktail party you went to and that dress. Ooooh! That black dress. It was fantastic. And that necklace. My God, you were gorgeous. Why didn't you tell me?"

"I don't know. It must have slipped my mind."

"Slipped your mind! *Oh!*" Patty exclaimed. Throwing up her hands, she stomped on ahead. She stopped at the table and took the sack from Erica. "Allow me." She looked at Erica. "Can you believe that? She doesn't even tell her best friend."

Everyone helped, and when her guests offered to make lunch, Kate stepped into her office. She checked for messages, and finding none that were urgent, she radioed Gene. "I need to get Ramrod and two other horses saddled up. My guests would like to go riding. Better make it Roy and Cally. They're pretty gentle."

"I'll have Bill do it. Would you mind if he rides along?"

"No, that's fine with me."

Following lunch, Kate looked at Patty. "You'll have to excuse us. Erica and Rachel want to go riding. Soon as we get the table cleared, we're going to head out."

Patty held up her hand. "Hold that," she said and bolted from the room. She could be heard running down the hall and up the grand staircase.

Confused, Rachel turned to Kate. "What's that all about?"

Kate shook her head. "I don't have a clue."

The three had just finished cleaning up in the kitchen when Patty returned. Kate stopped. Her neighbor was in jeans, a Western shirt, and a pair of old cowboy boots. "Where did you find all that?"

"The jeans and shirt are your brothers'. The boots are yours. I hope you don't mind, but I'd like to ride along."

"You would, would you?" Kate questioned. "No, I don't mind, but you haven't been on a horse in—"

Patty interrupted, "Yes, twenty years. But I still want to go along. Who knows, I might surprise you."

Kate grinned. "If you can ride, that'll surprise me." Stepping away, she telephoned the stable. "Bill, Patty is coming along. You'll need to saddle Muffin as well."

Patty glowed. "Is Bill going with us?"

Erica perked up. "Who's Bill?"

Patty answered, "He's an ex-Wall Streeter. He went through a nasty divorce and came out to Montana to get away from it all."

Rachel raised a questioning eyebrow. "You hire Eastern greenhorns?"

Kate shook her head. "I didn't. My foreman did. Bill knows how to ride. He's a hard worker and is learning fast."

Kate, with Erica beside her, led the way up the hill. Patty was next to Rachel, and the two were close behind. Kate smiled on hearing Patty's ramblings on, which drifted forward as they rode. As expected, Patty was flooding Rachel with fashion questions.

As they rode, Kate caught sight of Erica glancing back. At first, she was sure the actress was concerned with Patty's pestering Rachel until she realized Erica was focused farther back on Bill.

Erica swung her horse to the side. "Don't stop. I want to check out something. I'll catch up in a minute."

"No problem." After a couple minutes, Kate glanced back. Erica had eased in beside Bill, and he was gesturing with his hands as they talked.

On their way down, Rachel trotted up and motioned to Kate to move ahead. Once out of earshot, Rachel whispered, "Patty's trying, but she has absolutely no seat. I'm afraid we'll have to lift her off with a crane."

Back at the barn, Kate flung Ramrod's reins over a bar and grabbed hold of Patty's horse. "Hold up there. Let me give you a hand."

Grimacing, Patty tried to move but couldn't. "Oh God, I don't think I can get down."

"Don't worry, we'll get you down." Kate eased back on Muffin's bridle. "Down," she instructed, and Muffin sat back and then came down in the front. With the stirrups now at ground level, she and Bill eased Patty out of the saddle.

Patty tried to take a step but couldn't. "I don't think I'll be able to walk for a week."

Kate chuckled. "Don't worry, you'll be fine tomorrow."

19

Up early, Kate busied herself in her office. Minutes later, Erica came down dressed in jeans and a T-shirt. The actress had run a brush through her hair and done nothing else to enhance her appearance. Kate leaned back and looked her way. "Good morning."

Erica poured herself a coffee and looked at Kate. "We're leaving today, and I want to see Bill before I go." Her expression turned serious. "Do I look okay, or should I have put on some makeup?"

Kate studied the actress and then shook her head. "No, you look fine."

Erica stepped to the window and looked toward the bunkhouse. When she saw no sign of life, she asked, "Have I missed them? Have they already left?"

"No," Kate replied. "I suspect they're finishing breakfast, and Gene is still making out work assignments. They should be out in a couple of minutes. You'll have plenty of time to visit with Bill."

Close to an hour passed before Rachel entered the kitchen. "Good morning," she said. Her expression brightened when she saw the coffeepot. "Ah, coffee. Exactly what I need to get this old body going." She moaned. "It's been a quarter century since I've ridden, and my muscles are telling me I should do it more often."

Kate motioned toward the porch. "Erica has been visiting with Bill and just got back. I have one thing to do, and then I'll join you two."

Minutes later, with mug in hand, Kate took a seat across from her guests. "I'm sorry you have to leave so soon. I've enjoyed your visit. You've been a welcome break from my daily routine, and you're both welcome back anytime." Kate set her mug aside. "Patty phoned. She's a bit lame and not able to make it over, but she wanted me to tell you she really enjoyed her time with you and is looking forward to your next visit."

"We are too," Erica replied.

Later with breakfast over and their suitcases packed, Erica stopped beside the car. "Thanks. I needed to get away from the media and the not-so-polite fans. I'm already looking forward to next time."

Rachel stepped forward. "I'll send you the final mockups of the article as soon as I have all my notes and observations sorted out. This is going to be one of my best pieces."

With the good-byes said, the two disappeared over a distant rise. Kate's shoulders sagged. Right then, the idea of returning to an empty kitchen gave her a chill. Without her two new friends, her kitchen, like the rest of her house, would feel empty and cold. Instead, she'd work horses this morning.

Finished with her horses, she stopped on the porch and knocked the dust from her jeans as her father drove up. She waved to him. "Come on. I've eaten enough dust this morning. There's coffee in the kitchen. Let's get a cup."

"Bad news," Seth said. "I just heard the Wilsons sold out to that development company."

Kate whipped around. "You heard what? They sold out?"

"Yes," Seth replied. "When I heard it, I phoned Buck, and he said it's true. They sold out to that Wilderness Pines outfit. It was finalized late yesterday. He apologized. He didn't want to do it without telling you first, except he and Blanche had no other choice. They were told not to discuss it with anyone and had only a couple hours to make a decision."

Kate stomped her foot. "I can't believe it." She stepped to the window and looked in the direction of the Wilsons' ranch. "Wilderness bought their ranch? What on earth for?" She turned back to her father. "Wilson's place is miles from the nearest property they bought from Patty and Wylie. It doesn't make any sense."

"Sense or no sense, it's a done deal. According to Buck, they wanted to take possession immediately, and it was closed in less than an hour."

Fuming, Kate returned to the window. "This has to be another of Jarrett's tricks. He knew I wanted that land." Waving a fist, she punched the wall. "I'm sorry I ever met the son of a bitch."

"Have you talked to him since you've been home?"

"No, and I hope I never do."

⌗

Early the next morning, Kate stepped out on the porch just as Bill and Jody swung by and rolled to a stop. "Where to?" she called to them.

Bill called back, "We're going up to the calving sheds. A couple of cows are due any day. Going to see how they're doing."

"Good," she replied.

Behind them, Gene rolled up in one of their big trucks loaded with supplies and a couple of hands. He stopped when he saw her. Kate approached. Behind Gene was a second big truck with gear and the remainder of the hired help.

"Where are you and the crew off to?" she asked.

"We're heading up to the high range to help check watering tanks and chase down sickly stock."

"Great. See you at dinnertime," she said. Satisfied her day was off to a smooth start, she returned to her office. Seated at her desk, she busied herself with orders when her father rolled up. She hit Enter on her computer as her dad limped through the vestibule. "Good morning," she said and jumped up when she saw his pained expression. "You're limping, and not just a little. Let me help you."

"It's this damn hip," he said as she eased him into the chair. "I didn't get much sleep last night."

"I don't imagine you did," she said as she made him comfortable. "Pop, you have to get that hip taken care of."

"I know. I called the doc this morning, and he said we can't put it off any longer. He'd like to schedule my surgery next week if that fits in with your plans."

Kate straightened up. "Fits in with my plans! My plans are to get you well. The sooner, the better."

"I'll tell the doc to schedule it as soon as he can." He motioned toward the yard. "Where is everyone?"

"Bill and Jody are working the dairy calves, and Gene and the others are on their way to the high range."

No sooner were the words out of her mouth than Gene's truck raced down the hill and across the yard to her house. Dust boiled up as Gene bolted from the cab and into the house without knocking.

"What's happening?" Kate called as she spun around and raced to a window. "Has someone been hurt? Is one of the fields on fire?"

Gene pointed toward the mountains. "They won't let us cross."

Puzzled, Kate looked where he pointed and then back at him. "Who won't let you cross? Cross where?"

He pointed toward the high range. "Up at the meadow. That development company that bought Patty's place, Wilderness Pines. They say the meadow belongs to them. They've put up a fence and a gate and a big sign. They're demanding a toll of ten bucks per every animal we have up on the range before they'll let us pass. In addition, they want a hundred-dollar-per-vehicle toll each way."

Kate's jaw dropped. "That's outrageous." Twisting about, she looked at her father. "They can't do that, can they? We've been crossing there for over a century."

Seth settled back and slowly stroked his chin. "That is part of the land my dad sold off to Patty's grandpa. We had no written agreement that we could cross there. We simply did, and he let us."

153

Kate stared out toward her upper range. *This has to be Jarrett's way of getting even with me.* She looked at her father. "Where does this leave us? I have wranglers up there. They can probably make it another week or so with the supplies they have, but is there any other way up there?"

Her father stroked his chin. "There's an old county road north of the Wilsons. It'll get you up to the federal access road that runs south along the ridge to our upper range. It isn't much of a road. To get there is going to take six or seven hours in our big four-wheel drive."

At the window, Kate took a deep breath. *His mother warned me. She said Jarrett was ruthless and would stop at nothing to get what he wanted. This was obviously what he wanted.* She looked at her father. "Can they do this? Can they block us from crossing? Don't we have some legal rights to crossing that land? We've been doing it forever."

Seth pointed at the phone. "I don't know. I'm not an attorney. You better call Avery, see what he has to say."

Kate picked up the phone and motioned toward the coffeepot. "Go have some coffee. I suspect this is going to take more than a few minutes."

Gene and her father had drained the pot and made fresh by the time she took a chair across from them. "The good news is, yes, we have a legal right to that trail across the meadow. We've established that over the decades. The bad news is because there's another access to our high range, we'll have to go to court to establish our right to use the route we've been using for years. That can take days, weeks, or possibly even months. According to Avery, they could tie it up in court."

From down the hall came the sound of someone knocking on the front door. She looked at Gene. "Can you see who that is?" She turned back to her father. "I don't have that kind of time. We have to do something now so I can get supplies up to those wranglers and those cattle down in the fall."

Gene returned with a visitor. "This guy wants to see you."

154

"Hi. I'm Kate Clark," Kate said and extended her hand. When the nattily dressed man did not reciprocate, she pulled hers back.

He sneered. "Boy, do I have you. And don't try being nice to me now," the man said. Plopping his briefcase on the table, he pulled out some documents. "This is my deed to that strip of land you have to cross to get to your cattle. Here's our deed to the ranch to the north of you that we just purchased. I have you boxed in. We own the property to the north, west, and south of you. I have you locked out. You said no to us when we offered a premium price for your upper range, and now I have you."

"And who might you be?" her father asked.

Leering, he ignored her father and spoke directly to Kate, "I'm the guy you said no to. I'm Roger Gillie, the Wilderness Pines Development director of property acquisitions." He laughed. "That is the dumbest thing you ever did. I've had an aerial survey done. You have 15, 437 cows up there. I want ten dollars a head for every one of those stupid animals, plus ten dollars for every man you plan to send across *my* land. That comes to a 154,370 for the cattle alone, and I don't take checks. I want that money transferred to my personal account electronically today. If you don't, I'll never let you cross that land."

Kate caught sight of her father as he started to get to his feet. Bad hip and all she knew what he planned to do. His fists were clenched. Behind him, Gene too had clenched fists. She motioned to them to back off. "And if I don't pay?"

Gillie laughed. "Goddamn, you're dumb. If you don't pay, I'm going to put you out of business. You thought you were cute screwing the owner of the company. Well, I'll show you. You can't trade pussy for favors."

Red-faced, Kate exploded. "WHAT!"

He grinned. "We all knew he was balling you. That had to be the reason he told me to stay away and offer you so much. But I'll show him. I'm the attorney, and he's not. I told him in the beginning I could get you for less than current market price, and he wouldn't listen. My price now is fifty cents on the dollar." He shoved the documents back in his case. "That'll teach you not to say no to me."

Kate turned to Gene and pointed at the back door. "Get this son of a bitch out of here NOW!"

"With pleasure, boss." Gene grabbed Gillie. Jerking him off his feet, he wrestled him toward the back door.

Gillie squirmed about. "Get your hands off me, you moron." When he saw they were going toward the back of the house, his eyes grew large. "Hey, you stupid people, my car's the other way."

Kate led the way. "Have the boys take him to town. If they have to hog-tie him and gag him, do it. I want this miserable bastard off my property *now!*"

Gillie tried to jerk around. "Don't you dumb hicks understand English? My car's out front."

She pointed at the truck, with some of her wranglers in the back. "Forget his car. Throw him in the back and get him off my land."

"FORGET MY CAR!" Gillie screamed. "That's a $190,000 customized BMW. If you put a finger on it, I'll kill you."

Kate stopped at the edge of the porch and motioned to the men in the truck. "Tie this trespasser up and throw him in the back with your gear. Take him to the sheriff's office. I'll call Rawlins and have him arrested."

Her wranglers obliged. One stuffed a dirty grit-laden rag in his mouth while two others trussed him up with rope.

She looked at Gene. "You stay here. I need you to take care of his car." Together, they watched as the truck pulled away.

Gene looked at Kate. "What do you want me to do with the car?"

She pointed at a big-tired machine across the yard with a couple of long prongs out the front to pick up hay bales. "Pick it up with the hay-loader and throw it on the back of one of our flatbeds. Haul it to town and dump it on one of the side streets." Spinning around, she dashed for the door. There was no telling what effect Gillie had on her father. If she hadn't stopped him, she was sure her father would have ripped the little guy apart. She raced in and slid to a stop just as her father hung up the phone. "Give me the phone. I need to call Rawlins. I want the little bastard thrown in jail."

Seth shook his head. "No need. I just talked to him. I told him you consider Gillie a trespasser. He said he'd throw him in a cell and run him out of town in a couple days. He apologized. He just heard about the fence and gate. He said if he'd heard earlier, he would have tried to stop it. I told him that's okay. We'll handle the problem through the courts."

Red-faced, she looked at her father. "Pop, I didn't sleep with Jarrett." She settled back. "I did sleep in the same bed with him a couple times, but trust me, we didn't have sex."

"I believe you. No need to say more. The little guy is a jerk. We can handle the problem." The rumble of the front-end loader shook the windows as the big rig motored past the house toward the front. Within seconds, the sound of glass breaking and metal crunching could be heard. "I know this is your ranch, and I try not to butt in."

"You're not butting in," she said. The front-end loader went past the back door.

Seth turned and looked toward the sound. Gene had rammed the big prongs used to pick up the round hay bales through the windows of the BMW, and the car was bouncing along in front of the machine. He laughed. "What did you tell him to do with that car?"

"I told him to throw it on the back of a flatbed and haul it into town."

Seth grinned. "The more I get to know you, the more I love you. I like your style."

"I do have a bit of a flair, don't I?" She looked at her father. "You said you didn't want to butt in. What do you suggest?"

"Go to him."

Kate blinked. "I beg your pardon. Go to that little jerk?"

"No." He shook his head. "Not Gillie. Go see Sinclair."

Kate glared. "No way. I'm not going to him. He's trying to ruin me. I don't ever want to see him again."

Seth grabbed her arm. "Yes, you do. You have to confront him. We can handle the legal issues. I can make a few calls, and we can get this pushed through the court before you would have to truck any of the cattle down in the fall. This would be tried in a Montana court, and the Clarks have clout there."

She stared at her father. "So why should I go see him?"

"Because Gillie said he wanted the hundred and fifty thousand plus transferred to his personal account. You need to confront Jarrett. If he knew nothing of the toll and this is Gillie's idea, then he needs to know that. On the other hand, if Gillie is simply following Jarrett's orders and Jarrett is behind the fence and the gate and is trying to ruin you, then write him off. Trust me, you'll never be able to go on with your life until you get this resolved."

"I'll have to make sure he'll be in town," Kate said. "He travels a lot."

"You do that," Seth replied. "The sooner, the better."

In the morning, when her father hobbled in, he was quick to ask, "Is Jarrett going to be in town?" he said and dropped the mail on the table. "Do you have your plane reservations?"

She pointed at his hip. "Have you scheduled the surgery?"

"Yes. Surgery will be in a week." He stared at her. "Don't go trying to change the subject. Have you made your reservation to fly down to confront Sinclair?"

"Yes," she said. "I spoke to Lillian. He'll be in town tomorrow."

20

Having left the designer clothes Jarrett purchased in Los Angeles, she boarded the flight from Montana dressed in her customary dress: Western pants, tailored Western shirt, leather blazer, and cowboy boots. It was early afternoon when Kate's flight landed in Los Angeles. What little she needed for the one-night stay fit easily in a small carry-on. With no luggage to claim, she hailed a taxi and was off to the Sinclair building downtown. Seated in the back, she looked out and tried to decide what she was going to say. "I guess I'll just ask him flat out if he authorized the toll."

When the driver looked back in the mirror, she shook her head. "Never mind. I was just thinking out loud."

At the tower, Kate went directly to Jarrett's office. Stopping at Lillian's desk, she pointed at the door that bore his name. "I need to see him."

"By all means, Ms. Clark, except he stepped out for a few minutes. He should be back shortly." She took a key from her drawer. "While you're here, I'd appreciate it if you could separate what you wore and what can be returned. I haven't had a chance to do that." The woman handed Kate the key and pointed at a door off to the side. "This is a key to the apartment, and that door leads to the stairs that come out across from it."

Making her way down, Kate hesitated at the apartment door. The memories that lay on the other side caused her to pause. She took a deep breath and stepped inside. The apartment was as she remembered. Everything had been put in order. The bed was made. The door to the bathroom was open, and she could see fresh towels hanging on the rods. Where he had taped his notes, there was nothing. She opened the closet. The side she used was full. She checked the drawers, and her underwear and shorts were all there as well. She ran her fingers over the black dress. For a moment, the memories of that fantasy evening drifted back. The fabric was so elegant, and so were the people there. Just touching it made her feel warm all over again. About to take it from the hanger, she stopped. She shook her head. *Forget it. That's history. A page out of the past.*

Behind her, the door from the hall swung open. Kate turned. "It's you." She glowered.

"Yes, it's me," Jarrett replied. "Lillian said you'd be here."

"You have a lot of explaining to do," she snapped. "You're trying to put me out of business, and I want to know why."

"What?" Jarrett said with a puzzled expression. "I'm not trying to put you out of business. Where did you get that crazy idea?"

Kate stomped her foot. "How dare you call me crazy!"

Jarrett shook his head. "I'm not calling you crazy."

"Yes, you are. You just said so. I'm not crazy and quit insulting me."

"I'm not insulting you. Where did you come up with that silly conclusion?"

"First, I'm crazy, and now I'm silly. Goddamn, you're an insulting bastard. It isn't enough you're trying to destroy me financially, but you have to insult me as well?" She pointed at the door. "OUT! Get out of here! Get out of here now!" Grabbing him, she spun him around and pushed him toward the door. "Get out of my life!"

Jarrett pulled free. "I'm not trying to insult you." When she turned on him with clenched fists, he shook his head. "Oh, forget it. I'm tired of fighting with you. I have this for you," he said and held out a legal-sized envelope.

Seeing that, Kate exploded, "Of all the nerve." That envelope had to contain his demand for the hundred and fifty thousand plus for the cattle Gillie said had crossed his land. "You miserable skunk. You just couldn't send me a bill. You had to deliver it to me in person." She pointed at the door. "Out! Get out of here now!"

"What bill?" Jarrett questioned. Again, he tried to hand her the envelope, and when she flashed a fist, he tossed it on the bed. "I don't know what you're talking about." He pointed at the envelope. "I had what I believed was a great business plan we both could profit from, and it didn't work out. I guess I was wrong."

"Yes, you were wrong. You're trying to break up my ranch and hurt me financially. You're out to destroy me. Get out!" All but yelling, she pointed at the door. "I've had it with you. I don't ever want to see you again."

He backed toward the door. "If that's what you want, I'm gone."

"Yes! That's what I want. Now leave!" Pushing him, she slammed the door behind him.

With the door closed, she picked up the envelope and dropped down on the edge of the bed. Just like when her father quizzed her on Jarrett, she had overreacted. *Why does he always bring out the worst in me?*

Slumping back, she opened the envelope and pulled out three documents. She looked at each and froze. She tried to inhale but couldn't. For a few seconds, her body felt numb. Rather than a demand for the toll, what she found were the deeds to Wylie's, Patty's, and the Wilsons' ranches. She checked each quickly. Her name was at the top as *owner*. His signature was at the bottom. He had signed the three ranches over to her. Trying to inhale, she couldn't. Her heart pounded. What her great-grandfather had built was once again back together. She looked toward the floor above. About to follow, she stopped. She had to think. *What could have possessed you to have done such a thing? One minute, you wanted my upper range, and now you're giving it back. What's the catch? Those three ranches cost you millions. What can you want in return?*

Collecting the documents, she made her way to the floor above—*whomp, whomp, whomp*. The beat of helicopter blades could be heard as she climbed the stairs. "I need to talk to him," she said to Lillian and pointed at his office door.

"He's not here. He took off and is on the way to the airport."

Kate held out the deeds. "I need an explanation. He's given me the three ranches. What's the catch?"

Lillian appeared puzzled. "I'm not aware of any catch. From the moment he saw the pictures of you on horseback and in the lake, he was smitten. When he looked into your background, he was impressed. When he came back from Spokane and his trip out to your ranch, he was excited. He was in love. He believed the development project he had been working on could benefit both of you."

Kate shook her head. "I don't understand. Only yesterday, Gillie came to me demanding I pay a toll to cross his land, and now he's signed the properties over to me. What gives? Is Jarrett behind the toll Gillie demanded?"

"I'm not aware of any tolls," Lillian said. "I don't believe it was ever his intention to hurt you financially. He loves you too much."

"He what?" Kate blinked. Her jaw dropped. "Oh, really?" she said. "How do you know that?"

"I virtually raised him." The telephone rang. Lillian held up her hand. "Mrs. Lillenthaller here," she said. "Hold a second. I'm with her right now." She turned to Kate. "It's Erica Heath. Do you have a place to stay tonight?"

"Yes," Kate said. "I e-mailed her, and when I didn't hear back, I made a motel reservation out by the airport."

"No need. She's minutes away and wants you to stay with her."

Lillian turned back to the call. "Erica, we'll meet you at the apartment here in the building, floor 27, end of the hall." Lillian hung up and motioned to Kate. "Grab your stuff and let's go downstairs. You have some packing to do."

Kate looked toward the roof. "Do you have any idea where he went and when he'll be back?"

"He flew to the airport. He's going east. He has a boat race in a few days."

Kate followed Lillian to the apartment and watched as she pulled a large suitcase from the closet and laid it open on the bed. Returning to the closet, Lillian picked out a suit Jarrett had purchased for Kate and came back.

Kate tried to stop her. "I don't need any of those clothes. What I brought with me will get me through the night. I'm leaving early tomorrow."

Lillian nudged her aside. "These are the clothes the airline paid for and are yours to keep."

Kate tried to resist, but Lillian just kept pulling things from the closet and laying them in the suitcase.

There was a knock on the open door. Erica stepped in. "Oh God, it's good to see you." She beamed and gave Kate a hug.

Lillian pointed at the suitcase. "Give me a hand. We need to pack up her clothes."

Erica followed Lillian's lead and grabbed what was in one of the drawers.

Kate stepped forward. "I don't need any of that stuff. My flight is early tomorrow. I'll be out of your hair first thing in the morning."

Erica brushed past her. "Let's take it all and decide how long you're going to stay after you get to my house."

Kate spoke up, "But I can't stay. Dad's going in for surgery next week, and I need to get home to be with him"

"Fine," Erica replied. "Let's discuss that when we get to my place."

The sun was low when Erica handed Kate a glass of wine and led the way out to the patio. "Grab a chair."

Kate pulled out her cell phone. "I have to call Dad and tell him where I'm staying."

"If he isn't going to surgery until next week, that gives us four or five days to visit," Erica said. "Surely you can stay at least an extra day or two so I can show you the studio and where I work?"

Kate considered her offer. "I suppose I can spare a couple extra days."

"Excellent. I have tomorrow off, and we can hang out together."

Kate called her father, who was quick to point out she didn't need to come home. His nurse friend Hazel was going to take him to the hospital.

"But, Dad, I want to be there. What if something happens?"

"Nothing is going to happen. I'll be fine," he said. "I heard from the county clerk that Jarrett signed the three properties over to you. It sounds to me like he wasn't behind the toll after all. Go follow up on those offers from the medical school and research group. It might not require you move, and who knows, they could be fun. You've earned it." He hesitated. "Did you get a chance to see Jarrett?"

"Yes," she said and told how she blew up and told him to get out of her life. She continued. "I doubt those offers are still open."

"There's only one way to find out. You'll never know until you call them."

With the call over, Kate turned to Erica. "Dad said I should stay and hear if those offers are still open." She settled back. "He's made arrangements to get to the hospital," she said. "It's probably for the best. He's a terror whenever he's been hospitalized. He's the classic impatient patient."

"So it's settled," Erica said. "You're welcome to stay here as long as you want. Those follow-up calls will take a couple of days. Tomorrow you can come with me to the studio. It's my turn to show you around. After I give you a tour, we can have lunch on one of the sets. A friend of mine is in a Western being shot on the back lot." The telephone rang in Erica's kitchen. She excused herself.

Minutes later, Erica returned. "That was the studio. They've called an early-morning script conference. As usual, they're making last-minute changes. I'll leave you the keys to my other car and directions where to find me. We'll still do lunch."

The next morning, after Erica left, Kate dug out the business cards from the reception.

"Albert and Amelia Sinclair Research Foundation. Dr. Norman's office. Can I help you?" the receptionist asked.

"Yes," Kate said. "This is Kate Clark. Is Dr. Norman in?"

"Yes. What is this in regard to?"

"I met Dr. Norman at the anniversary reception, and he asked me to call the next time I was in town."

"Please hold." A minute passed, and the woman returned. "Dr. Norman is very busy right now. He suggested you call back in a week or so. I'll see if I can work you in then."

Kate stared at the phone. *That's a brush-off, if I ever heard one.* Thanking the woman, she lay Norman's card aside and dialed the number on the next card. The conversation was much the same. Dr. Carswell was busy, and his secretary suggested she call back in a couple weeks. She dialed Rolstadler's number. "I'm sorry, but Mr. Rolstadler won't be able to see you. He'll be unavailable for at least a week. You might want to try back then."

Kate pushed back from the table. *Well, so much for that.* Shaking her head, she stepped over to the window and looked toward Montana. "Like it or not, Dad, I'm on my way home."

With nothing to hold her in Los Angeles, Kate dressed in her Western clothes and went to see Erica at the studio.

Erica was quick to ask, "When's your first meeting?" She raised a curious eyebrow. "Surely you're not going to meet them dressed like that? I mean, Western pants and boots, isn't that a bit rustic?"

"There're no meetings. I phoned Norman, Carswell, and Rolstadler, and their secretaries brushed me off. At best, they'd try to work me in next week. I suspect because I told Jarrett off, the offers are dead." She scowled. "I never wanted their jobs in the first place. I've had it with these people and this damn town. I'm going home. I'll be leaving tonight."

Erica looked at her. "And that's that? Your mind is made up?"

"Yes, I'm going home. My ranch is back together, and I want to make that ride I have dreamed of from one end to the other." Kate pointed at the studio office building. "How did your meeting go? Everything okay?"

"No. That small part that Stanley was going to have for you has been written out. Stanley went back on his word as well. He's checking out a location, but as soon as he gets back, I'm going to have it out with him. He can't jerk you around like that."

Kate shook her head. "Don't get in a hassle over that. Your job is more important." She looked at the studio buildings. "Before I go, I'd still like to see where you work. Is that tour still in order?"

"It is." Erica pointed at her golf cart. "If we hurry, we can catch lunch with Miranda. You'll enjoy meeting her. After that, I'll give you the deluxe tour."

An hour later, lunch was nearly over. To Kate's left was the Academy Award-winning actress Erica Heath, and to her right was Miranda Wells, a polished performer who attained fame in situation-comedy roles. Miranda was dressed in a Western shirt, complete with scalloped trim and figure-hugging jeans and designer boots. Miranda looked her way. "I've heard from Erica that you're quite the horsewoman. Me, I'm the first to admit I don't understand those big animals. They scare me to death. I only took this part because of its romantic undertones, and well, the truth is, I need the work. I have bills to pay. I'm only scheduled to do the scenes where I trot the horse up and stop. The real riding will be done by a stunt person." She pointed at a palomino with a flowing mane and long, full tail. "What do you think of the horse I'm to ride? Isn't he beautiful?"

Kate studied him quickly. While the horse was beautiful, he was not a horse she'd have given to an inexperienced rider. A young stallion, he was jumpy and moved nervously at the least provocation. She considered saying something, except Miranda appeared anxious enough. "He's got great lines and should photograph well."

"Miranda," called the assistant director, "we're ready to shoot."

Kate and Erica watched as Miranda was helped into the saddle. The director approached. "I want you to trot over to that pickup and look down into the cab. When you don't see your cousin, show me concern. You need to know where he's gone. Do you understand?"

Miranda nodded.

"Fine. Get ready," he called out. "Roll 'em," and then "Action." He pointed at Miranda. "You're on. Now show me concern."

Miranda tapped the horse with her heels and nothing. It didn't move. Even *click, click* drew no response. The director ordered, "Get going," and gave the horse a slap. The stallion bolted. Miranda screeched. Someone yelled, "Watch out!" Off to the side, staging loaded with equipment swayed and tottered over. Lights and equipment crashed to the ground. The stallion reared. Miranda screamed. Some person yelled, "Help her."

The stallion bucked and bolted. Kate looked around, and no one was moving. "Shit," Kate muttered. Jumping up, she ran for the first available mount. Grabbing the saddle, she let out a commanding "yow!" The horse took off. Kicking off, Kate ran alongside and made a running start. Behind her, people were screaming. "Save her. Save her."

Ahead, the stallion bucked. Miranda held on, but barely. Kate hammered her horse. One more buck, and Miranda would be history. "Move!" she demanded, and her horse raced aheaderH. The stallion bucked again. Miranda went flying. Kate lunged out and caught her. "HOLD ON," she called to the actress and swung the slightly built woman around behind her. "You okay?"

Stammering, Miranda clung to her. Ignoring the young stallion, Kate brought her horse around and rode back to where it all began. People rushed up and helped Miranda down. Kate swung off, and Erica pulled her aside.

"What's up?" Kate asked.

Away from the rest, Erica whispered, "I just talked to the camera director. He got all that on HD digital. I told him to get copies to the local TV stations as fast as he can. What you did was fantastic. You saved Miranda, and maybe even the movie. Everyone will want to see that."

21

With the handshakes completed, Erica toured Kate through the studio. Erica's cell phone rang. "It's Rachel." Rachel's voice boomed forth. "You have to get Kate here immediately! All hell's broken loose. The local TV stations who received the copy of her saving Miranda have fed it to the networks. The national news programs are picking it up and are going to feature it as well. Kate is sizzling hot. My editor has been ringing me off the hook. We're pulling the cover on the edition that was going to press tonight and replacing it with Kate saving Miranda. I need her here NOW! I have to do an interview. How soon can you get her here?"

Erica grinned. "We're on our way." She pointed at the car Kate had driven to the studio. "Follow me."

Kate followed Erica to Jarrett's sprawling, half-timbered mansion. Parking, she surveyed the formidable structure. "Wow!" she whispered. *This is his house?* Wide-eyed, Kate tried to take it all in. *How big must Rachel's staff be to take over a building this large?* She followed Erica. "This is quite a house."

"Oh yeah, and this is only the end Rachel occupies. When you're through, I'm sure she'll give you a tour."

Rachel was quick to greet them. "God, you're hot. Your saving Miranda is the talk of the town." She led the way to her office. The four women there stood and cheered. "Not now," Rachel said. She cleared away a dress, two blouses, and a handful of papers from the chair beside her desk. "You'll have to excuse the way the room looks. We've been busting our butts meeting a deadline. Crunch time, you know. Come tomorrow, everything will be back to normal." Rachel settled in at her computer. "Tell me everything. I have to get this to the printer as fast as I can. What went through your mind for you to do what you did?"

Kate settled into the chair. Aside from herself, Erica, and Rachel, there were only four other women. *Where are all the people Jarrett was referring to? They must be in other rooms. Surely they can't put a national magazine together with a staff this small.* Kate turned back. "I don't know. There wasn't time to think. Miranda was in trouble. Everyone was standing around. There was a horse available, so I grabbed it. That's all there was to it." She turned on her cell phone. It had been off while she'd been on the set, and she just now noticed. No sooner on, and it rang. "It's Father." She motioned to Rachel. "Give me a minute. Hi, Dad. What's up?"

"I'll tell you what's up. Your saving that actress has caught everyone's attention. Our phone hasn't stopped ringing. All the major morning-show people have phoned, and so has CNN. They want you on their programs. The national late-night show people want you as well. I've been trying to get you. Where are you?"

"Sorry. I was touring the studio and switched off my phone."

Seth continued, "What do you want me to do? What should I tell them? Should I have them call you?"

Rachel overheard her father's question. "No! Don't give out your number," she said. "Have them call my office here. I'll keep a person on tonight and then cover it with my staff tomorrow."

Kate passed on the message, and the call was over.

Rachel continued, "How did you know to get on the horse that way? A running start is a pretty risky maneuver."

"The horse was facing where I needed to go, so I grabbed him and went. Miranda wasn't going to last much longer."

Rachel's eyes grew large. "But weren't you afraid the horse would run off without you?"

"Not with me holding on to the saddle," she said.

Rachel continued, "You've obviously done that type of mount before."

"Hundreds of times in riding exhibitions," Kate said. "It's a good attention-getter to open a demonstration."

Rachel looked up from her keyboard. "How were you able to grab Miranda out of the air? Doesn't that take a lot of strength?"

"I don't know. I train calf-roping horses. I rope and throw two-hundred-pound steers around. I suspect Miranda weighed quite a bit less."

"You've got a point," Rachel said. "How's Miranda doing?"

"The last I saw, she was shaken but will make it."

Rachel turned and addressed a person nearby. "You have my interview on your computer. You've heard our discussion. Adjust it and make it fit the space. Then get it to the printer." She motioned to Kate. "It's going to take an all-out effort to switch out the cover and one of the articles, but the printer assured me he can work miracles and start the run right after midnight." She grinned. "Our current month's issue will be out three days early, and with the help of FedEx, we'll scoop everyone and will be on the stands by midday tomorrow."

Kate questioned, "You're pulling the article you wrote about me in Montana and substituting what happened today instead?"

"No," Rachel replied. "The issue that's going to press tonight closed four weeks ago. The article on you up north is going to be featured in the following month's issue. That closes today. That's why we look so frazzled."

Erica stepped forward. "I told Kate when you finished with this, you would give her a tour of the house."

"By all means, let's do it," Rachel said. "Not counting the rooms in this wing that I occupy and the staff quarters over the garage, the main part of the house has ten bedrooms, fourteen bathrooms, of one form or another, a billiard room, a projection room, a game room, an exercise room the size of most small gyms, a basketball court, a bowling alley, a racquetball court, an office he seldom uses, a dining room that will seat two dozen, a living room that will accommodate twice that many, a commercial-sized kitchen, a library and two dens, and a wine cellar with over a thousand bottles. Jarrett's bedroom suite is in the turret at the far end." Rachel motioned to the women in the room. "And, Kate, this is my staff. They've helped me work on next month's article and have been dying to meet you." Rachel went around and introduced the four women.

Kate blinked. "And this is your complete staff? The five of you put the whole magazine together? Wow."

"What? Oh no," Rachel laughed. "The magazine is put together in New York. I'm only responsible for three fashion sections and my byline piece."

After touring Jarrett's house, Kate followed Erica in the other car. She slapped the steering wheel. *There's no way Rachel's four-person staff could have been noticed in a house that huge. The bastard. He's been manipulating me here too.* She slapped the steering wheel again. *I have only myself to blame. If he were in town, I'd let him have it.*

Back at Erica's, Kate watched as the actress went over the calls received so far. "I'm really not interested in doing those interviews."

"Maybe not, but this publicity will help Rachel's publisher sell more magazines. It'll be a big boost to Rachel's career, as well as generate great interest in the movie."

Kate slowly considered what she said. "Put that way, I'll do it. But I have a ranch to run, and when this is over, I'm going home."

"Whatever," Erica replied. "But let's see what happens once all this publicity plays out. Who knows, maybe Norman, Carswell, and Stanley will be interested in you on your own." Erica looked at her notes. "You're a hot news item, and it's been a bit of a juggling act to get you on all three networks the same morning, but Rachel pulled it off. There'll be back-to-back interviews done remote from the studio we were in today. They all want you in your Western clothes just as you were when you saved Miranda. As far as we're concerned, they can take that idea and shove it. While you can do all those cowboy things, you're a woman. Rachel's presenting you in her magazine as an intelligent modern-day woman, and that's what we're going to do as well. You'll have to get to bed soon. I'll be getting you up early to make it to the studio."

It was dark when Erica drove Kate to the studio. Dressed in one of the business suits she acquired on her first trip to Los Angeles, one interview followed on the heels of the next, and the morning flew by. By noon, Kate had done interviews with three major morning network shows, two cable channels, and a couple of national tabloids. Kate smiled. She was enjoying the attention. Up north when she roped a steer or trained a cutting horse or helped a mare bring a foal into the world, there was no fanfare, no applause; it was just another day on the job.

⁕

Rachel's office was handling the calls, so she came to the studio to update Kate. "You've another interview this afternoon. After that, the rest of the day will be free. I have you penciled in on a couple national late-night shows shot here in LA. One tapes at seven, and the other at ten o'clock. You'll be able to make both without rushing. I've contacted one of the design houses I've been featuring, and they are excited. They'll be knocking out two new creations. When you walk out, I want everyone's eyes to pop. Their designers and fitters will be here soon. The design house is excited you'll be wearing some of their originals on national television." She turned the page. "Norman called. He apologized. He didn't know what his secretary was thinking. He wants you to call him as soon as you can. Here's his number. Make him wait until after five. It'll serve him right." She continued, "Carswell called as well. He too was most apologetic. He wants you to phone him at your earliest convenience. He left his direct line."

The designers had come and gone. Alone, Kate reached for the phone and punched in Norman's number. "Ms. Clark, it's so nice of you to return my call. I have to apologize. My secretary misunderstood your name. I'd love to have you visit. Come tomorrow morning, and I'll give you a VIP tour, and then we can join everyone for lunch. Having you working with us will be a great addition."

Kate hesitated. *His secretary misunderstood my name? What was there not to understand?* She stared at the phone. *I haven't agreed to work for you.* "I'll see if I can work that in. I'm scheduled to do a talk show late tonight, and I'll have to see how I feel in the morning."

"Good. Call me when you get up, and we'll go from there."

With one call down, she dialed the dean at the university medical school. While the conversation was not exactly the same, he too was no less apologetic. Would she be available tomorrow? Kate said it would have to be the day after. He agreed, and the call was over.

<hr />

As requested by the first talk show production staff, Kate arrived dressed in what she had been wearing when she rescued Miranda: her Western shirt, twill pants, and cowboy boots. A few minutes prior to showtime, the host stopped by the dressing room.

"So you're the cowgirl from Montana who saved Miranda. You'll be the first person on. I'll do my monologue and then introduce you. We plan to show the last few seconds of the tape of you catching Miranda. I'll ask you how you did it, and well, we'll go from there. You'll be on no more than two minutes, and then I'll bring out my featured guest. I'll announce that you have to go, and you leave. Okay." Not waiting for a reply, he left and pulled the door closed.

Jane, the assistant Rachel had sent along, tripped the lock. "Quick, out of those clothes. We have to move fast."

Kate pulled off her pants and shirt, and Jane handed her the dress that Rachel's designers created. From outside the door came the familiar sound of the show's theme music. They could hear the roar of applause as the host was introduced. Any second, there would be a rap on the door, calling Kate to the stage. Jane zipped her up and stepped back. "God, you've got great legs," she said as Kate stepped into the high heels that went with the dress. "You'll knock their socks off. When you step through the curtain, remember to smile." There was the knock on the door. Jane tripped the latch. "You're on."

Poised at the curtain, Kate's pulse pounded. A stagehand wearing a headset was positioned to pull the curtain aside. Off to the side came a muted, "No, no, that won't work." Kate looked around as the stage manager ran up. He called to her in hushed tones. "Where's the cowboy outfit and boots? What's with the dress and fancy shoes? That won't work."

Jane stepped forward and whispered, "She spilled coffee on herself. This is the only other thing she has to wear."

"Damn!" he whispered. "If that's the case, we'll have to go with it."

The host could be heard. "Our first guest tonight, you saw on the evening news. Straight from Montana, the lady cowboy who saved Miranda Wells. Please welcome, Kate Clark."

The production assistant looked to Kate. He mouthed, "Showtime."

Kate took a deep breath and stepped toward the curtain. Her stomach churned. *I own a big cattle ranch, and I'm successful. I don't have to take a backseat to anyone.* The curtain parted, and she stepped through. The audience applauded. The host stood. "Ahhhh," he started to say and watched as she approached his desk. "You obviously don't wear something like that when you're working on your ranch."

Still smiling, Kate shook her head. "No. Up home, I wear jeans and a shirt and boots."

"Much like what you were wearing when you rescued Miranda." Kate affirmed.

He motioned toward the control room. "Run the tape."

At the end of her allotted time, the host reached over and tapped her arm. "You're an absolute delight. I know my guests will love to meet you. Can you possibly stay on for the rest of the show?"

Kate agreed and slid back on the sofa.

At the next show, the response was similar. As with the first host, he too encouraged her to stay. The hosts had loved her, and so had their audiences.

22

At the institution, Dr. Norman was quick to greet her. "I'm glad you could make it. I saw you last night on TV. You were quite a hit."

Kate looked at the man. *Before you were interested in me because Jarrett told you to be. Now you're interested because of my recent notoriety. You people are a bunch of jackals. Is everyone in LA like this?*

He led the way into a hallway marked Restricted. Their first stop was at a set of windows that looked in at a laboratory crowded with benches laden with equipment. Kate stepped forward. "What are they doing in there?"

"That's one of the labs where we synthesize cells that could aid in early identification of Alzheimer-altered cells."

Kate took a step toward the door. "That sounds exciting. Can we go in?"

Norman reached out and pulled her back. "Not today. They're close to completing their latest batch, and any interruption could be quite disruptive."

Kate's movement caught the eye of one of the people in the lab, who stepped to the door. "Hello, Ms. Clark," he said. "We heard you were going to visit us today."

Norman stepped forward. "Not now, Harry," he said and moved her along. "We're tight on time and have to keep going." He nudged Kate down the hall. "There's much more to see." He led the way and stopped at a window to another lab. His expression brightened.

"This is one of our ultraclean rooms. There are only a handful of clean rooms in the world that come close to the standards we have in there."

"Really!" Kate said. "What do they do in there that requires that level of cleanliness?"

"In there," he said as he moved her along, "that's where we do molecular research. We have some of the world's most powerful electron microscopes in that room."

"I've heard about them," Kate said and turned back. "I'd be interested to see how they work."

He chuckled. "That room is only open to those who work in there, myself and a couple others. It's quite a process to enter the space." With his hand to her back, he pushed her along.

They stopped at another window that looked into a room filled with people in street clothes at desks and partitioned workstations. Kate stepped up to the glass. *Should I even waste the time asking?* She shook her head. *Oh well, I'll give it a try.* "What do they do in there?"

"DNA and gene research," he tossed off. "A lot of high-tech number crunching. Pretty complex stuff. There's not much to see." Again, he nudged her along. "That might be my most promising avenue toward a solution, though."

Kate pulled away and stepped back. "I've spent years studying the genetic makeup of cattle in an effort to develop a heartier and leaner animal."

Norman laughed. "Oh heavens, what we do in there is far more complicated than that." Taking her arm, he moved down the hall. "We have to keep going. Lunch is about to be served, and everyone is waiting." He led the way toward a conference room on the main floor general office area.

She glanced at her watch. "I guess you're right. It is getting on toward noon. We better not keep the board members waiting."

Norman chuckled. "The board members? Oh heavens, no. We're not having lunch with the board of directors. They're very busy people. They can't drop everything to simply have lunch.

No. We'll be having lunch with some of the department heads and managers who can break away." He led the way into a conference room on the main floor with pale-green walls and bland commercial furniture. "Everyone, this is Kate Clark, the rancher from Montana who saved Miranda Wells. She's going to help us promote what we do here." Norman stepped aside as the caterer entered. "Lunch has arrived." Grinning, he looked at Kate. "I realize you raise cattle and are probably partial to eating beef, but we're into less red meat, so I've ordered baked sole." He snickered. "You do eat fish, don't you?"

Fella, you're starting to get under my skin. "Fresh sole, occasionally. Our local groceries are surprisingly well stocked, but I prefer the trout we catch on my ranch. Many run a good two feet or more in length." While that was a stretch, she'd had her fill of his snickers and high-handed attitude and decided to lay it on a little thick herself.

Jaws dropped. One man asked, "You've lakes with trout that big?"

Another quipped, "You go fishing a lot?"

"Every chance I get." While she didn't have the patience to stand on a riverbank with a pole in her hand, her foreman's son, Dusty, loved to fish and supplied them with all the trout they could eat.

"Enough fishing talk," Norman interjected. "Lunch is ready to be served." He motioned toward the caterer to begin. He pointed to Kate. "I'd like to use you and your newfound notoriety to raise awareness of what I do here. The old established medical foundations get all the headlines. I figure you can draw attention to my accomplishments. As we speak, I am having a publicity firm put together a couple ideas on how to get my work the recognition it deserves."

Little more was said as Dr. Norman hurriedly ate. Wiping his mouth, he pushed back from the table. "I have a phone call I have to make. I'll be right back."

With Norman gone and the door closed, a large man with big shoulders reached across the table. "Hi, I'm Brendon Herbert, associate director of operations. What do you think of our facility?"

Kate raised a critical brow. "What little I saw of it, I was impressed. I would've liked to have gone into some of the labs and visited with the people."

One of the other people spoke up, "Oh, he gave you the twenty-five-cent tour. A quick run down the hall and a 'thank you, ma'am.'"

"Something like that," she said. "He said he is on the verge of a major breakthrough."

Herbert responded, "A major breakthrough would be a bit of a push. What I can say, we're inching closer to a solution." He smiled. "Now, don't get me wrong. We'll eventually unravel the mystery around Alzheimer's. That much is a given," he said. "And by *we*, I mean the research community in general. Whether we do it or some university laboratory, here, or abroad has yet to be determined, but it will happen."

Another person chimed in, "Alzheimer's is the director's singular focus, but we've made significant discoveries in the possible treatment of Chiron's disease, arthritis, and gout that have been more or less brushed aside because they're not on his agenda."

Kate was about to ask why when everyone pulled back as Norman returned. He looked at Kate. "Did they talk your ears off?"

Looking at the people, she slowly smiled. "That, they did. They gave me an earful."

Norman stopped at the table. "I see you've finished. I need to spend a few minutes with you before you have to go."

While she wasn't finished, Kate glanced at her plate and then up at him. *I have to go? Since when? My whole afternoon has been left open for this meeting.*

Norman led the way to the top floor offices. On the way down the hall, she caught glimpses through some of the open doors. All the offices were richly paneled and elegantly furnished. Norman led the way into his office overlooking the city and around to behind his oversized all-glass desk. He pointed at the chair in front of his desk.

"Take a seat," he said. "The people I wanted here from a public relations firm aren't able to make it. No problem, though.

I'll explain what I'd like you to do. During your appearances on talk shows, I'd like you to mention the work I'm doing here and that I'm on the verge of whipping Alzheimer's. With all the aging baby boomers, it's becoming a major concern." Focusing on her, he rested his elbows on his desk. "It's going to be a few days until I can get exactly what I want you to say. When I get it, I'll give you a call. Okay?" Standing, he looked toward the door. "Now, if you'll excuse me, I have a ton of things that need my attention. Thank you for coming."

Kate blinked. *And that's it? Boom, bang, and out of here.* She reached for the door. *You impolite bastard. If you want publicity, you can promote yourself.* Stepping out, she looked to the left and then the right. She'd come from the left, so she decided to try the hall to the right. On her own, she might see some of the foundation Jarrett was so proud of. She turned a corner. The hall ahead was long. Some distance ahead, a woman in a black waitress uniform stood next to a cart laden with plates under metal covers.

On her way down the hall, Kate passed a set of double doors, one of which was partially open. A man's voice carried clearly through the opening. "The Dodgers are going to kill San Francisco. The Giants don't have a snowball's chance in hell of beating LA." Men laughed, and all appeared to talk at once, so many that she wasn't able to make out any one particular comment.

Kate approached the woman beside the cart. She motioned in the direction of the double doors. "Sounds like whoever's in that room back there are enjoying themselves."

"That's the board of directors. They're waiting for lunch." The woman lifted the cover from one of the plates. "We should eat so well. Lobster tail flown in special this morning. The finest steak from Montana that money can buy. The best fiddlehead ferns brought in from Tide Head, New Brunswick, late last night."

Kate studied what was on the plate. "That's a lot of food. That lobster tail alone is enough for two people with hearty appetites, as well as the steak."

The waitress shook her head. "Oh, they don't eat all this at one sitting." The woman pulled back the drape that hung around the cart and pointed at the take-home boxes on the bottom shelf.

Kate stepped aside as a second cart rolled up. It too had plates under metal covers. On one end of the cart were neat rows of liquor bottles of three different kinds and roughly a dozen of each.

A man stepped out from behind the double doors and looked their way. "Both carts are here, so let's get with it," he said. Scowling, he continued, "Let's get some service."

Kate looked to the waitress. "The elevator?"

The woman motioned. "Around the corner and just down the hall."

The man from the boardroom pointed at Kate as he addressed the woman pushing the lead cart. "Wasn't that, that lady cowboy who saved that actress?"

"I don't know. I didn't ask her name."

When Rachel heard Kate's afternoon was open, she set up a meeting with an energy drink company. The energy-drink people, like a number of other companies, wanted to capitalize on her recent fame. Unlike the offers Jarrett had arranged that would have required a full-time commitment, the corporate advertiser offers she was now receiving would be limited to a couple of daylong photo shoots every few months or so. The extra money they were offering was a windfall that would come in handy to make improvements on her ranch.

It was late afternoon when Kate got to Erica's. Happy to see her, Erica grabbed a wine bottle and a couple of glasses and headed for her patio.

"Good," Kate said. "I'm going to need more than one glass."

Erica stopped at the table. "How'd your meeting go at the medical foundation? Exciting?"

"Not really. Dr. Norman gave me a quickie tour pointing out this lab and that office, and that was it."

"Meeting the board of directors for lunch had to be better."

"I didn't meet the board. I had lunch with some of the department heads. They were very nice people and actually the high point of my visit. They weren't the board of directors, though. While we ate baked fish and some rice and peas, the board members had lobster, steak, and who knows what else."

Erica straightened up. "Then his offer of having you on the board fell through?"

"You got that right." Kate related how Norman wanted her to promote the good job he was doing.

Erica growled. "The arrogant bastard."

"Right," Kate responded. "He talked down to me every chance he got. I had half a mind to punch the smirking son of a bitch right in the mouth."

Erica grinned. "Why didn't you?"

Kate straightened up. "Down here, I'm trying to be a refined, proper woman and not some hard-nosed wrangler boss from Montana, but characters like that are trying my patience."

"And the rest of the afternoon, how did that go?" Erica asked.

Kate told her how she met with an energy-drink company.

"Sounds like you have everything under control," Erica said. "Stanley Rolstadler has jumped on the bandwagon as well. He pestered me all day to get you to come in. He assured me it hadn't been his intention to write you out of the movie." Erica hesitated. "Have you heard from Jarrett?"

Kate shook her head. "Not a word."

23

The next morning, Kate met with Dr. Carswell at the university medical school hospital. At the anniversary reception, he had spoken of how he would like to have her on the scholarship selection committee. That had obviously been something Jarrett had arranged. Now that Jarrett was not involved, she could only wonder what was behind his sudden interest.

Unlike the day before, Dr. Carswell went to great length to explain their state-of-the-art equipment and leading-edge facility. They stopped at nurse's stations and clinical labs where she talked with the staff at length. Following lunch with the executive board, Dr. Carswell tapped his water glass to get everyone's attention and then addressed Kate directly, "Unlike the near full-time commitment Jarrett had envisioned for you, we'd like to have you publicly involved in our recruitment program. Like all medical schools, we're interested in attracting the brightest and most promising student applicants. If by having you involved will give us an increased measure of visibility to attract those candidates, so much the better. What do you think? It is not a full-time position and will not require you to relocate."

So they will be trying to capitalize on my recent fame. There is no harm in that. "Yes. I will be glad to help you."

The next few days were a blur of activity. Stanley Rolstadler had her in more scenes than he'd originally planned. He had increased her involvement to include a few lines of dialogue and interaction with Erica. After five days of shooting, her part was complete. Stanley had asked her to come in an extra day in case scenes had to be reshot. None had to be, so she settled at a table with her laptop to catch up on ranch activity.

Jarrett approached and pointed at the chair beside her. "Is this taken?" he asked.

It's you. She glowered. "You've got a lot of explaining to do. In fact, you've got a lot of nerve coming here in the first place. I'm tired of your manipulations and tricks. I don't ever want to see you again."

Jarrett held up his hand. "Hey, I'm here in peace. I'm not here to get in a fight." He focused on her. "I have a couple of projects to inspect and, after that, another boat race. I'd like to have you come along. I want you to see what I do. I want you to get to know me better."

"I couldn't care less what you do." Kate snorted. "You're out of my life. Don't you understand? Now—" About to tell him to go, she caught herself. She sensed she might be on the verge of saying too much. Taking a breath, she eased back. "Just like that, you show up and expect me to drop everything so you can pick up like nothing has happened? Well, a lot has happened. First off—"

Jarrett signaled time-out. "Let's not argue." He looked at Stanley. "She's finished, today isn't she?"

"Yes," Rolstadler said.

"Fine," he said and motioned to her. "Come on. Grab your laptop and let's go somewhere where we can talk."

Reluctantly, she agreed. The least she could do was hear him out. Using the car Erica had lent her, she followed Jarrett to a Denny's not far from the studio. No sooner were they seated than she opened up. "You bought those three ranches and were ready to charge me a toll, and then boom, you signed the properties over to me. What the hell is going on?"

"The truth is, the moment I saw the pictures of you and that trip out to your ranch, I fell in love with you. I know that sounds a bit far-fetched but …"

"Bullshit," Kate blurted out. "Don't give me that crap. You're trying to tell me just like that, you saw some pictures of me and *boom!* you fell in love with me? Your…" Her voice trailed off. *What am I saying? Isn't that the same thing that happened to me when I saw his pictures in the magazine and in Spokane?* She slowly eased back. "Go on."

"I know that might sound crazy, but that's the truth," he said. "I fell in love with you. I know it happened fast, but I guess that's the way life is. I put together what I felt was a sound business deal that would benefit both of us, but I was mistaken. I'm sorry. After I bought the properties, I realized I might've hurt you instead. So rather than cause you grief, I signed them over to you. If I offended you, I apologize. You mean the world to me. Life is too short, and I'd like to spend every moment I can with you. Is there a crime in that?"

She stared into his eyes. He appeared sincere. *People can lie with their lips, but not so easily with their eyes. Could he be telling the truth?* Exhaling the breath she hadn't been aware she had been holding, she set her cup aside. "I'll have to think this over."

"What's there to think over?" he asked. "Can you go with me on my next business trip and then watch me race?"

She blinked. "Just like that, you want me to drop everything and go with you?"

"Well, sort of," he added. "Can you go with me on my next trip east? I'd really enjoy having you along."

"I can't right now," she said. "I'm swamped. In addition to handling ranch business, I have three commercials I have to shoot. Rachel has picked up a sportswear company that wants me. Maybe next time."

With everything Kate had to do, the time flew by. She had become comfortable in Los Angeles, which was something she never expected. With her evenings, free Jarrett was ever present. He took her to dinner and to shows at his restaurants and theaters. He took her to the symphony and introduced her to the conductor. Warmed to what he was doing, Kate sensed his overtures were genuine. Unlike in the past, she now believed he loved her. He was with her every chance he had. As the days rolled by, her feelings toward him grew.

Seated in his kitchen, she stared at him. It was late. The under-cabinet lights shone across the room. Finishing the second glass of wine, a warm feeling welled up within her. At first, she attributed it to the wine and then realized it wasn't that at all. This time, her feelings toward him were real. She had fallen in love.

He was talking about his latest project, but she wasn't listening. Nodding whenever she sensed he expected her to, she studied him. *Aside from that first week in Los Angeles, not once have you tried to get me in bed. How come?* She glanced down. *Is there something wrong with me? Don't you find me attractive?* Turning, she looked toward his bedroom suite. She knew what she had to do. She had to know if they were compatible. Picking up their wineglasses, she put them in the sink. Reaching out, she pulled him to his feet. "It's been a long day. Shall we call it a night?" With him in hand, she led the way to the master suite.

In the bedroom, Jarrett reached for the lights, but Kate shook her head. "Not now," she said. When their lips met, she kissed him softly. Easing back, she ran her tongue around her lips. He tasted as good now as she remembered from that first kiss aboard his plane. Tossing her blouse aside, she undid his shirt and pushed it off his shoulders. Her fingers trembled on feeling the hard muscles of his neck and chest. He was strong. He was powerful. He drew her close. He was excited. She could feel his erection against her as he unhooked her bra. She loosened her shorts and let them drop along with her panties. Reaching down, she took a hold of his jeans. Running the zipper down, she grabbed the waistband and pushed everything to the floor. Squatting down, she looked at his naked body. *Oh God, you're gorgeous.*

Standing, she pulled him onto the bed. His strong hands came up and over her breasts. His fingers caressed her nipples, sending a shock wave through her. They were raised and hard and felt like they were about to explode. Trembling, she pulled him between her legs. She gasped when they slowly became one.

How long they made love or how many times, she hadn't kept track. Awake on the bed, she stared at the ceiling. She was in love. She couldn't help herself. He was dozing beside her. *Can this be real?* she asked herself.

Constantly on the go, Jarrett was in town one day and out the next. When he was there, they spent every moment they could together. With breakfast over, following one of her many overnight stays, Jarrett set his cup aside. "Why don't you pack your things and move in here? I love you, and I think you love me."

Kate looked at him. *I don't know if I'm ready for that big a step. What'll I do if it doesn't work out?* She studied his eyes. He was expecting an answer. She slowly considered her response. "All my stuff is at Erica's. I've set up a small office there and am comfortable running things up north."

"Please consider this seriously." He focused on her. "Promise me."

"I promise."

Between trips to her ranch and commercials to shoot, the days melted away. Jarrett had been off inspecting another of his projects and had just returned. When he caught up with her at Erica's, they settled in at the patio table. "We're both in love," he said. "Why don't we take the plunge and get married?"

Kate blinked. "Just like that, you think we should get married?"

"Why not?" he asked. "We're in love. We're together every chance we get."

She studied him. That much was true. *I don't know. Sleeping with you is one thing. Marriage, that's quite another. If things don't work out, I'll end up a divorcee, forever questioning if I was at fault and if there was something I should have done differently.* She looked at him. *Worse yet, you could get killed racing that silly boat, and I'd end up a widow.*

She studied him. "I don't know. I'll have to think that through."

24

Days later, Jarrett returned to Los Angeles in time to accompany Kate to a showing of Phillip Claymore's paintings. Most of the gallery lights were out when Isabel walked Kate and Jarrett to the door. "I'm glad you two could make it. Your presence here meant the world to Phillip," she said and turned to Jarrett, "especially since you bought the two most expensive paintings."

"I can always use them in one of my restaurants," he said.

Jarrett led the way to the car. "As always, you look fabulous," he said. "You look comfortable in those fancy gowns."

"I am," Kate said. "I like the feel. The last time I was home, I actually felt uncomfortable in jeans and a Western shirt. I hate to say it, but I was looking forward to getting back here." She looked at him. "Does that mean I'm becoming citified?"

Jarrett grinned. "Don't get too uncomfortable in your Western duds."

"Why not?" she asked.

"Because you said you'd go with me on my next trip." He held the car door open. "You'll need to take along a little bit of everything. We'll be crawling around some construction sites. Then there are a couple of meetings I'll have you attend with me in boardrooms. That'll give you a feel for what I do for a living. Are you good with that?"

"I am," Kate acknowledged.

Packed for the weeklong trip, she walked directly from Jarrett's helicopter to his plane. While she'd been on flights before, this would be her first overnight experience. The plane would be their transportation, office, hotel, and dining room throughout the coming week. Kate stepped into the owner's stateroom. Laying her suitcase on the queen-sized bed, she checked the closet, and there was more than enough room for what she brought along. Likewise, there were sufficient drawers to hold what else. "Excellent," she mumbled. Next to it was the door to the bathroom. "Wow," she whispered. In addition to the polished granite countertop, there was a large vanity sink, a stand-alone toilet, and a full-sized shower. *Now, this is a bathroom.*

With her dresses hung and everything stowed, she went forward and stopped in the conference area. Jarrett was at the table. He had two laptops running and a large case bulging with files on the floor nearby.

"Aren't you flying the plane today?" she asked.

"No. Warren is. I have work to do." When she started to settle in at one of the swivel chairs across from him, he pointed toward the fixed seating ahead of the partition. "You'll have to sit up there. FAA regulations. The seats around the table don't have seat belts."

She looked toward the fixed seating and then at him. "Oh, then you'll be joining me there in a minute?"

"No, I'm staying here."

Settling in forward, Kate buckled up as the plane began to roll.

Sheryl stopped by. "Good. Your seat belt's secure."

Kate motioned in the direction of the conference area.

"Yes, I know," Sheryl whispered. "But who's going to tell him he can't sit there during takeoff?"

After they leveled off and the seat-belt light was out, Kate went back to Jarrett. "Getting a lot accomplished?"

"I am. It's a big project, and I want to make sure everything is still on schedule." Pausing, he looked at her. "I'm sorry I don't have time to visit, but I need to focus on this."

"Oh," she said and started toward the fixed seats forward.

He called to her, "The first site we'll be going to is little more than a block-square, four-story hole in the ground. You'll need to put on your ranch clothes."

After touring the site and meeting with the superintendent, Kate and Jarrett were off to their next meeting. Jarrett stopped in the stateroom doorway as she prepared to change. "Where to next?" she asked and took a seat on the bench next to the bath. The plane bounced sharply and made a violent jolt. She held on.

Jarrett's head snapped forward and back hard. He blinked and grabbed the door for support. Beads of perspiration formed on his brow. Trembling, he reached up and brushed the drops away. "Uh. An air pocket," he mumbled and slowly lowered himself onto the bed. Taking a breath, he turned toward her. "We're off to Oklahoma City and then to Pennsylvania. We should be in Oklahoma in an hour or so."

"Are you okay?" she asked and reached to offer a hand.

Shaking his head, he pushed her away. "Yes! I'm fine. I just had a little dizzy spell. I must have moved too fast."

Kate looked at him. This was another sharp jolt where his head snapped about like what happened when they first met. Back then, he had brushed it off as an old sports injury. Could this be the same? She studied him. His complexion was a little splotchy, but aside from that and his brief trembling, he appeared all right. She shrugged. *Maybe you're right.*

<hr />

The next morning, still in bed, Kate wiped the sleep from her eyes. The stateroom was dark. There was no engine noise nor the sound of wind rushing by the side of the plane. She reached down. The retention straps across the bed had been undone and laid off to the side. They were on the ground. The space beside her was empty. The door inched open. Jarrett stepped in. When he saw her awake, he switched on the bedside light. "Good morning," he said with a broad smile.

"Where are we?" she asked, sitting up.

"Western Pennsylvania. We landed an hour ago. I was supposed to wake you, except you looked so peaceful I couldn't bring myself to do it, so I made a special effort to land without a bump. Did I wake you?"

"No," she said and shook her head "I slept right through it." She looked about. "So what's the plan for today?"

"I'm building an office complex here that's behind schedule and costing me a fortune in overruns. I have a hard meeting ahead of me today. I won't have you stay, but I do want you to meet the key people involved. Soon as you're ready, we'll have breakfast here and be on our way."

Following her visit to the site and introduction to the super-intendent, Kate returned to the plane. She had ranch business to attend to.

After lunch aboard, she worked through the afternoon. It was going on six when Jarrett called. They were ordering pizza in and would be working late. After dinner aboard, Kate retired to bed. It was late when Jarrett crawled in beside her. She gave him a hug. "Did you accomplish a lot?"

"I did. I should get it wrapped up tomorrow," he said. "I promise the next stops will be better. Those projects are on schedule and running smoothly."

On the sixth day, they landed in Florida. His boat was in the water. All lean and with garish racing stripes along the side, it was down by the stern and up at the bow. The two control positions looked like jet-fighter cockpits complete with canopies. She shuddered. A surge of energy swept over her. The boat looked menacing even when it was sitting idle at the dock.

Dressed in matching racing suits, Jarrett helped her aboard. The canopies were open. He stopped at the one closest to the dock. "This is normally Warren's position. This is where you'll sit," Jarrett said and pointed at the single seat. "These positions are sealed units. The only way to talk to me will be to use the intercom built into the helmet. If there were a crash, these capsules would pop out. They're watertight and will float upright," he said. "As you can see, I've spared no expense making this the safest race boat on the water." He settled back. "I assure you I'm not out here trying to kill myself."

Strapped in, he brought the huge engines up to speed. Spray flashed by. Out on the ocean, the speedometer read 142 miles per hour. They were going faster on water than she had ever done on land.

An hour later on the dock, she looked down at the boat. "Wow, I didn't expect that," she stated. "I'm hooked."

He grinned. "Then you don't mind if I go racing?"

She nodded.

Back in Beverly Hills, Kate spent the night in Jarrett's house. Rachel had moved out days before, and they had the place to themselves. Breakfast was over. "You've seen what I do for a living, and you've experienced my racing firsthand."

Kate listened.

He continued, "So then there's no reason why we shouldn't get married." He looked at her. "I love you, and you love me. What say we fly over to Vegas today and do it?"

Kate blinked. "Just like that, you want to fly over to Las Vegas and get married?"

"Why not? There's a lull in our schedules. We're together every minute I'm in town," he said. "Lord knows we're compatible, so let's do it. We both want children. We're both a bit old-fashioned—no marriage, no commitment, no kids. So what do you think? If we're going to start a family, we better start pretty soon. I'm over forty and would like to be around while I can still enjoy their school years."

She looked at him. "Marriage would be wonderful, but why drop everything and fly over to Las Vegas today? What's the rush?"

"You know me. I'm the impatient one. When I make up my mind to do something, I do it." Standing smartly, he blinked and grabbed the table for support. His eyes drooped shut. Seconds passed before he slowly appeared to relax.

She reached for him. "You okay?"

"Yeah," he said. "I just got up too fast." Wiping his brow, he took a step back. "That old sports thing again."

"Oh," she replied. "Can't we wait a few days? I'd like to have Erica with me and some of the people I've been working with and my friends from up north, Patty and Dad especially."

Jarrett shook his head. "I've a bunch of commitments that'll take me away," Jarrett said. "When I get back, we can fly everyone up to the ranch for a big reception. So let's get married now privately and do the big blowout reception when I get back. Okay?"

Kate considered what he said and slowly agreed.

Dressed in the white cocktail dress she had not yet worn, they took the helicopter to the 757. Stepping into the plane, Kate was surprised when she saw there were people aboard. About to comment, Jarrett spoke up, "For everything to be legal, we'll need a couple of witnesses, so I'm bringing along my attorney and a gal from our legal department. When Lillian heard about the wedding, she insisted on coming too."

On the ground in Las Vegas, the ceremony was simple and quick. Swept up in the moment, Kate thought of their future together. They would each continue their professional commitments and, at the same time, work on starting a family. He wanted a boy, and she would be satisfied with a healthy child to inherit the ranch.

Returning to the plane, they were on their way to California when Jarrett ushered everyone into the conference room. "There are a few things we should do now that you're Mrs. Sinclair." He looked at her. "That does have a nice ring to it, doesn't it? *Mrs. Sinclair.*"

She nodded.

"Now to the matters at hand." He pointed to his attorney, who started pulling documents from his briefcase. "You're my wife now, and I need to have you registered officially as such. These documents designate you as legal codirector and co-owner of each of my operations. Yes, I know, California is a community property state, but at times, that has become clouded, and things have been known to get bogged down in court. With these, there will be no question you can speak with the same authority as me. This first document lists you as the codirector and joint owner of Sinclair Enterprises." He folded the multipage document open to the last page and pointed where she needed to sign.

"Must we do this now?" Kate asked. "I was hoping we could have a little champagne and celebrate. After all, this is our wedding day."

"Excellent point." Jarrett pressed the intercom button. "Sheryl, bring us champagne. We have some celebrating to do." He turned to Kate. "While we're waiting, let's start working on these papers. There are a lot of them to sign, and we may as well do it now. Come tomorrow, we'll both be too busy."

Kate scanned the document. Normally, she would read a contract before putting her signature at the bottom, but this was her wedding day, and Jarrett was now her husband, so she signed where he indicated.

Her signature was witnessed by Lillian and notarized by the woman from Jarrett's legal department. Sheryl stepped in with the champagne. As everyone sipped, he moved on to the next document that listed her as codirector and co-owner of AJS Foods. Without pausing, he moved on to all his development projects, theaters, movie production companies, and restaurants. There were documents that empowered her to act as a codirector in his medical foundation, the scholarship fund, and numerous other companies the likes of the one that produced the helicopters.

Kate was finishing signing the last document when Warren's voice came over the intercom. "Sir, we're in the pattern and ten minutes out from LAX. Everyone needs to be seated."

Back at his house, Kate glowed when the maid greeted her as Mrs. Sinclair. She was no longer Ms. Clark; she was now Mrs. Kate Sinclair. She mulled that over and tried Mrs. Katherine Sinclair. She nodded. She'd go with that. It was a bit more formal, but not too stuffy.

Walking through the house, she gave his arm an affectionate squeeze. "A one-week honeymoon somewhere would be wonderful. We've both been working hard, and this is the perfect excuse to go to that island you own in the Caribbean. What do you think?"

"I'd love to, except I have to leave tomorrow to demo our new helicopter."

"You do?" she asked. "Where to? The Himalayas? Mount Everest? I'd love to see if their mountains are anything like we have in Montana."

"No. Not this time. I'm going to South America. The Andes. The Columbians are interested in our latest chopper."

"Terrific!" Kate responded. "That sounds like fun. I've never been there either. Maybe we could go to Machu Picchu. I've always wanted to see it."

Somber-faced, he shook his head. "That's not possible. Mind you, I'd love to take you with, but this is going to be a whirlwind trip. They want me to demo our chopper in the backcountry. There are no roads out there or much of anything else. You would be better off staying here, and when I get back, you can come with me to the Chesapeake. I've been asked by a new race sponsor to do a demonstration. That'll take a couple days, and after that, we can fly down to the Bahamas or over to Hawaii and spend a week relaxing in the sun."

She looked at him. "When will that be, the race demonstration back east?"

"Two weeks from now."

She shook her head. "That won't work. I'm having a horse show up at the ranch then. It's my biggest sale event of the year. I have to be there."

"Okay. Then when I get back from the Chesapeake and you get back from your horse show, let's go to Hawaii and have a real honeymoon."

25

Three days later, there was a lull in activities. Kate had Warren's wife, Alice, along with Lillian, Erica, and Miranda, over for lunch. Rachel was in New York on business. After lunch, they moved to the patio for coffee. Miranda turned to Alice. "You say your husband flies with Mr. Sinclair. With him out of town, where's your husband? Home, I presume?"

"No," Alice responded with a troubled expression. "He's gone with him to South America. He's flying the second helicopter. The whole thing has me scared to death. To prove the helicopter's combat capability, they are having to go in after the number one drug lord in the area. If they can take him out, they'll get a big order. I'm frightened. It's a war zone down there, so they're armed to the teeth. Unfortunately, so are the people on the ground. I tried to get Warren to talk him out of—"

"WHAT!" Kate exploded. "They're going into a war zone with live ammunition?"

"Yes," Alice replied.

Kate glared at Lillian. "This is not some simple thing like rescuing a kid off a mountain?" Lillian nodded. Bolting from the table, Kate steamed off toward the pool. Everyone watched as she stomped back and forth. Turning, she came back and waved her wedding ring at Lillian. "Is that the reason behind that quickie marriage and all those documents he had me sign? There's a chance he could be killed, and he wants me to take over if he does?"

Lillian nooded. "Kate you have to understand, he loves you dearly. Otherwise, he wouldn't have made you co-owner of everything."

"GREAT! I could end up a widow, and I'm supposed to take solace in the fact he did this because he loved me. Forget it." She stomped off again. Spinning around, she came back. "He's up to his old tricks. He's manipulating me."

Lillian continued, "I've heard from the helicopter company. While the jungle is dense, they feel there should be no problem proving the value of the equipment without incident."

"Terrific." Kate stomped her foot. "What's that supposed to mean?" she stared at Lillian. "Where does that leave me, huh? Married less than a week, and I could end up a widow." She glared at Lillian. "This whole thing is a setup. He had to have known about the helicopter demonstration days ago."

"Weeks ago," Lillian replied.

Kate snarled. "Let me guess. He's been planning our wedding for about the same amount of time, right?" She glared at Lillian until she mouthed agreement.

***

The next two days were the worst Kate had ever spent. She was on the phone constantly with Lillian and the helicopter company. "What can you tell me?" she asked the manager of the helicopter company.

"Not much. They're still alive. I can assure you of that."

The sixth day came and went, as did the seventh. On the morning of the eighth, Lillian called. "I just heard from the helicopter company. He's fine. The demonstration was a huge success. They're on their way back to the capital to finalize the sale. He should be back here day after tomorrow."

Kate took a deep breath. She could breathe once again.

***

It was late afternoon when Kate went to Burbank to meet Jarrett when he flew in. With time to kill, she stopped by the hangar to look at the helicopters. She'd heard they had been damaged, and she wanted to see how badly. She approached the man at the office. "Hi. I'm Mrs. Sinclair. I'd like to look at the helicopters."

Stepping forward, he blocked her way into the hangar. "You can look at them, but there isn't much to see. They're filthy. We're still cleaning them up."

Sensing a stall, she pushed past him. In the hangar, light shone through the sides of the machines where it should have been solid. She looked at the man. "What are all those bullet holes?" She circled both and made a rough count. "There must be at least a couple dozen in each machine."

The man stepped forward. "Actually, there are thirty-seven in one and twenty-eight in the other. I counted them myself."

Kate leaned in through an open side door of one of the helicopters. "What's that?" she demanded on seeing what appeared to be blood next to the pilot seat. "Did my husband get shot!"

"No, ma'am, that's our fault. One of our technicians cut his hand on a piece of metal."

The hangar door opened, and a beam of light shot across the room. "I'm home," Jarrett announced. Running up, he grabbed her and held her tight. "Do I get a kiss?"

He got that and more. When their embrace ended, she pounded on his chest. "Don't you ever do anything like that again. They were trying to kill you."

He grinned. "They didn't, and I'm back."

"Couldn't you have at least phoned and told me you were okay?"

"I was exhausted. I was in a rush to get the contract signed and get out of that place." He gave her a hug. "Will you be able to go east with me when I make that racing demonstration?"

"No. I have that horse show to do. When you get back, let's go to Hawaii."

Kate's horse show was winding down. It had been a huge success with only two more horses to sell. Her father called from the small office in the corner of the arena. "Jarrett's on the phone."

"I'll be right there." Running to take the call, she checked the time. It was after two, which made it after four in the east.

Jarrett's voice was upbeat. "How's the show going?"

"Great. After the horse I'm presenting now, only one is left. How did the demonstration go?"

"I haven't run it yet," he said with a negative tone. "We should get everything straightened out shortly and run the demo at noon tomorrow. I'll call you when it's over."

It was after three o'clock the next day, and Jarrett still hadn't called. The last horse had sold and was in the buyer's trailer. The man was ready to leave. "Are you still rodeoing?" Kate asked.

"Every chance I get," he said.

Her father called from the back door of the house. "Telephone!"

"In a minute," Kate called back. "Lenny's about to leave."

Her father repeated, "You need to take this call *now*!"

There was something in his voice that gave her a chill. "Later," she said to Lenny and ran to the house. Bursting into the kitchen, her father handed her the phone. "It's Lillian."

"Kate here," she said and waited. There was no immediate response.

Seconds passed, and Lillian spoke. Her voice was barely above a whisper. "There's been an accident."

Kate shuddered. "How bad?"

"Bad. The boats collided. Jarrett was injured," Lillian said. "He has a concussion and a dislocated shoulder and a number of fractures. They're checking now for internal injuries, and we'll know more shortly." She paused. When she continued, her voice was barely above a whisper. "Warren was killed."

Kate collapsed into a chair.

"I've sent a plane up to get you, and it should be there in a couple hours. Alice's sister is taking the children, and she'll be heading east with me in the DC-9. We should be there a few hours after you."

Kate struggled to her feet. She repeated to her father what Lillian had said. She pointed toward the front of the house. "I need to pack."

When Kate arrived at the hospital, the tests had been completed, and Jarrett was back in his room. She gasped when she saw him. His head was swathed in gauze, and one arm and shoulder were tightly wrapped. Aside from his breathing on his own, he lay motionless in the bed. Kate kissed him. "Darling, I'm here." He did not respond. She kissed his limp form again and nothing. *Oh God, why did this have to happen to you?*

A nurse entered. "Mrs. Sinclair, the attending neurologist is in an office down the hall."

Kate kissed Jarrett and followed the nurse.

Seated in the office, the neurologist came quickly to the point. "Mrs. Sinclair, your husband has sustained a concussion. There's been some swelling of the brain, though not enough to warrant surgery at this time. He also incurred a broken shoulder and collarbone, along with multiple bruises. He has some scrapes and superficial injuries. We are checking him for internal injuries but won't know the outcome until later. I will advise you as soon as we know more."

"When will he wake up?" she asked.

The doctor slowly settled back. "I don't know," he said with a shake of his head. "He should be awake now. There is some trauma to the brain, although not that much."

Kate was quick to step in. "What's that supposed to mean? What's the problem? Why isn't he awake?"

"I don't know," the doctor replied. "I've gone through his medical history, and as near as I can determine, this is not the first major head trauma he has sustained. We know he experienced at least two major concussions in the past. The first one twenty-two years ago playing football in college. At the time, the school physician barred him from further contact sports. The next was some six years later when he took up racing sailboats. It appeared he stood up when he shouldn't have and was hit by the boom. That blow was severe. He was unconscious for most of a day."

Closing the file, he rested his arms on the table. "Mrs. Sinclair, you need to understand, concussions are cumulative. Each one does a little more damage. While I believe his chances of regaining consciousness are very good, you need to realize, people who have experienced multiple events to the brain are prone to contract chronic traumatic encephalopathy. CTE, as it is known, is a neurodegenerative disorder of the brain brought upon by multiple concussions, characterized by headaches, dizziness, mood swings, erratic behavior, and memory lapses. Those are changes that will have to be watched for in the future."

Focused, Kate studied the doctor. "Are you saying he'll get this chronic traumatic—CTE whatever?"

The doctor shook his head. "No, I'm not saying CTE happens to everyone who has had concussions. Many who have had multiple events go on to lead normal, healthy lives. With some, though, the CTE symptoms appear slowly and worsen with time. For those prone to CTE, ten or fifteen years will pass with no problem, and then suddenly the jerking of their head around abruptly or standing up too quickly or another innocent bump to the head can set them off. If they're lucky, they might only black out or gray out for a few seconds. If they're not, it could be the beginning of a downward spiral."

"That's not good, correct?" she asked.

The neurologist nodded.

Kate stopped. What came immediately to mind was when she was seated in the plane's stateroom and the aircraft made a sudden jolt. Jarrett's head snapped forward and back. For many seconds, he appeared dizzy and had to sit down. *Could that be what the doctor was talking about?*

"So you're saying if he's had prior occurrences of dizzy spells following a sudden jolt or something like that, his chances aren't good?"

"No, I'm saying nothing of the kind. I am saying I don't know what his chances are. Based on his general health and physical condition, I'd say his chances of a complete recovery are very good. He's extremely physically fit. When will he wake up? I don't have the answer. It could be in a few hours or a few days or even longer. We have no way to tell."

After the doctor left, Kate called Jarrett's crew chief to the office. A burly man with huge hairy arms, his name was Jedidiah Dramaderios, but everyone called him Bear.

"Bear, I need an explanation. I've seen his boat. I've ridden in it. The control positions are nearly indestructible. How did Jarrett get hit on the head? Why was Warren killed?"

The man eased his bulk into a chair. "They weren't in Jarrett's boat. They were in an open cockpit race boat substituted at the last minute. The sponsor wanted his company name painted on Jarrett's boat, and your husband refused." He leaned forward. "The two boats were running straight down the course. Your husband was three or four lengths ahead when he hit a swell. When the boat he was driving came down, it snapped hard over. We don't know if it hit something in the water or what. All we know is that Jarrett slumped forward, and his boat turned hard left in front of the trailing boat. The other driver did not have time to react. He hit them straight on. He hit Warren first, crushing his helmet and breaking his neck. He went on to hit Jarrett more a glancing blow."

He settled back. "If everything had gone as planned, it should have been a simple parallel speed run. Except for that rogue wave, the water wasn't unusually choppy. They were both good boats. You have to understand, though, at the speeds these boats run, accidents do happen," he said. "Your husband was lucky he wasn't hit by the other boat's outdrive or propeller. That would have been fatal." He straightened up. "Both Jarrett and Warren were airlifted here. And that's all I know."

Over the next two days, Kate slept at her husband's side as she maintained a twenty-four-hour vigil. Exhausted, she rubbed her eyes. There had been no change in his condition. A nursing assistant stepped in.

"Mrs. Sinclair, there's a call for you in the office down the hall."

It was her father. "Kate, honey, how's Jarrett?"

"No change."

Seth continued, "You've received two new large orders for dairy cows. We need to know where you want to put the cows once they're inseminated. We can fence off an area. We just need to know where."

Kate tried to think. If she were home, she'd jump into her pickup and stake out a site in a matter of minutes. With her not being there she'd have to make the choice from memory and right then she wasn't up to that. "Sorry Pop I'll have to get back to you."

Her father continued. He asked her specific questions about what she wanted to do with each horse she had in training. Without being there, she'd have to think that over as well. "I'll have to call you back."

With the call over, she knew what she had to do. She met with the neurologist. "Does my husband need to be in this hospital or any hospital right now?"

"No. Medically, he's stable. Aside from the fact he's still unconscious, we can't detect any physical damage to the brain. He can be moved to a long-term care facility."

"Excellent. I'm taking him home. I'm going to fly him to Montana and take care of him at my house."

The doctor shook his head. "You can transport him to Montana. That shouldn't be a problem. It's your caring for him that concerns me. I'm not questioning your ability. It's that he's going to require a lot of round-the-clock physical care. I strongly advise you put him in a long-term care facility convenient to your home."

"I live on a ranch. There's nothing convenient to my home. Anyway, I won't be doing the work. I'll hire nurses to cover 24-7. I have the space."

In less than a day, Gene had the dining-room furniture out and hospital equipment moved in. Nurses had been hired, and everything was ready for Jarrett's arrival. Two days after she'd spoken with the neurologist, Jarrett was in the room next to her kitchen. The trip had been arduous, but having him home was a relief. She was running ranch operations and was near him at the same time.

When the telephone rang, her father answered it and called from the kitchen. "It's Lillian, and it sounds urgent."

Lillian was the first to speak, "I've been doing as much as I can to run his businesses, but I can only do so much. I don't have the authority to make the major decisions. Also, the projects need to be inspected. As director of all his operations, you have the authority to do that. The 757 is up there. Can you break away and help us out down here?"

Kate looked in the direction of where Jarrett lay. She knew it would be wrong to let his businesses languish because he was temporarily incapacitated. It would double her workload, but what choice did she have? "Set a schedule," Kate said.

26

ate's first stop was Jarrett's office in Los Angeles. Settled in at his desk, she watched as Lillian opened the first of many files. "There's a problem with the framing of the stage in the new theater. It needs to open in less than two weeks, and the designer and theater manager are at loggerheads. The designer wants it one way, and the manager wants it another."

"I'll look into that first thing tomorrow."

Lillian set that file aside and pulled a check from the medical foundation file. "This needs to be signed."

Kate picked up a pen and stopped. Raising an eyebrow, she tapped on the check. "Five million dollars? Are they in need of some new equipment?"

"No." Lillian shook her head. "That's their bimonthly allotment. You know, to pay salaries, lights, water, and everything else."

Kate studied the check. What came to mind was the caterer with all the food and the take-home boxes. "Before I sign another of these, I want to see a report on their operating budget. I also want the personnel records of all the key managers, the administrative staff, and the members of the board of directors."

"I'll have that for your review on our trip east," Lillian said and moved on to Jarrett's major projects scattered around the country. All needed some measure of supervision.

Hours later, Kate finished with the last of Lillian's files. "I can see why Jarrett travels so much. He's a hands-on manager and oversees everything his company does."

It was early the next morning when Kate and Lillian arrived at the theater. Kate listened as the animated interior designer vigorously stated his position. "I insist the scrollwork I've designed flank each side of the stage. It ties all elements of my design together. It's the focal point of my whole concept."

The theater manager was equally vocal. "Those panels cut off too much view from the side and narrow the stage opening. This place is small enough without adding those needless decorations."

The designer exploded. "Needless decorations," he screamed.

Kate held up her hand for both men to stop. "One moment," she said. Without further comment, she walked over and checked the view from the seats off to the side. Still not speaking, she went to the next level up. Taking a seat in one of the boxes, she looked toward the stage. "Take that scrollwork down. I agree it blocks too much of the view from the side. The people sitting along the sides came to see a play, the whole play. Reinstall it above the curtain."

"What?" The designer snorted. "So they miss a few feet of the show, no big deal. What do they expect from a twenty-buck ticket? Carnegie Hall?"

Kate spun around. "To a lot of the people who come here, that twenty-buck ticket is a big deal. I say the scrollwork goes on the proscenium arch or out in the garbage. Which do you want? I don't have all day."

Momentarily speechless, the designer cowered back. "I never looked at it that way. More people would get a better view of my work if I put it on the arch above the curtain."

"Fine," Kate said. She mouthed to Lillian, "Problem solved."

Kate buckled in as the 757 taxied to the runway. Grabbing the phone, she called home. "Dolores, how's Jarrett? Any news?"

"Sorry. Nothing new. Hazel has assured us Mr. Sinclair is on the mend and should be okay."

"Oh God, I hope she's right."

The jetliner lifted off and headed east. Kate closed her eyes and pictured Jarrett lying in bed. *I should be there beside him, but no, I'm off tending to his business projects. What a way to run a marriage.* There was a bong and the seat-belt light went out.

Moving to the conference table, Lillian followed. She laid Jarrett's notes out for their first stop. "This job is ahead of schedule and on budget. The central issue will be the planning for the upcoming dedication ceremony."

"That's straightforward enough," Kate said. She set that aside and picked up the medical foundation file. Focusing on the financial section, she zeroed in on the catering report. "These numbers are ridiculous. The lunches cost over eight hundred dollars per person. The liquor and wine alone is over six hundred per each. Who are these people on the board? Are they friends of Jarrett's?"

Lillian shook her head. "No. They're people Norman chose."

"Really?" Kate looked at Lillian in a questioning way. "Does Jarrett go to these bimonthly meetings?"

Again, Lillian shook her head. "No. He's too busy. Dr. Norman reports to him every month or so."

Kate looked down at the file. She could only imagine what Norman's reports were like after listening to him expound on what a great job he was doing. "What's your take on Norman?"

"He's a conceited, pompous ass," Lillian said. "Granted, he might be a brilliant researcher and one of the foremost authorities on Alzheimer's, but he has an ego bigger than a barn door. Ever since Jarrett stopped going to the board meetings, all the costs, including the catering, have skyrocketed. He keeps telling Jarrett what marvelous progress he's making, and Jarrett keeps signing the checks."

"And Jarrett believes him?" Kate asked, to which Lillian agreed.

One of the flight attendants stepped around the corner of the Plexiglas partition. "Mrs. Sinclair, we're approaching Phoenix and will be landing shortly."

On the ground, Kate stepped to the door of the plane dressed in one of the business outfits Jarrett had helped pick out. People at the private jet terminal crowded forward. All appeared anxious to see who the woman was who arrived in the huge private jet. Warmed by the attention, Kate made her way down the stairs.

Leon Martin, project superintendent, was at the base to greet her. A slightly built man with a stern expression, he had a reputation of being aggressive. Kate eyed him quickly. *Can't be any worse than some of my rancher competition.* She smiled. "I've read the reports, and I am pleased to see you're finishing a month ahead of schedule and under budget."

"I like to keep on top of my projects," he was quick to respond.

"So I've heard," Kate replied.

It was late when Kate completed her inspection and review of the upcoming dedication. Back aboard, she looked across at Lillian. "Get a lot accomplished?" she asked.

"Got caught up on all the correspondence," she said. "And you? Did the inspection go well?"

"It did. The dedication is in a couple weeks, and I'll need to be here," Kate said as she settled in. The big jet rolled and she was off to St. Louis.

The next day, Kate met the project manager in charge of the renovation of an office tower complex Jarrett had purchased in St. Louis. Following that meeting, it was off to upstate Pennsylvania. She and Lillian enjoyed dinner in flight. High over Middle America, Kate set her dinner dishes aside. "I'm finished," she said to Sheryl. With the table cleared, Kate laid out the medical foundation file. "I've gone through the dossiers of the members of the board of directors. Where did Norman come up with these people? I mean a golf pro, a tennis instructor, a salesman of exotic cars, a charter boat skipper, a flying instructor, a yoga instructor, a ski school manager." She tapped on the stack of files. "And the list goes on and on." She looked at Lillian. "These are hardly people I'd expect to see on the board of a medical research foundation. What do they do other than eat a lot of expensive food and cart away free booze twice a month? Do they actually make any decisions concerning the foundation?"

Lillian shook her head. "The actual direction of the foundation is dictated by Jarrett. Once the foundation began to gain recognition and Jarrett moved his focus to other projects, Norman moved in his cronies. These board members aren't really needed. You can remove who you want and appoint who you want. You're the boss."

Kate smiled. "How about that?"

27

On the ground in Pennsylvania, snow had fallen overnight, and the sight of it pushed off to the side caused Kate to shiver. The people on the ramp were bundled up. Flaps on their wool caps were pulled over their ears. She looked at Lillian. "Do you want to come with?" The woman shook her head.

"I guess it's up to me," Kate said. Pulling her coat tight, she stepped to the door. At the base of the stairs, she was met by Jarrett's northeast contact, Sheldon Burgart, a heavy-set gentleman with gray hair.

"Welcome, Mrs. Sinclair." He motioned toward his car. "Let's get in out of the cold. How's your husband doing?"

"Nothing has changed." Sliding in, she waited until he was settled. "How's Gordon doing? Has he made any progress turning the project around?"

Sheldon shook his head. "No. The project is four more days behind schedule and two more percentage points over budget."

Approaching the project, Sheldon slowed as they entered the site. Kate pointed at the cranes, loaders, and dozers parked off to the side. "Stop there. I want to check something." Jumping out, she approached the man standing next to one of the idle machines. "Are you one of the operators?"

"No, ma'am." He pointed at a work trailer. "The operators are in there."

"Thank you." Bolting up the stairs, she entered the double-wide without knocking. The room was filled with men in work clothes. Some were playing cards. Others were visiting or busy with coffee and a doughnut. All looked up when she entered.

"Good morning, gentlemen. I'm Mrs. Sinclair."

"We know who you are," said the man closest to the door. "We've all seen you on TV and in the news."

She pointed toward the machines outside. "Why are you fellows in here and not out there working?"

A man off to the side spoke up, "Because he hasn't told us what to do yet."

A cold blast hit her from behind as Sheldon entered. "Who is the he you're referring to?"

The man continued, "Gordon Miller. The boss man. We don't move until he tells us to."

She looked at the man. "Is that some union thing?"

"It's no union thing. It's a Gordon thing. No one moves on this project without his direction."

She looked at the men. "Is that right? Superintendent Miller runs every detail on this job?"

The men nodded. She looked at Sheldon and pointed at the door. "That has to stop. Let's get to the meeting."

On entering the portable office, Gordon Miller greeted her and directed her toward a woman seated nearby. "Can I have my secretary get you coffee? We also have some rolls. They're very tasty. The Pennsylvania Dutch around here really know how to bake."

"Thank you, no," Kate replied. She pointed toward his office. "Why's the job four more days behind schedule and two more percentage points over budget?"

He stopped at his desk. "Well, now, that's a very complicated question, and there are no simple answers. I might add this is a very complex construction project, and I don't have the time to explain the basics of construction to you. I suggest we wait until your husband can be here."

212

"My husband can't be here, and I want some answers now. Why's the job four more days behind schedule and two more percentage points over budget?"

He typed a command into his computer and a flowchart came up on the wall monitor. "Prior to your husband's last visit, a shipment of wrong materials was delivered that I didn't catch. When they arrived, I was too busy to check the packing list against the requisition before telling the driver where to drop the load. Unfortunately, by the time the materials were found and the mistake discovered, we were that much further behind." He pointed out the window. "And the weather hasn't been any help. Working in this snow slows us down."

"Is snow unusual around here this time of the year?"

"No." Slouching back, his shoulders sagged. "Every time you people demand one of these meetings, it puts me that much further behind. It takes me a day to prepare. Then there's the meeting. The last one lasted a day and a half. I'll admit, I was a nervous wreck afterward. Following that it took me over a day to get everything back together and find out where I was before being interrupted. And there are your four days."

Kate's expression didn't change.

"Now can I show you around the project as I make the work assignments?"

Kate stepped aside. "No. That won't be necessary. Go out and get the crews working."

Minutes later, Kate settled into the car without comment. Sheldon glanced her way as they drove from the site. "What do you think? Do you think he can pull it out?"

"No," she said. "He's in over his head. I'm going to replace him. I'll have another person up here in a couple of days. I have to get this project turned around."

Airborne, Kate flew on to her next appointment. The meeting in Pennsylvania had taken less time than planned, which gave her time to catch up on ranch activity. "How's he doing?" Kate asked when she got her father on the phone.

"Unchanged," was his brief reply.

The next morning, she was greeted with temperatures more comfortable than Pennsylvania. It was warm along the Carolina coast. Some months before, the area had been devastated by a hurricane and needed tourism to get back on its feet.

The men and women from the governor's office and the office of economic development stood when she entered the room. With the introductions completed, the director of economic development began, "What your husband plans to do here is exactly the economic boost this community needs. The resort he is proposing will kick-start our way to recovery." He expounded on all they would do to expedite the project. He assured her the governor would personally oversee the permitting process and make sure everything went smoothly. "All we need now is your signature on the contracts."

Kate raised a cautious eyebrow. *Whoa there*, she said to herself. *Let's slow down a bit.* She looked at the anxious faces and sensed they were trying to push for a quick decision. *You need us more than we need you. Let's see how far I can get you to bend.* "To go forward with this project, we'll need to see some major tax concessions." When the director appeared about to speak, she held up her hand. "I know you've offered a two-year break on property taxes. Unfortunately, that's not enough. As I see it, we'll need a 100 percent ten-year relaxation of all taxes."

"What?" The director's face blanched. "Your husband and I had discussed a property tax break on the order of two years and nothing more. You're new to this project, and you don't understand the economics. We can't afford to do what you ask." Pushing back from the table, he started to get up. "We'll just have to wait until we can talk to your husband."

Kate motioned for him to sit. "My husband can't be here. As co-owner of Sinclair Enterprises, I can and will be making the final decision." She opened her folder. "As I see it, the anticipated 150,000 plus person per month increase in tourism should net the state well over six million per month in new sales tax revenue alone. That, combined with the 800 new jobs we're planning and all the income taxes those people will pay, the state can well afford to give me the tax break I require."

The director shook his head. "Those population numbers are way out of line. Your calculations are ridiculous. You obviously don't understand what we're doing here."

Kate made with a confident smile. *Bullshit. I've done my homework. Let's see if you have done yours.* Still smiling, she pointed at the stack of papers she'd brought along. "If the projected tourism numbers I used are wrong, which I copied from these, your own press releases, I better call the newspapers and TV stations and tell them you exaggerated the project's potential. I'm sure they'll be interested to know their governor is leading them on. That should go over big during the coming election." Turning, she made a move toward the telephone next to her.

The director lurched forward, almost onto the table. "Stop!" he called out. "No need to make any hasty calls." He motioned for her to move away from the phone. "There's no way we can sell ten years to the governor and the voters. That much I can assure you." He looked at the people with him. "We might be able to sell, what, eight years." He zeroed in on each person and moved on only after he received a nod of acceptance. "And that's the best we can do."

Kate looked at the director. "If you can sell eight years, we might have a deal. Get back to me as soon as you know for sure."

Kate glowed on her way back to the plane. There was a good chance she had just saved the company over fifty million dollars. *Not a bad morning's work if I say so myself.*

Back on the plane, there was little time to celebrate as she was off to one meeting after another. It was late Friday when she landed in Los Angeles long enough to drop Lillian off and fly to Montana to be with her husband.

Exhausted, she dropped into the chair beside his bed. His breathing was slow and rhythmical. She looked over at the doctor who had come out to meet with her. "I'm sorry I can't tell you when I think he will wake up, but based on his vital signs, he is improving," the doctor said. "We just have to be patient. Recovery from head trauma takes time."

Late Sunday, Kate stopped by Jarrett. "I'm off again," she said. "There's the dedication in Phoenix early tomorrow, and then I'll be going to Los Angeles for the opening of the new theater. After that, Lillian has me on the go. All I know is I'll be gone all week."

Following the dedication and ceremonial ribbon cutting in Phoenix, Kate met with Leon Martin. "Wrap this up as soon as you can. I have another project for you. It is behind schedule and over budget."

Kate returned to the plane for the trip to Los Angeles and the theater dedication. Seated at the conference table, she set the medical foundation file aside and reached for the phone. "Lillian, I am calling from the plane. I've decided I'm going to replace Norman with Brandon Herbert if he'll take the job. Call Dr. Herbert and set up a meeting tomorrow morning at the house."

Kate put the file away. With nothing else pending, she stepped into the galley. There was no one there, so she knocked on the door and stepped into the crew lounge. Janine looked up. "Can I help you?"

"I'd like a glass of wine. It's been a long day." She pointed at the book that was on the seat beside Janine. "Is that any good?"

"Yes, ma'am. It's by a new author. I just finished it, and you're welcome to borrow it. Take a seat, and I'll bring the wine."

It was midmorning when Dr. Herbert arrived at the house. Settling in at the patio, she came right to the point. "I think Dr. Norman needs to be replaced, and I'd like you to take over as director."

Whistling softly, Dr. Herbert leaned back in the chair. "After our lunch the other day, we sensed you were a no-nonsense kind of person. We figured when Jarrett was injured and you took over, some changes might be in store." He straightened up. "I'm flattered you've chosen me. If it's okay, I'd like to think this over a day or two. Regardless of whom you choose, Condon is going to fight. He feels the foundation is his."

"Thank you. I'll keep that in mind."

Following breakfast the next morning, Kate went to the office she had set up in Jarrett's house. The theater opening and dedication had been a big success. The theater patrons loved the decor. The telephone rang. It was Dr. Herbert. "Good morning, Mrs. Sinclair. I've decided. I'll take the job."

"Excellent." Setting the phone down, she stared off toward the city. *The easy part is over. Now the hard part. I have to confront Condon Norman.*

"Good afternoon, Condon. It's good of you to meet with me on such short notice," she said as she settled into a chair in front of his desk. "I've given considerable thought to the foundation, to its direction, its budget, and its future. I've decided I have to make a change. I have to ask you to step aside."

Norman did not move. He did not blink. His expression appeared frozen. Suddenly his eyes grew large. His cheeks flushed red. "You want me to do what! No way! This is my institution, and no cowgirl from Montana is going to order me around. I run this place. You think that wedding ring gives you a right to tell me what to do? Forget it. When I finish with you, you'll be ruined. I'll squash you like a bug." He pointed at the door. "Get out of here."

Kate had had it with him. "Now, you listen to me. I'm the legal co-owner and director of all my husband's operations. If you challenge me, I'll saddle you with enough legal expenses to keep you broke the rest of your life." She pointed at the door. "As of now, you're out. I've had it with your expensive board meeting lunches and your single-minded research. You're welcome to stay on as head of Alzheimer's studies. As overall director, you're out. Dr. Herbert will be taking over. I've brought along the head-office facilities people, and they're ready to move you out and him in. So do you step aside peacefully, or do I have security put you out on the street?"

Norman's jaw muscles worked and made hard ridges under his scarlet cheeks. Many seconds passed before he slowly stepped back. "Okay."

"Fine," she replied and left.

Outside, she glanced back at the building. While he agreed, she suspected she hadn't heard the last from Condon Norman. He wasn't the type to give up easily.

With no time to ponder Norman's next move, she was off to another meeting and project review. After a while, she lost track of where she was or even the day. Working straight through the weekend, Kate returned to California, exhausted. In Los Angeles, she went directly to the house. A maid greeted her. "Good afternoon, Mrs. Sinclair. It's nice to see you home."

"It's great to be back," Kate struggled to say as she made her way to the kitchen. Taking a seat at the table, she addressed the woman, "I'm beat. I don't want any phone calls or visitors. Understood?" Kate focused. "Turn everyone away."

"Yes, ma'am," the woman said.

Unable to reach Kate by phone, Rachel came in search of her friend. Bypassing the staff, she let herself in. Kate was in the kitchen, slumped over at the table. There were dark circles under her eyes, and her complexion was pale. The maid stepped forward. She whispered, "Madame has left orders she doesn't want to be disturbed."

Kate heard and looked up. Seeing Rachel, she nodded. "She's okay. Let her stay."

The telephone rang. The maid answered and looked to Kate. "It's Mrs. Lillenthaller. She wants to talk to you."

"Tell her I'll call later."

Rachel reached for the phone. "I know Lillian. I'll talk to her."

Lillian was quick to point out, "Kate's late for a meeting at the helicopter company."

"Sorry, Lillian, she's exhausted," Rachel replied. "She can't make the meeting. Get the 757 ready. I'm taking her home."

It was late when they got to the ranch. Kate insisted on going to Jarrett. Taking a seat next to his bed, she promptly fell asleep.

The next morning, the sun was beginning to break over the horizon. Snowflakes flew by the window of the bedroom Rachel had used. The wind howled. Rachel descended the stairs in the great mansion and stopped at the bottom. The nurse was standing outside the room where Jarrett lay. She held up a finger, signaling for quiet. Rachel tiptoed forward and gasped. Kate was in the chair beside Jarrett's bed. She was slumped over with her head on the mattress. Jarrett's eyes were closed. His hand was on Kate's head. He was stroking her gently.

Within hours, the house was alive with activity. Hazel was there, and so was Seth. Patty was busy in the kitchen making lunch. Wylie had come over to help with chores. Doc Perry was there and smiled when he returned to the kitchen. "He's doing better than expected. I had him sitting up. I even swung him around and had him dangle his legs off the edge of the bed. He's stiff, as can be expected. He's going to need a lot of PT, but he should recover."

The next day, Wylie stopped by and helped Jarrett get from his bed to a chair in the kitchen. Kate stepped around and held on to her man.

Jarrett looked up. "Where's Lillian have you off to next? Is there anything I need to take care of?"

"Not now. I've got everything handled." Kate leaned down and kissed him on the cheek. "Our first order of business is to get you back to LA. You'll be needing physical therapy." Jarrett shook his head. She looked at him. "Are you saying no to the physical therapy or to LA?"

Jarrett was slow to respond. When he did, his facial movements were forced. "I'm saying no to LA, at least for right now." He took a breath and slowly continued, "As I see it, I have to master getting out of bed by myself and making it around the main floor on my own. After that, I want to work on making it upstairs." He looked up at her. "Following that, I'll be ready to return to California. When I get back to the office, I'll have to hit the ground running." Squeezing Kate's hand, he grinned. "Hey, it's not every day I get to explore a gorgeous antebellum mansion on my own."

Kate looked down. The usual glow in his expression wasn't there, nor was the spark in his movements. *Must be because he just woke up. I'll give him a few days to get back on his feet.* Patting his shoulder, she chuckled. "Try not to get lost."

28

Jarrett continued his rehab at the ranch. Kate made stops in Florida, South Carolina, and Georgia and was finishing her meeting in Western Pennsylvania. "Leon." She smiled. "Moving you here from Arizona was what this project needed. You should have this turned around by Christmas."

"I plan to," Leon replied.

Airborne, she settled in. She picked up the book Janine had given her. It had been weeks since she had been able to read a book without interruption, and she wanted to finish.

It was dark outside when Sheryl stepped out from the galley. "Mrs. Sinclair, we're approaching LAX and should be landing shortly." She looked down at what Kate had set aside. "I read that. Isn't that a great story? It'd make a good movie."

"I agree," Kate replied. Reaching for the phone, she called Lillian. She told her of the book she had been reading and how she felt it would make a good motion picture. "I'd like to pick up the move rights. It's by a local author. See if he's in town and can meet me tomorrow."

Kate delayed her trip north a day and welcomed the author at Jarrett's office downtown. "I asked you here because I'm interested in buying the movie rights to your book. Are they still available?"

"They are."

"Excellent. Can I deal with you directly, or do you have an agent?"

"I had an agent, but she retired."

"Okay," she said and slid a contract across to the man. "Prior to your coming, I had our legal department draw up a standard agreement. It's nothing exotic and has no hidden clauses. I've put in a dollar amount, and you can tell me what you think."

He studied the document and slowly reached into his coat for a pen.

"Whoa, there." Kate smiled. "You're welcome to take it and have it reviewed by an attorney."

He shook his head. "I'm satisfied," he replied.

After the meeting, Kate helicoptered to the airport and the 757. Still in a skirt and high heels, she shivered when they landed. Montana was covered with a blanket of white. With her coat pulled tight, she made her way from the plane. On the tarmac, she looked toward the break in the chain-link fence. "It can't be," she called out when she saw Jarrett. Racing to him, she gave him a hug. "You're driving now. You must be ready to go back to work."

"Not so fast," he said and pointed at his bandaged ankle. "I slid on the ice and twisted it badly. Gene drove me in. Dolores is in town, and he's going to ride back with her."

Kate looked down. "Is anything broken?"

"Nah," he said. "Doc Perry x-rayed it. He said it'll take time for the swelling to go down, but it should be okay."

Settled in behind the wheel, Kate looked at Jarrett. "I'm sorry I'm late. I bought the movie rights to a book. I had Lillian hunt down the author. I met with him this morning." Exhaling slowly, she continued, "What I need to know is…what do I do now?"

"Describe the story."

She did and concluded, "It's about two sisters who are forced to examine their relationship with each other and their father, who's terminally ill. It's a powerful book. I figured the two sisters could be played by Erica and Miranda and the father by Phillip Claymore."

Jarrett nodded. "It sounds like you've really looked into this."

"I have."

"In that case, take it to Stanley and see what he has to say," he said. "Tell him you'd like him to make the movie and go from there."

On Monday, Kate's first stop was Stanley's office. "How's AJ doing?" he asked.

"Better," she replied. "He wants to rehab a few more days up north before he heads south." She pulled the book from her bag and stood it on his desk. "I bought the film rights to this. I think it'll make a powerful movie. I discussed it with Jarrett, and he told me to bring it to you. I'd like to hear what you think. If you agree it's good, I'd like to have you make the movie."

He thumbed it quickly and set it aside. "I'll get to it tonight."

The next morning, Kate was still at the house when the telephone rang. It was Stanley.

"I've read the book. Can you meet me in my office this morning?"

Seated before him, she watched as Stanley tapped on the book. "Do you have any actors in mind for the parts?"

"Yes. I'd like to see Erica Heath and Miranda Wells play the two sisters and Phillip Claymore play the father."

"That has-been." He chortled. Pausing, his expression eased. "You might be right. Phillip just might be the ideal choice to play the father. He can pull in the older generation who remember him from days past." Stanley tapped on the book. "You bought a hell of a book. I read it last night. I couldn't put it down. I'm only sorry you found it first. How soon do you want us to begin?"

"As soon as possible."

223

Leaning back, he focused on her. "Now, that's the tough part. It'll be a number of months before we can get to your book." He told her how he and Jarrett had the movie they were making right then to finish and then another ready to go into production. "I won't be able to start yours for at least a year and a half, or possibly longer. Is that okay?"

Kate paused. That was not what she had wanted to hear. "I guess so," she reluctantly replied.

<hr>

Four days before Christmas, Kate finished back east and swung by Los Angeles to pick up the presents she'd purchased. Lillian was widowed and had no children, so she invited her to celebrate Christmas with her up north. She would also have picked up Erica and Rachel, but they had gone north in the DC-9.

Back in Montana, she stomped off the snow on her way through the vestibule. Her father was seated at the kitchen table and was quick to greet her. "What's with the fancy clothes?"

She looked down. "I didn't have a chance to change," she said as she pulled off her coat and tossed it on a nearby chair. She looked at Lillian. "That handsome brute who chose not to greet his only daughter with a merry Christmas or welcome home is my father."

"Sorry. When I saw you all dressed up, you took my breath away. Merry Christmas," he said and reached to help Lillian with her coat. When their eyes met, they slowly smiled.

Kate picked up on the warmth in her father's expression. Not since before her mother's illness had she seen such joy in her father's face. She nodded. Bringing Lillian along had been a good idea.

Jarrett grabbed Kate and gave her a kiss. Behind him, Isabel Howard stepped into the room and busied herself on a cutting board next to the sink. On seeing her, Kate whispered, "What's she doing here?"

Isabel's voice boomed from across the way. "I heard that, young lady." She grinned. "I'm cooking."

"Yes, I can see you're cooking," Kate said.

Jarrett held Kate out and gave her shake. "Tell me, what do you have in your attic?"

"Ah," Kate hesitated. "I don't know. It's been months or even a year or more since I've been up there." She shrugged. "A bunch of old junk, I guess."

Jarrett shook her again. "A bunch of old junk! Boy, do you have that wrong. The place is filled with your grandfather's paintings. His studio was up there." He stepped back and held up his hand. "I apologize. I went up there the other day exploring. I started looking through the rooms and discovered stacks and stacks of paintings. When I saw them, I phoned Isabel and told her she had to drop everything and get up here. She came up with Erica and Rachel."

Isabel put down the knife and wiped her hands on her apron. "Young lady, your grandfather, without question, has produced some of the finest and most spectacular Western paintings I have ever seen. Not only was he a fantastic artist, he was also one of the most prolific. Erica and Rachel have been helping me catalog what you have up there. So far, we've found enough paintings to do at least three major showings. You have an absolute fortune up there."

The remaining days before Christmas flew by. Erica and Bill were inseparable. Seated in her office, Kate looked up when Jarrett entered the room. "I need some fresh air," she said. "I need to check on the cattle brought down from the upper range. Do you want to come along?"

"Sounds good to me," Jarrett said.

Bundling up, he followed her to the equipment shed. Kate pointed at two ATVs. "Let's take these." She cranked up the engine and led the way out into the open. Jarrett followed. Not to be out-done, he leaned back and ripped the throttle wide open. The engine roared. His machine reared back, tossing him to the frozen ground. He bounced hard, hitting his head.

Whipping around, Kate skidded back. "Are you okay?"

Getting up, Jarrett brushed the ice crystals from his hair. "Yeah, I'm fine," he mumbled and got back on the machine. "You go on. I've got the hang of this now. I'll race you." Leaning into the machine, he gunned the throttle and shot ahead.

"Watch out for that—rut," she called to him, but it was too late.

Hitting the rut, Jarrett's machine bounced high and landed with a thud. Momentarily airborne, Jarrett came down hard. His ankle snapped back. Slumped over, he writhed in pain.

Kate motored up. "Hurt yourself?"

"Damn it, yes," he exclaimed. "I twisted my ankle again." He pushed himself upright and trembled as he looked toward the lower range. "I'm cold, and I need to get off this foot."

Back in the kitchen, he limped as he made his way across the room. He pulled down the ibuprofen bottle and shook out a couple of tablets. "That cold air gave me a beast of a headache."

Recalling the neurologist's warnings about blows to the head, she asked, "You banged your head on the ground. Are you okay?"

"Yes, I'm okay," he shot back. His nostrils flared angrily. "It's the cold air," he growled.

Kate looked at him. This was definitely not his normal behavior. He was sharp and crisp. "Are you sure we shouldn't get you to the doctor to get that bump checked out?"

"No," he fired back. "It's the cold air, I told you. There's nothing wrong with my head."

29

The day after Christmas, Lillian, Erica, Rachel, and Isabel flew back to Los Angeles. Alone with Jarrett, Kate glowed. Two of her three goals had been attained. She was married to the man she loved, and he was with her on the ranch. The only thing missing were children, and they were working on that. On the morning of January 2, Kate and Jarrett went to the airport. Jarrett was off the ibuprofen and wanted to get back to work. His ankle had healed, and he no longer needed a cane.

Gene was driving. "So you two are heading back to the big city?" he said.

"That we are," Kate replied. *And not a day too soon. After a week of looking at the walls and the snow-covered hills, I'm ready to get on the plane and fly anywhere, even to the North Pole if we had business there.* Kate turned to Jarrett as they approached the plane. "I suppose you're going to do your usual walk around preflight check?"

He shook his head. "No, not today," he said. "Watching four bowl games yesterday has given me a hell of a headache. I'm going to lie down. Call me when we're ready to land."

"Ah yes, I will," she said and frowned questioningly. That was so unlike him. He always wanted to personally check over the plane before they took off. She paused. *Maybe he's not totally well. Could we be leaving the ranch too soon?*

Home in Beverly Hills and on their way in from the garage, Kate gave his arm a squeeze. "God, I'm glad we're home." She snickered. "I'll race you to the bedroom. The first one there gets to be on top."

"Not tonight," he muttered. "I've a splitting headache."

The next morning, Kate was the first down in the kitchen. She prepared the coffee and settled back against the counter with a mug. When he entered, she greeted him with a kiss. "How's my darling this morning? Are you recovered from all that football?"

Jarrett did not respond.

She pointed toward the counter. "I've made coffee, and it's hot and fresh."

Jarrett snapped around and looked to the end of the counter where his coffeemaker normally sat. Wincing, his eyelids drooped shut. Grabbing the counter, he held on. Seconds passed, and he slowly took a breath. Straightening up, his eyes opened. Trembling, he pointed at the empty space at the far end of the long granite slab. "Where's the coffeemaker?" he demanded. Before Kate could reply, he growled, "Where's my coffeemaker?"

Kate blinked. This was so unlike him. It had caught her off guard. Frowning, she pointed at an area close to one of the sinks. "I moved it closer to the water. I can move it back if you'd like."

"Yes, I'd like." He snorted. "Who told you, you could move it in the first place? This is my house and my kitchen, and the coffeemaker belongs where I put it."

She winced. *Whatever you say*. Picking up the appliance, she moved it back. "There. It's back where it belongs."

"Fine!" Jarrett snapped. Stepping to the refrigerator, he jerked open the door.

Kate watched as he stared inside. *What are you doing? You drink your coffee black*. A minute passed, and he slowly relaxed. Empty-handed, he closed the door and walked back to where the coffeemaker had been when he entered the room. Not finding it next to the sink, he turned and found it a dozen or more feet away at the end of the counter. "Huh, there it is," he grumbled. "How did it get way over there?"

"Ah." Kate shrugged. "I guess it just did." She studied him. *What's going on? You've never acted like this before.*

Jarrett poured himself a cup and smiled. "What's with the glum expression?" He kissed her. "It's too nice to sit in here. Let's go out by the pool. It's going to be a marvelous day." He chortled. "I do miss the snow, though, don't you?"

Kate stared. His bouncing from subject to subject caused her to pause. *Could this be early signs of that CTE downward-spiral thing the neurologist warned me about? Am I losing my husband? Do I need to get him to a doctor?*

Dressed for work, they entered the garage. With fifteen vehicles to choose from, Kate dashed ahead and reached for the driver's door of a Mercedes sedan. "Shall we take this one?" she asked as she prepared to get in and drive.

"No," Jarrett replied and stepped up to the driver side of a black Chrysler 300. "I feel more like this one. Something that really snorts."

Kate hurried to where he stood. "Here, let me drive."

"*No*," he barked and pushed her away. "I know how to drive."

"Yes, I know you do," she replied. "But shouldn't we wait until after you see a doctor?"

He glared. "See a doctor? See a doctor for what?" He snorted. "I'm not sick." Climbing in, he pointed at the other side. "If you're coming with, get in."

She did. No sooner in than he slammed the gas to the floor. Peeling out, she grabbed on as he weaved their way through traffic. Minutes later, he screeched to a stop in the office garage. Jarrett beamed as he led the way to the elevator.

Waving at Lillian, he entered his office. Settled in, he beamed as he ran his hands over the polished wood surface of his desk. "Damn!" Jarrett exclaimed. "It feels great to be back."

Lillian's voice burst from the intercom, "Kate, O'Neil from Carolina is on line one."

Jarrett reached for the phone. "I'll take the call. Which line did you say he's on?"

"Sorry, Jarrett," Lillian explained. "I told him you were here. He is glad to hear you're back, but he wants to talk to Kate."

"He does, does he?" Jarrett retorted. He glared at Kate and pointed at the telephone. "Take the damn call." He snorted. "I'm going to the studio."

Before she could respond, he was out the door. *What's wrong now?* Kate asked as she started after him. After a couple of steps, she stopped when Lillian's voice came over the intercom, "Kate. O'Neil is waiting on line one."

Kate looked back at the desk and reached for the telephone. *Business comes first.* "Mrs. Sinclair here."

"Mrs. Sinclair, we met with the governor and key legislative members, and everyone's in agreement. We need your project, and if we have to give you the eight years of tax relief you require, we'll have to do it. We're going with you."

Yes, Kate mouthed and thumped the desk. Ecstatic, she knew Jarrett would be pleased. She'd only told him she was waiting on the people from Carolina to make a decision and hadn't told him she demanded four times more in tax relief than he had negotiated. Thanking the man, she dashed to see Lillian. "Did he say anything on his way out?"

"Jarrett?" Lillian asked.

"Yes," Kate said.

"Nothing other than snorting that he was the boss and was going to the studio."

⚜

It was late when Jarrett got home. Kate was in bed. He slid in beside her. Not yet asleep, she looked his way. Still confused by his earlier outburst, she didn't know how to approach him. She needed to get him to a doctor, but how? At the last instant, she decided to play it safe. "How'd everything go with Stanley?"

Jarrett slid close to her. "Huh? Oh, Stanley. It went well. He's on schedule and only slightly over budget."

She raised up on an elbow. "Did Stanley discuss my book?"

"He mentioned it," Jarrett said. "I told him to talk it over with you. It's your project." Reaching out, his strong hands stroked her body. "Forget Stan. I want you." One hand started at her shoulder and ended up between her legs. Caressing her gently, he kissed her. Excited, she forgot what had been on her mind and succumbed to his passionate advances.

The next morning, Jarrett pushed the big Chrysler to the limit on their drive to the office. Once again, Kate held on. In the office, he settled in and looked at her. "How is the Carolina project coming? Did they finally agree to the two years of tax concessions I requested?" He grinned.

Kate straightened up. "No. I didn't get the two years, I—"

Snapping forward, he hit the desk with a fist. "You didn't get it! *Goddamn it!*" he roared. "Don't tell me you settled for nothing! Son of a bitch." He hit the desk again. "I worked hard to get them to agree to two years, and you pissed it all away. I should never have left a woman in charge. That's going to cost me a fortune." His eyes flared. "Don't you know anything about business?"

Kate slapped the desk with the flat of her hand. The sound exploded like a rifle shot. "If you'd let me finish, you would have learned I told them we needed ten years of zero tax liability to make the project viable. They came back with eight years. I saved you over fifty million dollars in taxes alone." Now on her feet, she planted her hands on the edge of his desk and, leaning forward, glared down at him. "Don't you ever tell me I don't understand business. And don't you ever talk to me like that again."

Jarrett blinked. His head snapped back. His jaw muscles flexed. He studied her. He tried to speak, but only garbled sounds came out. Moments later, he swallowed hard and made a noticeable effort to speak. Taking his time, he enunciated each word slowly. "I find it hard to believe that you talked them into eight years," he said, brushing perspiration from his cheek. "I worked hard to get two."

Kate focused on him. "Well, I did. I showed them how we're going to increase their tax revenue to more than offset what I want. They insisted I was wrong until I pointed out I'd used the numbers they'd released to the press. I told them I was prepared to call a news conference and explain how we were no longer interested because they and the governor had lied to us."

Jarrett's jaw dropped. His expression froze. "You...you...you said what!" he stuttered. "You could have blown the whole deal." He glared at her. "Don't ever try that again. I work hard to put these programs together, and I don't need you fouling them up with amateur maneuvers."

"Amateur maneuvers?" she roared. "I accomplished more than you did. You put me in charge, and I did a damn good job. I saved you fifty million dollars. Admit it."

Cowering back, he brushed more perspiration from his face. Many seconds passed, and he slowly nodded. "Okay, you did a good job, but from now on, I'm the boss. You stick to running your ranch. I don't tell you what to do up there, so don't tell me what to do down here. Understood?"

Before Kate could respond, Lillian's voice came from the intercom. "Jarrett, remind Kate she's scheduled to fly to Sacramento in an hour. She has that meeting with the state's facilities people. Do you feel up to going along?"

"Yes, I feel up to going along," Jarrett shot back. "And why shouldn't I? I'm well." He looked toward the roof. "When do you have me scheduled to fly to the airport?"

"The helicopter will be here shortly," Lillian replied.

30

On the ground in Sacramento, Jarrett was the first down the stairs from his plane. "Good afternoon, Mr. Sinclair," the superintendent said and looked past him for Kate. "I was expecting Mrs. Sinclair. The facilities people want to meet with her and discuss her decorating ideas."

"They do, do they? Well, they're going to meet with me. The first team is back on the field. I'm over my accident, and I'm in charge."

At the project, the superintendent led the way into the meeting room. Before he could introduce those in attendance, Nadia Edmonds raced up and embraced Jarrett. "It's so nice to see you survived that horrific accident," she said and gave him a very affectionate squeeze. A stylishly dressed woman in her midforties, she pulled him tight and pressed her breasts hard against his chest.

Kate picked up on Nadia's advance. She glared. *Back off, lady. He's married.*

Ignoring Kate's sinister look, Nadia continued, "How long were you unconscious, two months? That must have been an awful ordeal."

Jarrett shrugged. "It was more like six weeks, but that was long enough," he replied.

"Oh, you poor man. I'm sure it was," Nadia said. Patting his chest, she sparkled affectionately. "Well, you stay here and take it easy while we steal your wife. She was up here a few weeks ago and made some outstanding suggestions. We've discussed them and want to make sure we're all in agreement."

Jarrett tried to follow but was quickly forced to bring up the rear. Nadia led the way with Kate at her side and the governor's wife and department directors close behind. Jarrett called to Kate. "You go discuss paint colors and fabric swatches. I'll meet you back at the plane."

It was late when Kate returned to the plane. No sooner was she aboard than Jarrett's voice boomed from the overhead speaker. "Close the door, and everyone be seated."

Moments later, the engines could be heard as they roared up to speed. When the plane leveled off, the flight attendant approached Kate. "Do you want to go forward and watch from the cockpit?"

"No," Kate replied. "We covered a lot, and I need to get it into my laptop while it's still fresh in my mind."

A half hour out of Los Angeles, Janine stepped into the conference room. "Mrs. Sinclair," she began. "Good. I see you stowed your computer. We're approaching LA and will be landing—"

Bang!—the plane snapped hard over. The engines screamed. Janine went tumbling and ended up against the down-side wall.

Kate grabbed on. "What the hell?" she called out. With a hold of the conference table, she looked toward Janine just as a commuter jet flashed dangerously close by the windows. Seconds later, the 757 snapped back level, and the engine sound backed off. Getting up, Kate reached out to help Janine. "Are you okay?" she asked and pulled the woman to her feet. "Is anything broken?"

Steadying herself, Janine looked down. "I don't think so," she said and felt around to make sure.

Sheryl burst into the room. "Are you two okay?"

"Yeah, I think so," Kate said and looked toward the front of the plane. "What was that all about? We passed close enough to that other plane that I could see people in the windows."

"I don't know, but I'll find out." Sheryl disappeared and, a minute later, was back. "Apparently, Mr. Sinclair missed a call from air traffic control."

Upon landing, Jarrett was heavy on the gas as they squealed from the parking lot. Kate held on. "Darling, aren't we going a little fast?"

He grinned. "You know me, always in a hurry. Life is too short. We can't waste a minute."

"Yes, I know," Kate agreed, grabbing the door to keep from being tossed about. "But I would like to live a little longer. Can't we slow down a bit?"

"If you insist," he said and eased back on the gas.

On their way in from the garage, Kate hooked her arm around his. "We have both been working hard. Why don't we take a week off and go someplace fun like Hawaii? There's nothing doing up north, and your projects are running smoothly. So can we take that belated honeymoon?"

Jarrett considered what she said and slowly nodded.

⟡

The next morning, out over the Pacific, Jarrett was seated in the left front seat. With the California coast behind them, Jarrett's copilot let Kate take his place. Unhurried, Jarrett explained the flight instruments and how he was using them to navigate across the featureless ocean. She smiled. He was like he had been on that first flight back from Spokane, warm and friendly. She studied him as he talked. *Why can't you always be like this?*

In Honolulu, they passed the luxury resorts in Waikiki and motored directly to a beachfront home on Diamond Head Road. Kate gasped. The living-room window wall had been rolled aside, giving her an unrestricted view of the ocean. The warm breeze that wafted in was filled with the sounds of the surf breaking on the sand a few yards away.

Jarrett stepped up and wrapped his arms around her from behind. "What do you think of the place?" Jarrett asked proudly. "Quite something, huh?"

"Yes, it is," Kate said. Wide-eyed, she turned in his arms and gave him a kiss. She licked her lips. He tasted as good now as he did that first time in Montana. "Do you come here often?" she asked.

He shook his head. "I haven't been here in years. Rachel uses it when she shoots in Hawaii."

Settled in, they took a long walk on the beach. The next morning, they helicoptered north to Dillingham Field. Jarrett pointed at the plane without an engine. "The winds are good, and I thought we'd go sailing."

While Kate had seen pictures of gliders, she'd never seen one up close. When she did, she was a bit taken aback by how fragile they appeared with their long slender wings and sleek wasplike body. Seated behind him, she looked past his shoulder as the towplane took them aloft. Minutes into the flight, Jarrett reached down and pulled the release lever. The little plane jolted. She gasped. Her stomach felt like it popped up into her throat. She looked out. They were gliding. There was no noise other than the wind rushing by the side of the plane. Jarrett banked, and they swooped down over the north shore lagoon. The shallow waters inside the coral reef were a light blue green in color. From a couple hundred feet up, she could see to the bottom.

"Look," Jarrett called out, "there's a turtle. It must be a couple feet across."

An hour later, after many passes over the lagoon, they glided in and hit the runway with a thud. The plane shook as they rumbled to a stop. Kate sat and stared. When Jarrett didn't move, she tapped him on the shoulder. "What do we do now?" she asked.

Turning, he looked her way. "We get out. I was waiting to see if the winds would pick up, but they didn't. It wouldn't be any fun going up again."

To Kate, one hour seemed to melt into the next. Between sailing and gliding and snorkeling trips to Maui and Lanai, the week disappeared. To her, their time in Hawaii was over too soon.

Home in Beverly Hills, she was up early and into the office she had set up. After a week of being away, she had a ton of ranch e-mails and phone messages to answer.

Jarrett stopped by her desk. "You appear to have plenty to keep you busy," he said. "Me, I'm off to the office. I've some business to take care of, and I'll see you there for lunch, okay?"

Kate nodded without looking up.

It was after twelve when Jarrett phoned. "Where are you?" he asked. "It's going on twelve-thirty. Weren't you coming down so we could go to lunch?"

Kate looked at the time. "Oh, honey, I'm sorry," she said. "I'm swamped. I have too much to do. Maybe tomorrow."

"We won't be in town tomorrow," Jarrett said. "We'll be on the road. I have to check on the Minneapolis project and the building in St. Louis. From there, to Houston and on the way back, a stop in Albuquerque to review the progress on the office tower. You're coming along?"

Kate shook her head. "I'm sorry, hon, I can't," she said.

"You're not?" he replied. His tone had changed. "We were having such a good time in Hawaii. I was hoping we could continue it this week."

"Yes, I know, darling, and I appreciate the offer, but I need to get caught up," she said. "This once, can you go the trip alone?"

Jarrett did not immediately answer. "I guess so," he said slowly. "If you can't come, I guess you can't."

It was midweek when Kate received a call from the building superintendent in St. Louis. "Mrs. Sinclair, I have to advise you, your husband tripped on the stairs and fell. We were painting, and he caught his foot on a drop cloth and took a nasty tumble. He landed on his back and hit his head on the way down. We took him to the emergency room and got him checked out. He protested, but state industrial and workman's comp required us to do it. My corporate office required we call and advise family members whenever there is an accident. Be assured the ER doctor examined him thoroughly. Other than a couple of bruises to his tailbone and arm and a bump on his head, they couldn't find anything else wrong. The doctor released him and said he's okay."

"Thank you for calling," she said. Hanging up, she immediately dialed Jarrett. Was this one of those bumps to the head the neurologist had advised her she needed to be concerned about? "I just heard from the building superintendent in St. Louis. He said you fell and hit your head. Are you okay?"

"Yes! I'm okay," Jarrett shot back. His voice was gruff, not the least like he was when he left LA.

Kate blinked. "Why are you so brusque? Why are you yelling at me? Is something wrong?"

"I'm not yelling," Jarrett came back. "And no, I'm not brusque," he growled. "Nothing's wrong."

Kate tried to decide what to do next. "Are you cutting your trip short and heading home? You really should have that bump to the head checked out by a specialist."

"No," Jarrett replied. "I don't need any specialist." He snorted. "And I'm not cutting my trip short. I'm off to Houston and then to Albuquerque. I'll call you when I'm ready to come home." *Click*, and the call was over.

Kate stared at the phone. He had changed. This was not the person she'd said good-bye to three days before. *Could that fall have been one of those bumps the neurologist had warned me about?* She tried to think. *How do I get him back? He needs to see a specialist.*

Friday afternoon, Jarrett called from Houston.

"Are you on your way home?" Kate asked.

"No," he said. "The oil people want to show me their wells. I'll call you when I get to Albuquerque."

Kate blinked. Something was definitely different. He was not his warm, considerate self. *I'm losing him. What can I do? He won't listen to reason and go to a doctor.*

Monday afternoon, Jarrett called from Albuquerque. "Hi, honey, how's it going?" he asked. His voice was strained.

"Jarrett, you sound exhausted," she said. "You really need to come home. You sound beat."

"I am," he replied. "I've cut my meeting short today, and I'm going to bed as soon as we're finished on the phone. I need a good night's sleep."

It was noon the next day when Jarrett called. "A couple of properties have come to my attention," he said. Unlike the day before, his voice was warm and friendly. "I need to fly east and check them out. One is in upstate New York a half-hour north of Albany. The other's outside of Atlanta."

"Just yesterday, you were tired and heading home," Kate countered.

"I was," he replied. "But after twelve hours in bed, I'm rested." He chuckled. "I had a great sleep last night." There was life and energy in his voice. "I'll be home after I check these out."

Kate smiled. He sounded like his old self. "Can I come with?" she asked. "I'm all caught up."

"No," he replied. "I don't have time to fly back to pick you up. These properties are hot."

Late Friday, Jarrett called.

"How was your day?" she asked. "Does the property in New York look promising?"

"It does. It's great." His tone was upbeat and filled with energy. "I'm meeting with the sellers again and should have a deal. Come Tuesday, I'm off to Atlanta."

"Atlanta. After New York, I was hoping you might be on your way home. I miss you."

"I know," Jarrett said. "But the property in Atlanta is hot, and I really should check it out while I'm back here."

Kate sighed. "Then after Atlanta, you'll be coming home?"

"No," he replied. "I am going to swing down and check on the new boat in Florida. Bear is having problems."

Frustrated, she tapped on the desk. "Will you be coming home after that?"

"Of course," Jarrett replied.

On Saturday, Kate went to the gallery. It was late when Isabel dimmed the lights and locked up. "Thank you for coming. Saturday is always one of my busiest days." She pointed toward her office. "I am planning on wrapping my hand around a dry martini. Care to join me?"

Kate shook her head. "Thanks, but I'm exhausted. I need to get home and off my feet."

Kate wasn't home five minutes when the doorbell rang. Her pulse quickened. *Who could that be?* No one had called from the gate, so how did they get in? Kate peeked out and relaxed. It was Rachel.

"To what do I owe this visit?" Kate asked.

"I was in the area," Rachel said. "I've misplaced a couple sketches, and I thought they might still be here."

Kate led the way to her old workroom. Aside from the bare workstations, the room was empty. "I guess I wasted a trip," Rachel said. "They aren't here."

Kate led the way back to the kitchen. "I was getting ready to relax with a glass of wine. Care to join me?"

Rachel glowed. "Love to."

Kate poured the wine and stepped over to the kitchen table. "The last time we talked, you said you had a photo shoot back east? Was that canceled?" she asked as she settled in across from her friend.

"No," Rachel replied. "We were at Saratoga Springs, New York, Wednesday and Thursday, and we finished up late yesterday. We grabbed a commercial flight back last night. I left Margo behind. She wanted to visit with a friend, so she's staying the weekend." She paused. "You remember Margo? She's the model I use in my outdoor shoots. She's very athletic and loves to ski. She has blonde hair and…" Rachel's voice trailed off. She studied Kate. "Yes," she said. "She's tall and looks a lot like you. From a distance, you two would be hard to tell apart."

Kate frowned quizzically. "Saratoga Springs? Where's that?" she asked.

"Thirty minutes north of Albany," Rachel said and looked at her watch. "Oh my, sorry," she said. "Got to run. Thanks for the wine." She motioned for Kate to remain seated. "I know my way out."

Kate blinked. She looked at the wineglass that hadn't been touched. She shook her head. *She didn't come here to get sketches she had to know weren't here.* She looked at the door and then back at the glass. *So why did you come?* she asked herself. *So Margo looks a lot like me. What's that supposed to mean?* She stopped. *Her photo shoot had been thirty minutes north of Albany. That's where the property was that Jarrett was interested in.* She grabbed her phone. *Something's not right.* She tapped in Rachel's number.

The phone rang and rang, and then voice mail clicked in. "Thank you for calling. I'm not available right now. Please leave your name and phone number, and I will call you back."

Kate settled back in the chair. *Obviously, you don't want to talk right now.*

31

ome Monday evening, Jarrett called. His tone was upbeat. "I met with the owners, and they've agreed to my offer." He chuckled. "We have a deal. All that's left is signing the papers."

Kate couldn't be happier. "So you're still in New York?"

"Yes. I should be leaving tomorrow," he replied.

Kate stared at the phone. *If Margo stayed behind to spend a weekend with a friend, could Jarrett have been that friend?* She stopped. *Rachel, look what you have me doing.* She settled back. *Stop worrying. He's your husband.*

When Kate did not respond, Jarrett continued, "Are you still there?"

"Yes," she replied. "I'm here. When will you be going south?"

"As soon as the ink's dry tomorrow," he stated. "I'll be in Atlanta tomorrow night. I'll be busy all day Wednesday and into the evening checking over the property and looking at comps. If I don't call, that's the reason. I need to get a feel of the area. I might not call until late Thursday or early Friday when I get to Florida."

"I would like it if we could spend more time together," she said. "After all, we're married." About to say more, she stopped. He traveled a lot. She knew that from before they were married. *I guess this is what I have to expect.*

On her way into Jarrett's office on Wednesday, Kate stopped to say hi to Lillian. "Anything this morning?" Kate asked.

Lillian looked down at her appointment pad. "You might check with that Edmonds woman in Sacramento on their painting and decorating progress. It's been a couple weeks since you were there."

Settling in at Jarrett's desk, she dialed Nadia's office. "Hi. This is Mrs. Sinclair. Is Nadia there?"

"Ms. Edmonds left last night for a meeting of state building managers in Atlanta," the receptionist stated. "She'll be flying back Friday and be in the office Monday."

Kate stared at the phone. *Nadia and Jarrett will be in Atlanta at the same time.* Her brow furrowed. *That could be coincidental. Then again, maybe not.* She tapped on the desk. *Rachel, this is getting to be too much. Look what you have me doing. I'm getting paranoid. First, you have me all worked up about Margo, and now I'm getting wound up over Nadia.* Scowling, she shoved back from the desk. *Atlanta's a huge city. He probably doesn't even know she's there.*

❦

A couple of days later, Jarrett called from Florida. "Bear has run into some problems with the new boat that need my attention. I'm going to stay on an extra few days. I should be back by Tuesday, Wednesday at the latest. I'll keep you posted."

"How was that property in Atlanta?" Kate asked.

"What?" he asked. "Oh, the property in Atlanta? It wasn't what the sellers represented it to be. It was too far out of town. It'll take years for the city to get close enough to make it desirable."

Couldn't you have figured that out before you went down there? Isn't that what satellite images are for? About to question him, a light flashed on her phone. Someone was at the front gate. She checked the closed-circuit TV and pressed the button. "Jarrett, honey, I have a dinner engagement, and I have to go."

"What!" he responded. "Are you seeing other people when I'm not around?"

Kate blinked. "No. I'm not seeing other people," she said. "I'm going out with folks from AJS. Karl Schneider and his fiancée and a couple of the AJS regional people are stopping by, and we're going to dinner."

"Oh," he replied. "That's okay."

"What do you mean, that's okay?" The doorbell rang again. "Oh, forget it! We'll discuss this when you get home. Good night," she said and slammed the phone down.

Kate opened the door. "Hi, Karl," she said and looked past him. To her surprise, his car was empty. "Where are Melissa, Bill, and Jim?" she asked.

"Melissa is off with a girlfriend. She wanted to come with but knew we'd end up spending the whole evening talking beef purchases. That would have bored her to death," he said. "Bill wasn't feeling well and decided to stay in the motel, and Jim is off visiting his sister in Long Beach. That leaves only me. Are you okay with that?"

"Of course," she said. He was engaged and wasn't likely to make a pass at the boss's wife. "Where're we going?"

Taking her arm, he led the way to the car. "I know this place in Hollywood. Their music is fantastic, and the food is good."

Leaving Jarrett's house, Karl turned toward Hollywood. A block or so back, a nondescript minivan pulled away from the curb and slipped in behind them.

Miles later at the restaurant, Karl leaned back in the booth. "Enough talking about beef purchases. We do that all the time at work. Let's talk about you. I've seen you in those commercials. Are you having fun?"

"I am. I'm having a ball. The extra money is coming in handy to do some of the projects around the ranch."

Karl focused on her. "In all the years I've known you, this is the first time we've ever had dinner together. We should have done this years ago."

"Agreed," she said. "We shouldn't let another five years pass before we do this again." Reaching over, she gave his arm a friendly squeeze.

Monday morning, Kate had something she needed to discuss with Erica, so she swung by the studio and caught the actress between takes. "I have the film rights to that book I've told you about. I've talked with Stanley Rolstadler, and he's interested in the project. I'd like to consider Forrest Pendleton for one of the parts, but I heard quite a row developed between Forrest and Stanley toward the end of that movie you and Forrest did with him. Do you think Forrest would be a good choice?"

"It all depends on who you ask," Erica said. "Stanley, I'm sure, will have a negative opinion. He wanted to shoot a scene one way, and Forrest disagreed. Stanley shot the scene his way. When your husband saw the rushes, he ordered the scene reshot. End of incident."

Kate continued, "I think Forrest would be perfect for the part of the neighbor. What do you think?"

"I agree," Erica said.

"Do you think he'll do it if Stanley's involved?" Kate asked.

There was a knock on the dressing-room door. "Ms. Heath? You're needed on the set."

Standing, she grabbed her script pages. "I'll be right there," she called back. She turned to Kate. "There's only one way to find out. Call him." She gave Kate Forrest's number. "Take him to dinner and see what you think."

Forrest was between scenes when Kate called and only had a couple minutes to talk. "I've bought the movie rights to a book, and

I'm mulling over who might best fill some of the roles. Any chance we can meet for dinner?"

"Yes," he replied. "I'm finished today before five. Tomorrow morning, I'll be on location and will be out of town for the next few weeks. If we meet today, it'll have to be an early dinner."

"Then let's do it this afternoon at my place," Kate said. "We can barbeque a couple of steaks and have dinner out by the pool." She gave Forrest directions, and the call was over.

It was going on six when Forrest drove up. She led the way to the patio. With the barbecue preheated, she put the meat on the grill. When she saw he appeared ill at ease, she winked. "Relax," she said. "I'm a friend." She pointed at the bottle of tequila. "Erica said that is your drink."

Eased by her smile, he relaxed and reached for the bottle. "You got that right," he said and poured himself a glass.

Closing the barbeque, Kate turned to Forrest. "Regarding those movie rights, I'm planning on having Stanley do the picture. I heard you and he had words toward the end of that last movie you did with him. What can you tell me?"

Forrest downed a big swallow of Tequila. "Yeah, I heard you bought the rights to a book." He took another gulp and wiped his lips. "Have you spoken to Stanley about me?"

"No," she replied. "I wanted to hear what you had to say first."

"I appreciate that," he said. He told her how Stanley wanted a scene shot one way, and he disagreed. "Well! He ordered me to do it his way and to keep my job, I had no choice. When your husband saw the rushes, he ordered the scene be reshot. The way he told Stanley to shoot it was exactly the way I had pushed for all along. In an effort to save his ass, Stanley told your husband he'd shot the scene the way I wanted to play the character. As a result, your husband put me on notice that no more disagreements would be tolerated."

Kate turned the steaks. "Here's my problem. I'd like to have you in the movie. I also want this project to be a success. Stanley is the best. I want him doing the picture."

246

Forrest drained the glass and pointed at the tequila bottle. "Okay?"

"By all means."

He splashed more in his glass. "Stanley is a good director. And with your husband's supervision, he's put out some very successful work. But hey, there's no shortage of great directors in this town. The director of the picture I'm in right now is considered one of the best. When he heard you'd bought the rights to that book, he was upset he hadn't gotten to it first. According to him, done right, that book will make a great movie."

Kate's interest piqued. "Who's this director you're working with?"

"Aaron Seigelman," Forrest replied.

Kate raised a questioning brow. "I've never heard of him. Has he done anything important?"

"Has he done anything important?" Forrest laughed. "Yes," he replied with a broad smile. "Aaron is considered one of the best directors right now. He isn't as flamboyant as Stanley, but every movie he's made in the last fifteen years has made money, big money. He's highly respected and definitely someone to be taken seriously."

Between bites, Forrest rambled on about Aaron Seigelman and the picture he was in. Kate hung on his every word. She was becoming exposed to the movie business, and what she was hearing fascinated her. She smiled. *All sorts of new avenues are opening up. With luck, I might not have to wait a year and a half to get my movie made.*

Kate picked up the tequila to refill Forrest's glass.

"Whoa, there," he said and put an unsteady hand over his glass. "I've 'ad enough." Getting to his feet, he wavered about. "In fact, I've probably 'ad too much and talked ta much." He looked at his watch. "Wow, I've got to get going. It's a long drive to my house, and I have that early call, so I had better be on my way."

Reaching out, Kate steadied him. "Where's your house?" When he told her, Kate pulled him back. "Why, that's way out in the valley.

247

You're in no condition to drive. I'll call a cab. You have to get home and pack."

He shook his head. "I'm already packed. We were supposed to have left today. My suitcases are in my car."

"If that's the case, I insist you stay here." She walked him through the kitchen and called to a maid. "Make up a room. Mr. Pendleton will be staying the night." She looked at the actor. "You can assure your girlfriend or wife that everything is on the up-and-up. This is a very big house, and we're not alone."

He grinned a bit sheepishly. "I'll explain it to Ronnie. I'm sure he'll understand."

⁂

Kate was up early to see Forrest off. "Thanks. I enjoyed our visit. So you think Aaron Seigelman would be interested?"

Forrest pulled out his cell phone and gave her his number. "Call him yourself. He'll be in town the next couple days. I'm sure he'll take your call."

With Forrest gone, she glanced at the sky. It was still dark. Too early to call Seigelman. In her office, she checked her computer. Jarrett had sent her an e-mail. "There is a problem with the freshwater system on my island in the Bahamas I have to look into. I won't be home today." *Damn! Another delay*, Kate concluded.

Arriving at Jarrett's office downtown, she stopped at Lillian's desk. "Anything this morning?"

"No, not yet," Lillian replied.

Kate looked about to see who might be listening. With no one close, she whispered to Lillian. "I need the name of a good ob-gyn. I have something I need to have checked out."

"Dr. Carswell is one of the best," Lillian said.

Kate shook her head. "He and Jarrett are too close."

"Oh," Lillian replied. Grabbing a notepad, she wrote down a name and phone number. "This is my doctor."

Kate looked toward Jarrett's office. "Nadia Edmonds should be back. I'll give her a call." In Jarrett's office, she dialed Nadia's office in Sacramento. "Hi, this is Mrs. Sinclair. Can I speak to Nadia?"

"I'm sorry, Mrs. Sinclair," the receptionist said. "Ms. Edmonds has decided to stay on another day. She won't be back until tomorrow."

Kate continued, "When she gets in, tell her I called."

Still at Jarrett's desk, she dialed the number Forrest had given her. Aaron Seigelman was on another call, so she left her name and number.

Moments later, Lillian burst into the room. "What's up?" Kate asked as Lillian pushed the door closed smartly.

Lillian pointed at the telephone on Jarrett's desk. "Aaron Seigelman phoned and said he was returning your call." She stared at Kate. "Are you considering having Seigelman do your book?"

"Maybe," Kate said. "Jarrett and Stanley are involved with other projects and won't be available for eighteen months or more."

"Seigelman is an excellent choice," Lillian said. "But whatever you do, don't use the phones in this office to make calls like that. With all the business deals Jarrett discusses, all calls in and out are automatically recorded. Fortunately, after Seigelman called back, I was able to erase your call to him."

Kate frowned questioningly.

Lillian continued, "When Jarrett first became interested in movies and approached some of the established producers and directors, they were less than receptive. Aaron Seigelman was one of those who didn't take him seriously. Jarrett has never forgotten. If you want to talk to Seigelman, call him on your cell phone. I told him you were on another line and would call him back. If you choose to meet him, do it somewhere other than here. Jarrett is going to explode if he finds out you're even considering Seigelman."

So let him explode. He's off doing his thing. I can do mine. With Lillian gone, she pulled out her cell phone and called Seigelman. "Good morning. This is Mrs. Katherine Sinclair. Aaron Seigelman, please."

"This is Aaron," the man replied.

Kate continued, "I bought the movie rights to a book, and Forrest Pendleton suggested I give you a call."

"Yes, I heard that you bought the rights to that book, but I'm surprised to hear from you. I assumed Jarrett would have wanted to control that production himself. Done properly, it should make an extremely profitable movie." Pausing, he cleared his throat. "But why are you calling me? Why aren't you going with Stanley and your husband?"

Kate explained how Jarrett and Stanley were tied up on other projects and wouldn't be available for a year and a half. Also, she wanted to use Forrest, and he and Stanley had words. "So Forrest suggested I call you."

"Interesting," Aaron replied. "The movie I'm shooting right now should wrap by the middle of next month. I'll be available after that. Are you considering producing the project yourself?"

About to say no, she looked at the phone. *I hadn't actually considered producing the movie myself, but now that you mention it, there is no reason why I can't.* "Sort of, but with the help of others," she said. "I'm new at this game."

"No problem," Aaron said. "I can put the people together you'll need to make it a success. I know Jarrett well, and if he gets wind of this, he's going to have a fit. He's still peeved that I once turned him down, so I suggest that until you decide if you want to go with me, or anyone else for that matter, the preliminary meetings should be somewhere private. If you can come up with the place, I'll get the people together."

"Great," Kate said, and the call was over. She leaned back and considered her options. *I have a longtime supplier of feeding equipment south of Los Angeles. I'm sure he has a conference room I can borrow.*

Lillian called on the intercom, "Kate, an e-mail just came in from Jarrett for you. It's on the computer behind his desk."

Sorry, honey, I've been trying to reach you all over. There's been a change. I'll be flying in early tomorrow and going straight to the Newport Yacht Harbor. Fletcher has a new America's Cup boat he wants to check out. If he can beat me with his new boat, he's confident he might have a winner. You can watch from my yacht. Afterward, we can take it over to Catalina for a couple days of R and R.

Jarrett

32

At the yacht harbor, Kate was directed to a gleaming white vessel at the end of a long dock. *Wow*, she mouthed. *What is this? A small cruise ship?* she questioned as she ascended the boarding stairs. "Hello, Mrs. Sinclair," the stewardess said. "Welcome aboard. The captain is waiting for you upstairs."

Kate followed her direction and was met in the pilothouse by a man in uniform.

"Good morning, Mrs. Sinclair. I'm Captain Jensen. If you'll accompany me to the wing of the bridge, you can watch us depart."

Kate did, and in no time, they were heading for open waters. A mile or so offshore, the yacht anchored. "We are one end of the start-finish line," the captain explained and pointed out the buoy that made up the other end of the line. "Those two buoys in the distance are the turning buoys they have to race around."

Kate watched two eighty-foot sailboats with great tall masts pirouette before them jockeying for position. The captain dropped a flag and squeezed the trigger on a handheld horn. Both boats snapped around toward the imaginary start line. Jarrett was first across the line in Fletcher's old boat. Within minutes, the sailboats were well down the course. Kate watched as the two boats all but faded from view.

Several hours later, the two boats approached the finish line. Fletcher was ahead, but not by much. Jarrett's boat was closing. He was alongside Fletcher and was forcing him into a collision course with the boat she was on. Less than a couple boat lengths from the yacht, Fletcher yelled. His voice carried across the water. "Bear off! Goddamn it. I've right away." Jarrett didn't. To avoid a collision, Fletcher swung away, sliding by the yacht with mere inches to spare.

With the race over, the yacht she was on returned to the harbor. Docked, Kate quickly made her way to the narrow work pier as the two sailboats were towed in. Being the owner of the syndicate, Fletcher and his boat were the first to arrive. Fletcher jumped off and ran her way.

"Boy, have I got a bone to pick with your husband. His cutting me off damn near cost me my new boat." Grabbing her arm, he walked to his car. "I know we were planning a debriefing session, but I'm too worked up to even be in the same room with him."

Jerking the door open, Fletcher slid in. "Tell him that I had an emergency and had to rush off." Peeling out, he shot ahead and screeched to a stop. He called to her, "I almost forgot. My wife wanted me to apologize to you. She tried to say hello when you and Jarrett were skiing in Vermont a week and a half ago. She said she called to you when she was coming off the lift, but you and Jarrett had already started down and apparently didn't hear. When she saw you two that evening in the hotel, you were so intimate in a corner of the lounge she didn't want to intrude."

Kate cringed. "Yes, thank her. I appreciate that." Her eyes narrowed as Fletcher dug out. Behind her, Jarrett and the boat he was on was approaching the dock. She glared at him. *You have a lot of explaining to do.* She fumed. *Not hard to guess who that friend was that Rachel said Margo stayed behind to be with.* Her eyes closed down into angry slits. *If what Fletcher's wife said is true, then you're cheating on me.*

Leaping to the dock, Jarrett raced up and kissed her. He looked toward the exit. "What's going on? Fletcher lit out of here like his tail was on fire."

A crewman ran by on the narrow work pier, almost knocking her into the water. "Sorry, miss," the crewman called out.

Jarrett jumped back toward the sailboat. "Watch those lines! You!" he commanded. "Let go of that backstay." That said, he turned and looked toward the exit. "Where'd Fletch go in such a hurry? We were supposed to have drinks and a debriefing aboard the yacht."

"He had an emergency."

"An emergency?" Jarrett asked. "What kind of emergency?"

"I don't know. That's all he said." She looked around. They needed to talk. Men were everywhere, swarming over the sailboats.

Jarrett stepped away. "I said watch that backstay. Now do it." He pointed at one of the other men. "You, on Fletcher's boat. Careful with the boom vang." He turned to Kate. Just then, the shackle on the end of a heavy lifting line swung dangerously close to her head. Jarrett grabbed the cable and ran to attach the shackle to the boat. "I'll get this one," he called to the men near the other three cables. "You three do the others."

Kate stepped back. Her pallor was poor, and her disposition worse. Crewmen were everywhere. Fletcher's boat was swinging through the air. The other was waiting to be picked up. *This is not the place to confront you about infidelity.* She looked toward the yacht at the end of the dock. That boat too was swarming with crewmen, busy hosing it down. *That could take hours.*

Kate looked about. *Before I confront him, I'd better make sure I'm right. I need proof he was cheating, and only Rachel can supply that. If Fletcher's wife was mistaken, then what? He could accuse me of not trusting him.*

Jarrett grabbed Kate's shoulders. "You don't look good. Did the boat ride disagree with you?"

"Yes," she said and pointed at his yacht. "You and your crew go have your debriefing. I have to get home. I'm not feeling well."

He studied her. "Do you want me to drive you? The debriefing can wait."

She shook her head. "No. Go have your meeting. I can drive myself."

"Whatever you say." He pointed toward the yacht. "After the meeting, I was planning on us going over to Catalina. If you're not feeling well, we can always do that some other day."

"Yes, some other day," she replied. "When you finish here, I'll see you when you get back from Catalina."

Heading out, Kate punched in Rachel's number. "Hi, Rach. It's me, Kate. I'm heading north from Newport. I need to discuss something with you. Are you at home?"

"Yes," Rachel responded. "I'll see you when you get here."

Kate dropped the phone on the seat and focused on the road. The drive to Beverly Hills was long and would give her time to think. The phone rang. It was Aaron Seigelman. "Hello. Kate Clark here." Right then, she did not feel all that married.

"Kate, I've one day left in town. How would getting together tomorrow morning sound? I have some people I'd like you to meet."

"Tomorrow will work fine," Kate said. "I'll make the arrangements and call you back."

After two quick calls, she was set to meet Seigelman in the morning.

Upon arriving at Rachel's, Kate settled in at the breakfast bar. "I heard from someone that his wife thought she saw me and Jarrett in Vermont a week and a half ago. We both know I wasn't there, so who was he with? Was it that model you said stayed behind who looked like me? Was that what you were trying to tell me when you came by the other day?"

"Yes," Rachel said. "Margo stayed on, and the two of them went to Vermont to do some skiing and whatever else." She settled back against the counter. "I know I probably should have told you straight out. I'm sorry."

"Yes, you should have told me," Kate said. "Is this a first-time incident or a frequent occurrence?"

"Prior to meeting you, there was no shortage of female movie hopefuls anxious to be auditioned. He bedded so many aboard the plane and his yacht back then, even the crews lost count. I got tired of his wandering ways and broke off our relationship. Oh, I stayed on at his house, but that was only because I liked the address, and he liked my watching over the place. After meeting you, he stopped chasing around, at least as near as I can tell. What information I have is hearsay, but from what the girls aboard the plane and the household staff have said, he's been faithful."

Kate focused on Rachel. "Prior to our getting married or after?" she asked.

"Both," Rachel said. "Before you got married and while you two were going together, he was too busy with his business deals to have played around much. When you two got married, he was off to South America and then back east to do that demonstration."

Kate stared. "So when did he pick up on his old ways?"

"When he flew us east to Saratoga Springs. That's when he talked Margo into staying on after the shoot was over."

Confused, Kate looked at the woman. "He flew you and your crew to Albany from Albuquerque?"

Rachel shook her head. "We weren't in Albuquerque. He flew back to LA to get us. Didn't you know that?"

Kate scowled. "No, I didn't know that."

Rachel continued, "He phoned me shortly after he arrived in Albuquerque. He knew about my shoot in Saratoga Springs and asked if we needed a lift. I said we could use one, so he flew back special to pick us up before he went east. I asked if you were going along, and he said you were too busy to be bothered with anything he did."

"That's a lie," Kate said. "When he called and told me of his trip to New York, I asked to go along, and he told me he didn't have time to swing by to pick me up." Kate got to her feet. "Was there ever any property he was interested in, in New York?"

"Yes," Rachel said. "He was busy with that during the day, but in the evening, he and Margo were a number." Rachel looked at Kate. "Since he's come back from his rehab up at your ranch, I've noticed a change. He's been moody, and especially after his fall in St. Louis, he's been…well, different. He's not the same person he was before that race-demo incident. It's nothing I can really put my finger on other than when he used to fly us around, he'd be friendly and full of spirit. This time, he was charming one minute, and the next brusque and sullen."

Kate looked at Rachel. "Have there been any others other than Margo?"

"There's the woman from the governor's office in Sacramento. I believe her name is—"

"Nadia Edmonds." Kate's eyes narrowed.

"Yes," Rachel said. "Nadia. I heard from one of the flight attendants that Nadia met up with him in Atlanta. Sheryl said they were real cozy in Atlanta aboard the plane and in the Bahamas. He dropped her in Sacramento on his way back to LA."

33

Kate slowed as she approached Jarrett's driveway. *The neurologist had warned me to watch out for attitude swings. This has to be what he meant.* She recalled what Rachel said: "He's not the same person he was before the accident. Since St. Louis, he's been different." Kate eased off on the gas. *Could this be the beginning of that downward-spiral thing?* She looked at the dark half-timbered structure. *This is your house. This isn't our house. You never shared this with me. In fact, you shared very little with me.*

In the bedroom, she grabbed clothes from the closet and laid them into the large suitcase Lillian had bought. As she worked, she called Lillian on the speakerphone on the nightstand beside the big bed. "I need a flight to the ranch. What do you have available?"

"The DC-9 is ready," Lillian replied. "When do you want to leave?"

"As soon as poss—" Kate stopped. "Hold off on that. I have an appointment with Seigelman tomorrow. I'll know more after that." She looked at the phone and flinched. "Lillian, I might have made a mistake. I used the house phone here and mentioned Seigelman by name. If he has this recorded, I'm in trouble."

"No, you're okay," Lillian said. "He never wanted a record of his calls from the house, and I switched off the recorder here when I saw the number come up."

"Thank you." Kate grabbed more clothes from the closet. "I'm packing what I can carry. I need to get away and think. I'm

258

going to stay with Erica tonight. I called her, and the room is still available."

With suitcase in tow and her laptop under her arm, she walked through the house to the car. The garage attendant was off, so the gardener had a hose out and was washing it down. "Afternoon, ma'am," he said. "Are ya going somewhere?" he asked when he saw the suitcase and laptop.

"Yes," Kate replied. "While Mr. Sinclair is away, I'm going to visit friends." She pointed at the car. "You don't have to wash it. I'm in a bit of a hurry."

<hr />

The next morning, Kate dressed in one of her business suits. Parked in front of her supplier's building, she watched as Seigelman drove up in his '70s Rolls Royce with the square castle-like grill. Not far behind, his associates followed in a Cadillac limousine. Out on the street, the older minivan stopped in sight of where she parked.

"Hello, Kate. I'm Aaron Seigelman, and these are the people I'd like you to meet." As he spoke, Seigelman went around and introduced each person. All were specialists is some phase of motion-picture production.

With the introductions completed, Kate led the way into the building and to the conference room. Seigelman began, "I have to admit, you bought a heck of a book. The story is gripping and has the makings of an interesting movie. Do you have any actors in mind for the parts?"

"Yes, Erica Heath and Miranda Wells for the two female leads and Phillip Claymore for the father."

"Excellent choices," Aaron replied. "Erica and Miranda are both seasoned professionals and will add body to their roles. Phillip Claymore is the first name that came to my mind as well. And for the neighbor?"

"For the neighbor, I was thinking of Forrest Pendleton."

"Again, an excellent choice," he said. "I sense we are going to have fun working together."

The meeting continued, and Seigelman spelled out what he and his associates were prepared to do. "How does everything sound so far?" he asked.

"A bit overwhelming, but it sounds good to me," she said. "I can't wait to get started."

"Neither can we," Seigelman replied. "Then it is agreed," he said with a shake of hands. "I'll get the contracts drawn up and have my people jump on this right away. We'll be ready to start as soon as I finish with my current project."

On her way north to the city, Kate grabbed her cell phone and called Lillian. "Cancel the flight north. I have a problem. It appears Jarrett's up to his old ways and is cheating on me. I have to confront him. Running home to Montana isn't going to solve my problem. I've never run away from problems before, and I'm not about to start now."

"Just letting you know when you canceled going with him on the yacht, he and his sailing buddies sailed over to Catalina for a little R and R, and they weren't alone."

Kate squinted. "They weren't?"

"Right," Lillian replied. "Before they left, he called up some female hopefuls. The head stewardess on the yacht just phoned me. She's livid. She and the rest of the female help aboard think the world of you. They're so mad they're all ready to quit."

Kate's cell phone beeped. "Hold on, Lillian. I have another call coming in." She hesitated. "Forget it. The freeway is a mess. I'll call you back after I finish this next call." She pressed the button. "Kate here."

Jarrett's voice blasted from her earbuds. "Good. I finally caught up with you. You must be feeling better."

"Yes," she replied. "Where are you?"

"I'm still on the yacht. We're preparing to leave Catalina. I telephoned the house, and you weren't there. The staff said you were going to visit some friends. Which friends? You told me you weren't feeling well and needed to be alone."

"I was with Erica," Kate replied.

Jarrett's voice boomed forth. "You call that being alone? Who else were you with?"

Kate glared. "What's that supposed to mean? Are you accusing me of doing something behind your back?"

"Forget it," Jarrett said. "Anyway, you seem much better. I'm glad because now I won't have to drop everything and dash home. Ramsey Titus of Titus Tactical Specialties is aboard. He's one of the sponsors of Fletcher's new boat. TTS is out of Idaho, and they're throwing a special kickoff celebration in Sun Valley. He wants a few of us to go there to talk racing. It'll only be for a couple days. Will you be okay?"

"Yes, I'll be fine," she stated. "I'll see you when you get back." Snapping the phone shut, she dropped it on the seat. She stared out at the traffic. *That smells. In fact, it stinks*, she thought and swung off the freeway toward his office tower downtown.

Minutes later, she had Lillian follow her into Jarrett's office. "I heard from Jarrett. He and his pals are on their way back from Catalina and are going to Sun Valley. He said a kickoff celebration is being thrown by Titus Tactical Specialties. I'm guessing the young ladies are still with him and are going to accompany him and his pals to Idaho. Is there any way to find out?"

Lillian pulled out her cell phone. "Give me a couple minutes, and I'll have an answer." Lillian took a seat on the sofa. When she completed her calls, she stepped over to Kate. "I caught Sheryl aboard the plane when they were about to take off, and the answer is yes. He and the skipper and tactician from Fletcher's boat are aboard. She said there are two other men with him wearing TTS jackets. In addition, there are five young ladies along. According to Sheryl, everyone appeared very friendly. I phoned the manager at Sun Valley and asked if Titus Technical Specialties planned a kickoff celebration, and he said there are no corporate meetings of that nature scheduled today or tomorrow. He said he knew of TTS. If they are having a celebration, his guess was they are probably having it in the condominiums they own a mile or so down the road."

Kate glared. *The son of a bitch.* She looked away and then back at Lillian. "I need time alone to think. I don't want to stay with Erica and hash this over with her, and I don't want to go up to the ranch and try to explain this to Father. I have to get away. Do you have any suggestions?"

"Yes," Lillian said. "Melvin and I had a small beach house up the coast past San Simeon. I haven't been there much since Melvin passed away, but you're welcome to use it. If you'd like, I'll call my neighbors up there and have them open it up. They watch over it for me."

"Do it," Kate said.

34

Hours later, Kate turned off the coast highway onto a driveway that wound its way through the trees. Seasoned with the freshness of the spray off the ocean and the call of the gulls, it was like another world. Some distance in, she rolled to a stop in front of a small cabin. The man on the porch greeted her as she approached. "Hi. I'm Mark," he said. He pointed in the direction of a cottage, just visible through the trees. "My folks live there and they watch over Lillian's place for her. They had to leave for a few days so I came down to help out," he said, extending his hand in greeting. "And you must be Mrs. Sinclair."

"Yes," she replied and checked him quickly. He was tall, at least as tall as she and appeared to be about her age. His build was average and his smile friendly. "Forget the Mrs. stuff, Kate will be fine."

"Well, then Kate," he said and led the way inside. "This is the living room. Lillian called and asked me to come over and open it up so I raised the blinds, turned up the heat and built a fire in the fireplace." Continuing, he pointed at the kitchen. "I hope Lillian reminded you to pick up groceries on your way up. The cupboards are empty."

Kate shook her head. "I don't believe she did."

"That's unfortunate as the only grocery close by is closed for the day." He settled back. "I know this is going to sound a bit forward, but if you'd like you're welcome to join me for dinner at our local bistro. I just got in this afternoon and I'm not into cooking this evening and had planned to eat out."

Kate looked toward the kitchen. "The cupboards are really empty?" she asked.

"Yes," he nodded and opened a couple doors to prove it.

She sighed. "Okay. If you'll give me a few minutes to unpack, I'll be ready to go."

Finding the bedroom, she unpacked the few things she brought along. Alone, she stared out at the ocean. Aside from the gulls floating by, little else was stirring. *Yes. This is really alone. Maybe too alone.*

Later, seated in the restaurant, Mark's expression brightened when their eyes met. "Tell me about yourself. I know you do those commercials. I've seen you on TV."

Kate fingered her wedding ring. *What should I say? Should I tell him I'm married to a scoundrel who thinks nothing of having affairs and is off on a sex binge as we speak?* She pondered that and decided her problems were hers. "I have a ranch in Montana, and I raise cattle and horses."

He continued, "But those commercials, are you having fun?"

"I am," she said. "The work is easy, and the money's good." There was warmth in his expression, and she relaxed. "And you? What do you do?"

"Me, I'm the sales manager of a computer chip supplier in Menlo Park. We specialize in chips that go into industrial applications like drill presses, milling machines, and industrial tools."

"And your family? Did they stay behind while you came down to look after your folks' house?"

He shook his head. "I don't have a family, at least not a wife and kids." He paused. "I was married once. We were pretty young at the time. We grew apart and divorced a year or so later." An older woman stepped out from behind the counter and walked their way. Mark whispered to Kate, "The owner."

"Hi there, Mark," she said when she stopped at their table. "Where are your folks?" She looked about and, not seeing them, turned back. "They were here for lunch today and said I'd see them again at dinner."

"They had business in the city they had to take care of," Mark replied.

"Really?" The woman said. "They said nothing to me about that. It must have come up rather sudden."

"It did," Mark replied.

"Oh," the woman remarked. She studied Kate and motioned toward the people seated at the counter. "My friends and I are wondering, are you that rancher from Montana who rescued the actress? You sure look like her."

"Yes," Kate said and looked across at Mark. *So your folks left in a hurry, and you came down quickly to take over.* She nodded. *Sounds like Lillian might have had a hand in this.* She grinned. *Oh well, he's nice and has kept my mind off Jarrett.*

⋘ ⋙

Following breakfast the next morning, compliments of some cereal and milk Mark lent her, Kate went down to the beach for a walk. She watched as the water raced up the sand and coasted back out. *Not unlike my relationship with Jarrett. One day he's with me, and the next he's with who knows who.* Looking down, she kicked at the foam left behind. *What am I going to do?* She studied the situation. *There's no apologizing for adultery.* She took a deep breath and let it out slowly. *First off, I have to confront him. He's probably going to explode, but what choice do I have?* She looked out at the ocean and slowly considered her options. *My life will go on. Not as I had envisioned it, but it will go on.*

On her way up the hill to Lillian's cabin, Mark called to her, "Care to join me for dinner? There's plenty in the folks' pantry, and I'm not a bad cook."

"Why not?" Kate said.

The sun was still up when she walked the narrow trail through the woods to the cottage next door. Mark led the way to the glassed-in porch. He pointed at a wine bottle. "Can I pour you a glass?"

Kate shook her head. "I know I had wine last night, but I shouldn't have."

"No problem," he said. "I have Diet Coke, regular Coke, and water."

With dinner over, they visited until after dark. Stifling a yawn, she glanced toward Lillian's cabin. "It's late, and I need to get up early tomorrow and head back to the city. The dinner was lovely."

Mark walked her home through the woods. It was dark, with only the light from the two cottages to guide the way. Stopping on the porch, she unlocked the door. "I had a wonderful evening. Thank you."

Reaching out, he brushed her cheek with a friendly kiss. "I had a wonderful time as well."

Click. From somewhere in the dark came a sound. Kate looked about. "Did you hear that?" She cocked her head and listened. *Click.* "Yes, there it goes again," she said. "It sounds like a camera shutter."

Mark listened. "Yeah, I heard it too." He looked up just as a breeze off the ocean rustled the branches nearby. "That's it," he said. "It must be the wind rustling the trees."

"You're probably right," she agreed. Stepping inside, she locked the door. *So much for a relaxing evening out. Now back to reality.*

Pulling off her coat, she tossed it on the sofa. Unbuttoning her blouse, she flung it open as she started toward the bedroom. *Bam, bam, bam*—came a pounding on the front door. Spinning around, she grabbed for the latch, and the door was locked. "Who's there?" she called out.

"It's me, Mark. Open up. I'm bleeding."

"You're what!" she exclaimed. Letting go of her blouse, she jerked open the door. There was dirt on his face, blood was running from his nose, and a cut near his scalp. Grabbing him, she pulled him in and bolted the door behind him. "What the hell happened to you?"

He pointed toward the woods between the two houses. "I ran into some guy in the dark with a camera. When I confronted him, he punched me. I must have hit a branch or rock on my way down." Blood was oozing between his fingers and trickling down his face.

"Oh God, we've got to get you cleaned up." Ignoring her open blouse, she pushed him toward the kitchen. She set him down and shoved a handful of paper towels under his nose. A quick search of the drawers produced a first aid kit.

"Tell me what happened," she said as she attended to his nose and cut near his hairline. "You said some guy with a camera attacked you in the woods?"

"Ouch! Yes," he called out.

"I'm trying to be as gentle as I can, but go on."

"When he confronted me, I demanded an explanation. He told me it was none of my business and punched me. Like I said, I must have hit something on the way down. When I got up, he was gone."

With the scalp wound bandaged, she buttoned her blouse and took a step back. A little blood was still dripping from his nose. Mark checked the paper towel. "It looks like the bleeding is stopping. It's time for me to go home."

Kate grabbed her coat. "I'll walk you there."

"No," he stated. "You'll do nothing of the kind."

When he tried to resist, she grabbed a hunk of wood from the box next to the fireplace. "If whoever is out there so much as sneezes in my direction, I'll split his head open with this."

35

The next morning, Kate returned to Los Angeles. The long drive gave her time to think. *He's sick, or is he?* She stared out at the traffic. *Infidelity was not one of the characteristics the neurologist spoke of. Either way, he can forget about apologizing. He's violated my trust. He's done it once, or twice, or possibly even more. That's inexcusable. There's no going on.*

Minutes out from his office tower, her cell phone rang. "Good morning, Lillian, what's up?"

"You have to get back here right now. The stuff is about to hit the fan. Jarrett had an incident on his drive in this morning. I'll explain when you get here. Jack Rainer, his security goon, is here and gloating over the photos he's taken. I overheard him brag about how he's caught you red-handed, whatever that's supposed to mean. And Condon Norman has cut his trip short to the International Alzheimer's Convention. He's on his way here and is demanding to see Jarrett. Where are you?"

"I'm seconds away. I'll be there momentarily." Kate turned into the garage.

Someone was parked outside the garage attendant's office and was pointing at the side of an Audi. "That son of a bitch sideswiped me. Look at the damage he's done. I don't give a god damn if he dozed off at the wheel. That's his problem. I want my car repaired and now."

The attendant tried to calm him. "Sir, you'll be taken care of. The insurance people are on their way here and will put everything in order."

"They damn well better," the man demanded.

That had to be one of the problems, Kate concluded. At the top floor, she stopped at Lillian's desk. The woman grabbed an envelope and shoved Kate into an empty office nearby. "God, what a morning," Lillian said and snapped the lock closed. "I have a guy downstairs whose car Jarrett sideswiped on his way in. The man was parked at the curb, and apparently, Jarrett hit him. There were a dozen people waiting to cross the street who will attest to that. I suspect he blacked out like he's been doing lately. When I suggested he needed to see a doctor, he just about ripped my head off. I phoned the insurance company, and they're sending people down. With luck, he won't get sued." She pointed in the direction of Jarrett's office. "His security goon with a camera is in his office right now. I heard him say he had pictures of you."

"Pictures of me? What kind of pictures?" Kate asked.

"I don't know. All he said was he had the goods on you."

"So that's the man who punched Mark last night."

Lillian appeared puzzled. "What?"

Kate said, "I'll tell you later. Go on."

"Jarrett has changed," Lillian said. "He's not the same person I raised. I've tried to get him to a doctor and can't. After I heard from Sheryl, I realized things had deteriorated, and your marriage was being threatened. I consider you my daughter-in-law, and I love you dearly. I don't want to see you get hurt, so I had Erica get one of the photographers who's always hounding her to follow him. I know you didn't authorize this, but I had pictures taken of him in Sun Valley." She pulled photos from the envelope and handed them to Kate. She motioned toward Jarrett's office. "I have a feeling things are going to get ugly in there. In case they do, you'll need ammunition to defend yourself."

269

The first picture was of Jarrett and four other men and five young women shoulder deep in a hot tub.

"Go on. Trust me, they get worse." She stepped back and left Kate to scan through the stack.

The second was of Jarrett and some blonde alone, chin deep in the water, kissing. The next was of the two of them on their feet. They were naked. Obviously standing on one of the submerged bench seats, they were knee deep in the water. In the next, he was seated on the edge of the tub, and she was on his lap, facing him with her legs wrapped around him. Kate's complexion paled as she thumbed quickly through the rest. Lillian was right; the pictures got worse. She didn't say anything as she slid them back in the envelope.

He's not just cheating on me, he's making a mockery of our relationship. She looked at Lillian. "You said Dr. Norman's coming here?"

"Yes, he's been carrying on that he and Jarrett had some private understanding, and you had no authority to fire him." *Bam, bam, bam*—someone was outside the office door. Lillian tripped the lock.

Jarrett stormed in. "What the hell are you doing in here? Are you two conspiring behind my back?"

"No," Lillian said. "I was discussing your accident with Kate and phoning the insurance people. They said they would be here shortly. We don't need someone suing you."

"Suing me? What the hell for? He ran into me. I've telephoned the cops. I'm going to have him arrested." He pointed at Kate. "You! Get into my office now." He gave her a shove and looked back at Lillian. "I'll deal with you next." He stepped into his office and flung the door closed. Kate looked around. They were alone. Jarrett stomped over to his desk. It was covered with pictures.

"God, you're something else. Jack was right. You are a slut. I never should have married you." He pointed at the pictures. "He got the goods on you. It's obvious when the cat's away, the mouse will play. Here you are with Karl in the restaurant giving him a hug. Lord only knows what you two were doing under the table." He sneered.

"I've taken care of that. I'm firing the bastard." He moved on to the next. "Here you're entertaining the actor I used in that movie. I gave Forrest his big break. I can make 'em, and I can break 'em, and that's exactly what I'm going to do. I can only guess what you two did in my house when he spent the night."

While he spoke, Jarrett's attorney stepped in with Lillian close behind. Jarrett glared. He pointed at the desk. "These pictures were taken only hours ago. You were with some guy in that cabin." He sneered. "My man took care of that. He punched his lights out." He continued, "Not only are you playing around behind my back, you're trying to swindle me as well. You felt you were cute sneaking off to rendezvous with Seigelman. You didn't think I'd notice? Well, I did, and my man has you cold. He's been following you everywhere you go. You went around behind my back and arranged for someone to make my movie?"

Kate's nostrils flared. "Your movie?"

"Yes! My movie, you cheating bitch. You bought the rights to it with my money so that makes the rights mine and mine alone. I'll decide who'll make my movie."

"Listen here, buster!" Kate said. "I bought those movie rights with a check drawn on my account in my bank in Montana." She glared at him. "For your information, while you were rehabbing up at the ranch, I was running your goddamn businesses. I saved you millions. Don't you dare call me names."

"I'll call you anything I want. I'm the boss. You're nothing. This is a community property state. Half of those movie rights are automatically mine. I'm keeping your half and giving part of my half to Stanley. We're going to do the movie, and you're out." Snapping around, he reached out and made like he was going to push her away. His eyelids drooped, and he slumped back against his desk. Perspiration trickled down his forehead. He held on. After many seconds, he slowly let go. He cleared his throat and pointed for her to go. "Out," he gurgled. "Do you hear me? Get out!" Raising a hand, he swung at her face.

Kate ducked and caught his hand in midflight. In the past, she would never have had the strength to overpower him. Today she deflected his blow with little to no effort. He was weak. His pallor was poor. She studied him. "Oh God, we need to get you to a doctor."

"Bullshit! I don't need any goddamn doctors. I'm fine." He sneered.

"No, you're not! We need to get you to a specialist." She reached out to help him into a chair.

Flailing about, he pushed her away. "Don't touch me. Get out of my way!" He snorted and pointed at the door. "You're out of my life. Now leave!"

Pulling back, Kate straightened up. "Not so fast," she said and swept the pictures he had laid on the desk onto the floor. "Explain these," she said as she pulled the pictures from the envelope and laid them out for him to see.

Studying each, Jarrett grinned. His smile quickly faded, and his face turned crimson. "Where did you get these? You went checking up on me behind my back? Is that what you did? How dare you do that? What I do on my time is my business and none of your business."

Kate exploded, "None of my business? I beg your pardon! I'm your wife."

"Damn right, it's none of your business. You don't tell me what to do. I tell you what you can do. I own you. I gave you that ranch property, and I'm taking it back." He pointed at the door. "Get out of here before I throw you out."

Kate didn't move. "You're not getting rid of me that easy."

"Yes, I am." He turned to his attorney. "I want you to cancel all those contracts she signed. I'm retaking control of my business. I want her out. And cancel those deeds I gave her. I'm taking that property back. I own half of her ranch, and I'm going to build my resort." He turned to Lillian. "Where's my helicopter?"

"On the roof."

"Good." He collected the pictures Kate had spread out. "My friend and I are going to Tahoe for two days to do a little skiing and a lot of sex." He grinned. "She'll love these pictures." He pointed at his attorney. "She's out. I want those cancellation orders ready for my signature when I get back."

Kate watched as he shuffled from the room. "He's sick," she whispered to Lillian. Squatting down, she started to pick up the pictures.

His attorney stepped up and stared down at her. "You heard him, you need to leave. You're no longer welcome here."

Kate stood and reached out to hand him the pictures she'd collected. Inches from his fingers, she let the pictures go, and they fluttered to the floor. "In that case, pick them up yourself."

"You insolent bitch!" he remarked.

Kate sneered. "I'll remember that."

Lillian grabbed her and pulled her from the room. With the door closed, she directed Kate to the empty office. "Don't let him get under your skin. He's a jerk, just like that security goon. If it were up to me, I'd fire the both of them."

Kate quickly asked, "Can he take the property back? Can he break up my ranch?"

"Yes, I believe he can," Lillian said. "I just now received access to those deeds to the three ranches he gave you. I studied it, and the wording was a little strange, and now I know why. It's stated that if you two married and then separated for any reason, ownership of the property would revert to him. If that happened, he can build his development without your approval."

Kate tried to take a breath but couldn't. "He planned this all along," she managed to say. Clearing her throat, she continued, "There were strings attached. I was too trusting and didn't read what he had me sign."

"Kate, I'm sorry," Lillian replied. "He's sick. He's not himself. Regarding the movie rights, those are yours. You purchased them with a check on your bank. He can huff and puff all he wants, but I'm sure a judge would rule in your favor."

Kate took a step toward the door. "I guess that's it."

Lillian tripped the latch and stepped out into her office. Condon Norman charged up and pointed at Jarrett's office. "Where is he? I need to see him now."

"He's gone skiing," Lillian replied. "You'll have to wait until he gets back in two days."

Norman leered at Kate. "When he gets back, we'll settle this once and for all." Reaching out, he thumped Kate hard on the chest with a rigid outstretched finger. "You're playing hardball with the big boys now, little girl, and you struck out." Laughing, he charged from the room.

Kate looked toward Jarrett's office. "He's sick, and there's no turning back." She turned toward the door. "I'm going to the house and get the rest of my things."

36

Kate gathered the last of her belongings in Jarrett's house and stopped in the doorway to his bedroom. *Had our nights together ever been real?* Confused, she stared at the bed. *Did you ever love me, or did you use me like so many others you've used in the past?* She tried to think but couldn't come up with an answer.

Shaken, she loaded the car and looked toward Montana. *There's always my ranch, or at least what'll be left of it after he takes over.* Drained of all feelings, she slid in behind the wheel. *I've failed my family and my father.* She stopped. *Mostly, I've failed myself. How could I have been so stupid?*

Settled in at Erica's, she shook her head when Erica brought out a bottle of wine. "No wine right now."

"After today, I expect you'd want me to stick a straw in the bottle and let you go to it."

"Not now, and not for the next few months. Okay?" Kate replied.

Erica looked at the empty wineglass and then studied her friend. Her pallor was poor and her complexion blotchy. "When are you due?" she asked.

Kate did not reply.

"Does he know you're expecting?" Erica continued.

Kate shook her head. "No. I only found out a few days ago," she said when her cell phone rang. She checked the caller ID. "It's Jarrett. I wonder what the bastard wants now."

His voice was weak. Kate pressed the phone to her ear. "Take care of the business. Don't let it fail." There was noise in the background. "I love you. I always will."

"What?" Kate called to him. There was no response. There was the sound of a jet taking off. People were yelling. There was a clunk, and the phone went silent.

Erica looked at her. "What was that all about?"

"I don't know," Kate said. "It was definitely Jarrett. He said not to let the business fail and he loved me, and that was it. There were people yelling, and then the phone cut out."

Kate called him back, and when his voice mail clicked in, she laid the phone aside. She looked at Erica. "I don't know what's going on."

"Tell me what happened in his office. Did you use the pictures Lillian had me get the paparazzi to take?"

"Yes," Kate said and related her experience with Jarrett. "Can you believe he had the gall to tell me what he did on his time was his business?" Kate looked down when her cell phone rang. She checked the caller ID. "Hi, Lillian. What's up?"

There was a long silence. "Jarrett's dead."

"Jarrett's what! Dead?"

"Yes." Lillian's voice broke. "He was doing a preflight under the plane. Someone saw him step up into a wheel well and then slump back down. He had a hold of the strut and appeared to be making a cell phone call when he fell backward, hitting his head on the concrete. When they got to him, he wasn't breathing. They tried to revive him but couldn't. He was pronounced dead at the scene."

Kate struggled with her emotions as she worked through the next few days. Arrangements had to be made, and she had to make them. Focused on his businesses, she reviewed every project and put management teams in place. With the last one taken care of, she settled back in what was now her office. Lillian joined her. "Kate, you have to realize, he loved you very much. And yes, he planned his development from the time he received the aerial photos, but when he saw the pictures of you, he would stare at them every chance he got. When he came back from that meeting in Spokane and the trip out to your ranch, he was changed. He was happy. He was smiling. He said he was in love and was going to marry you."

Kate pushed back. "I'm finding that hard to believe. If he loved me so much, why did he try to ruin me?"

Lillian shook her head. "I don't think he tried to do anything of the kind. I know he felt that once you two were married, what was his would be yours, and vice versa."

Kate struggled with her emotions. "He planned to marry me almost from the beginning? Why couldn't he have shared that with me?"

"That was Jarrett. That was the way he worked. It was his nature not to discuss or share with others what he planned until he was ready to move. Difficult as it may seem, he loved you, and you'll just have to wipe his actions of late from your mind. He was sick and not himself."

Kate looked at the woman. "That makes his passing even worse. I was starting to hate him, and now I know that was wrong. He loved me." She wiped the tears from her cheeks. "Where do I go from here?"

<hr>

Following the funeral, a meeting was set in a judge's chamber. Present were Kate, Lillian, Albert and Amelia Sinclair, Jarrett's attorney, and Condon Norman, who demanded he be allowed to attend.

The judge looked to Jarrett's attorney. "May I have the will?"

The attorney pulled a document from his case. Norman grabbed the papers and shook them at Kate before handing them to the judge. He glared at Kate. "I told you the foundation was mine, and now you're going to see."

The judge scanned the document. "This is indeed a will. It is signed and notarized. It's dated five years ago." He folded it open and prepared to read.

Lillian pulled an envelope from her handbag and handed it to the judge. "I think you might want to see this first." Across the face of the envelope was written, "To be opened only in the event of my death." Across the flap on the back, Jarrett's signature was across the seal. Lillian looked at Kate. "He executed this the morning after you two came back from Hawaii. When he came in that morning, he was the happiest I'd ever seen him."

The judge looked at the envelope and examined the seal. He turned to his secretary. "You're a witness the envelope has been sealed and the signature has not been disturbed." She studied it and nodded. He held the envelope up for all to see. "I am now breaking the seal." He opened the envelope and pulled out the document. The judge mumbled as he glanced down the sheet. "Being of sound mind, I, Albert Jarrett Sinclair, do hereby"—etcetera, etcetera, mumble, mumble, mumble. He continued down the will. He stopped at the bottom. "This will is dated and signed. It has been witnessed and notarized." He checked the will handed him by Norman. "This will is dated roughly five years ago." He checked the date of the will handed him by Lillian. "Yes, this will is dated about three weeks before his death." He looked at the attorney. "Do you have a later will?"

The man shook his head.

Norman leaned forward and rapped on the desk. "Come on, Judge. Quit stalling. Read what he has to say." He grinned at Kate. "Now you'll see."

"Being of sound—"

Norman interrupted again, "Forget all that. Get to the point."

The judge scanned down the document. "I bequeath to Albert and Amelia Sinclair an income of one quarter of a million dollars per year for as long as either shall live. I bequeath to Lillian

Lillenthaller, who has always stood by me, her present salary and benefits for as long as she shall live. I bequeath the balance of my estate, my businesses, developments, properties, personal belongings, and the Albert and Amelia Sinclair Research Foundation to"—the judge turned the page and carefully folded it flat—"my wife, Katherine Clairolyn Clark Sinclair." The judge looked at Kate and set the document aside. "Young lady, you are the principal beneficiary of his estate."

Norman grabbed for the document. The judge pulled it back. "What about me? He told me if he died, the foundation would be mine."

The judge directed him to Kate. "You'll have to take that up with her."

A day following the reading of the will, Norman demanded a meeting. In what was now Kate's office, he leaned across the desk. "I insist on being reinstated. Jarrett promised me if anything happened to him, the research foundation would be mine."

"That's not what he stated in his will."

"Forget what is in the will. He and I had a private agreement." He pointed at Lillian seated beside Kate's desk. "Check through his notes. He kept fastidious notes of everything. He was compulsive that way."

Kate looked at Lillian. "Was there anything stating that in any of Jarrett's notes?"

Lillian shook her head.

Kate stood. "Then it's settled," she said and stepped out from behind the desk. She looked at Norman. "Strike three," she said.

"What?" Norman questioned.

"You heard me, strike three. You're out. You're fired."

"Fired!" he roared. "You can't fire me." He reached out with a finger to thump her on the chest.

Kate grabbed it and bent it back painfully, almost breaking it in the process. "Yes, I can, and I just did." Spinning him around, she jammed his hand up behind his back. With a hold of that hand and a firm grip on his collar, she marched him toward the door. As she did, she called to Lillian, "Call security and have them meet me at the elevator."

When Kate returned, she dusted off her hands. "That takes care of that problem," she said as she approached Lillian. "Is the jet available? There's something I want to do."

"Yes. The helicopter is on the roof, and the jet is fueled and ready to go." Lillian looked at the woman she respected and had grown to love. "There is?" Lillian questioned.

"Yes. I need to go to the ranch." Reaching down, Kate stroked the next generation Clark that was growing within her. "We need to fly up to the Montana and make that first ride together from one end of the restored ranch to the other."

CPSIA information can be obtained
at www.ICGtesting.com
Printed in the USA
LVHW091115070619
620403LV00057B/329/P

9 781640 798151